To Su

My Island Cafe

A HONEYCOMB BEACH NOVEL

VALERIE BUCHANAN

Valerie

Sea Glass Books LLC

Copyright © 2025 by Valerie Buchanan.

ISBN – 979-8-9862532-9-9

Sea Glass Books LLC

Special thanks to Maggie Morris, The Indie Editor

Chapter 1

Daily Mantra

October Sinclair sat at the enormous handcrafted writing desk wedged between her bed and the closet door. Still damp from her shower, she basked in front of the fan, which tossed out cool air like a tempest. The computer screen held the information she needed. Each morning before work, she ritually recorded her account balance in her journal.

Every penny of her twenty-four thousand, one hundred and nine dollars, and eighty-eight cents was there. It was more than money. It was her way out of Honeycomb Beach. It was a way to see the world.

She signed out of the online bank, reached for her spiral-bound productivity journal and a fine-tipped pen, then entered the date and time before constructing her goals for the day.

Today, I will gain one more sale at the newspaper. I will eat less sugar and bypass Glen's Bakery on my way to work but will treat myself to a new roast of coffee at the Island Café. Today, I'm one step closer to my dream. I will reach my goal of $36,000. Italy, here I come.

The journal heaved with the places she wanted to visit, the food she wanted to taste, and the music she wanted to dance to. She used tape to hold the spine together, as her dreams, daily mantras, and visions for her future burst from every colorful page. She wrote in it every morning like clockwork, a habit she'd started shortly after her mother died, as a way of controlling something. Anything. Her newest vision board held glossy photos that would make her dreams a reality someday. Words like *Success*, *Achieve*, *Voyager* were among the words she used to describe her future. Her travel expenses would include a new wardrobe, so she cut out ideal outfits, mostly of Italian design, from the *Vogue* and *Glamour* magazines she'd swiped from the dentist's office. To be the ultimate tourist would require her to blend in, not jump out as if she didn't belong. She would meet new people, eat exotic food, and walk on unfamiliar streets. October Sinclair would finally be free from the mundane and boring confines of Honeycomb Beach. She closed her eyes and inhaled a couple of long, deep breaths and proclaimed her daily mantra.

"I deserve success." She stopped when there was a knock on the bedroom door.

Summer Young stepped into the bedroom wearing a pink robe with her hair under a tightly wrapped terry towel. She was a social butterfly who loved people and hanging out at the beach. Her job title, Social Science Collection Development Support Specialist, was a mouthful. She worked at the library. The name itself made October envious, but she loved her friend and would want nothing but the best for her. And Summer would always want the best for October. Even if it meant leaving. Her roommate sat on the bed and waited for October to finish up her journal entry.

"Still up for dinner tonight?" Summer said. The two roommates had dinner almost every night after Summer finished up at the library and October got done with her job at the *Honeycomb Beach Times*.

October had calculated all the money she'd spent on eating out. She'd be a lot closer to her goal if she hadn't eaten her way through an eighth of her potential savings, but they were best friends, and it was what they'd always done. And she didn't want to ruin it.

"Of course. Why wouldn't I be?"

Summer patted October on the shoulder and kissed her on the top of the head. A motherly gesture they'd begun in high school.

"I'll meet you at Jack's Tiki Bar then." Summer left October there and closed the door behind her. October looked up at the framed poster of Tuscany, the same one that decorated the wall at her office, and wished she were there now. Her hometown was a beautiful place but also a place where everything stayed the same.

She slid the journal into a drawer and drew out a book she'd been reading but was unable to finish. *When the Night Leaves You* was a bestseller years ago. October stared at the cover and brushed a finger over the author's name. Lillian Sinclair. The large yellow font should have brought her joy.

The name Sinclair implied a penchant for poetry or novel writing, which October had tried with no luck and was a constant reminder of her mother's criticism. After one hundred and fifty-two submissions and a handful of dry, unhelpful letters implying that she lacked her mother's unique storytelling ability, October had thrown away her manuscripts and attended a community college for a degree in liberal arts.

She made twenty dollars an hour at the newspaper.

It was a pittance compared to what her mother must have gotten paid for her novel. No one discussed money, and after her mother's death, a letter to the town's lawyer had revealed her intention to use her royalties for other purposes.

Her father had taken it badly. October had gotten a piece of her mother's income: twenty thousand, which she immediately put away in her bank account. Her father had sold the house and left Honeycomb Beach for a new life in California.

She tossed the book back into her mother's desk and closed the drawer.

Chapter 2

Peruvian Blend

I t was almost seven thirty. October finished her makeup and hair, then dressed as if she were going out for a day in Italy, with a simple floral skirt and lightweight top, a hat to block the sun, and her favorite pair of sneakers for walking long distances. She bypassed Glen's Bakery, keeping her promise to avoid the decadent confections, took a shortcut through the kite store parking lot, passed the little mom and pop grocery, and crossed the road to the Island Café on Main Street, where the familiar sign Come in for a Jolt greeted her.

The interior popped with canary yellow, cerulean blue, and a flash of grass green, a setting as energizing as the coffee beans she inhaled. A jolt indeed.

Bridgette, the proprietor, was wiping down the counter flanked by yellow leather stools in a long row.

"I'd like to try something exotic this morning," October said. "What do you recommend?"

October slid onto one of the shiny leather seats while Bridgette contemplated the perfect grounds.

"Would you like to try a nice medium roast from Peru? I just made some."

October hadn't considered Peru as a travel destination. It sounded fun, but she was set on Italy. Luckily, coffee could take her places that her wallet couldn't, so she ordered the exotic blend.

Bridgette poured the coffee into a large to-go cup, one where both hands were necessary. October inhaled the chocolate aroma with a hint of something fruity. It was just what she needed to start another new day.

"This one's on the house," Bridgette said. "For being my first customer today."

"First customer prize. That's so nice." October looked up at the parquet ceiling, fantasizing about being draped in colorful falling streamers. Nothing happened.

"I was bummed to hear that your newspaper decided not to interview me," Bridgette said. "It would have been good for business. We just got a new shipment of coffee beans."

"That's odd," October said. "I'll talk to Alice."

"I saw her last night," Bridgette said. "She was coming around the corner as I was locking up."

"Did she say anything?"

"Just that she couldn't do the article. That she might be leaving."

October had heard nothing of the sort. There must have been a mix-up. "I'm sure we can do the interview," she said, knowing that the paper needed the news.

The Island Café was a lovely place, and it deserved recognition. The interview cancellation made it a bad time to ask Bridgette about the ad. She'd come back another time. Her advertisers had been dropping out lately. Maybe it was that it was summer, or that it was hurricane season, or that Clive, her boss, had raised the cost of ad space in the last month. Whatever it was, it was making her job more difficult.

"I'll see what I can do about the interview," October said, paying her bill.

There was no way Alice was leaving. The paper needed her. And why hadn't Alice said anything?

Chapter 3

The Newspaper

October crossed the road to the *Honeycomb Beach Times*. It was an old cement building, once painted orange but now faded to the shade of a Creamsicle. The office was just shy of three hundred square feet, but it looked larger inside. A wall sliced the room in two. Clive had one whole side to himself, the side where light poured through the south-facing windows. On the other side of the room, a long desk with two drawers and two swivel chairs stared at the wall. Also sharing their side was the coffee pot, a little refrigerator, and a tiny microwave. The sole inviting feature was a small side yard with several palm trees. No one used it.

October inserted the key Clive entrusted her with and let herself in, switched on the overhead lights, and gingerly lifted and clipped the two cheap blinds that covered the windows. The sun painted the wall with a broad swath of gold.

She plopped into her office chair, ready to get to work, but acknowledged the emptiness. Gone were Alice's favorite magazines: *Coastal Living*, *Key Life*, and *Flamingo*. Alice had taken the heart-shaped tin that held her pens, her lollipops, nail files, and the slender vial of vanilla travel spray that October inhaled

7

every day right before Alice's lunch break. The frame with her college degree in English was gone, along with the familiar coffee tumbler and half-used packets of sugar and dehydrated creamers that left a slight powdery residue where they had been. The only thing Alice had bequeathed to the newsroom was a potted hibiscus plant with a giant red flower that had made October sneeze since the day Alice had placed it on her desk.

October chucked it into the trash.

There were tons of things that October would have liked to have known about Alice besides the fact she was quitting. She'd always yearned to know whether Alice's last name was truly English. Her degree was in English. October admired the name, but it appeared fake somehow. Now she would never know.

Unlike Alice, everyone knew all about the Sinclair name in Honeycomb Beach. Her mother's book *When the Night Leaves You*, had swiftly become a bestseller and received a nod from Oprah. Lillian Sinclair had died of a rare heart condition in 2013, when October was sixteen. She had found her mother dead in her study, sitting in a chair, clenching a glass of sherry with a romance novel on her lap. Aside from being shocked about her mother's sudden death, she was quite shocked to find her reading a romance. She'd never portrayed those traits in her marriage. Seldom did her mother say the word *love* to anyone.

October shook off her questions and mother's memory when Clive arrived at eight o'clock, earlier than usual. She wanted to know more about why Alice left and hoped he'd still honor the commitment to Bridgette to cover the story.

"Good morning, Clive," she said when he entered. He kept on his sunglasses and propped his surfboard outside the door.

"Can you come to my office?" he said.

She followed in behind him, took a seat opposite his desk, and waited for him to take a soda out of his backpack, drink part of it down, burp, then slump into his seat.

Clive used to be good looking, but now he neglected to comb his hair, his pants were wrinkled, and his once striking and youthful face looked tired. The beard he'd recently started growing had gray strands in pieces. Gone were the days when he'd arrive clean shaven with a sports jacket even in the death of summer.

"There's something I've got to tell you," he said.

She waited for him to say it, but she already knew.

Chapter 4

Alice

B efore he could get to the point, Clive adjusted the fan on his desk, turning it too far, and a stack of papers blew like startled birds whipping through the air. October shot up from her chair and helped retrieve them so he could get to what he wanted to say. That Alice had quit.

He slapped the papers he'd collected from the floor on his desk in a pile.

"Alice quit," he said.

"I know. I saw Bridgette at the Island Café. She told me she saw Alice."

"Don't know about that part," Clive said while October tidied up her stack of papers and laid them neatly on his desk.

Alice had mentioned plenty of times how she'd rather be doing something else and headed out for a two-hour lunch most days of the week, something Clive allowed. Her writing was good, but October had often considered that if Alice had searched deeper for content, the paper would have more substance, but what substance was there in her tiny beach town? October had a sinking feeling in her chest. She and Clive were the only ones left, and he didn't appear to care anymore.

"Where's she going?" October said.

"No idea."

October repressed her resentment. She was probably going somewhere interesting, somewhere exciting.

"I met her here last night," Clive said, "after I'd been at the Beachside Grille. She wanted to get her things."

Alice and October had worked together, but they weren't friends. Still, it bothered October that Alice didn't even have the decency to say goodbye.

"I don't know why she quit, but that's the way it goes," he said.

Didn't he have a right to know? October had already explained to him that someday she would leave for Italy. It was just good etiquette. In her opinion, Clive used to run things with a clear head. Lately, he appeared to be giving up. He sat down and swiveled his chair back and forth, back and forth, making October dizzy.

When October finally reached her goal and could travel to Italy, she'd give him the proper two weeks' notice. Like people are supposed to do. Maybe it was old school, but she wanted a going away party, a celebration. With cake. That's how it's done. Not like this.

Alice's sudden departure was a concern. Who would interview the locals? Who would write the content?

They both sat in silence, the news having appeared to stun them both. Alice was Honeycomb Beach's version of a proper journalist. Mostly punctual, fairly curious, and getting any story that she could find in a town where nothing ever happened.

"The final articles for the paper are due," October said, not that it was any surprise to Clive. "What story was she working on?"

"I didn't ask. She always got things to me."

"Do we have enough content for the paper?"

He shook his head.

"What are we going to do then?"

It was getting too close to the deadline to find enough stories. Nothing was happening in town, no events, no neighborhood garage sales. Alice, Clive, and October had managed the paper like clockwork. While Alice wrote articles and October obtained advertisers, Clive paid the bills and kept the paper running. Now it was all falling apart.

Clive was slipping. His father had run the paper for years and finally retired, leaving the work for his only son. But his initial interest in the newspaper was being taken over by his love for surfing.

"Check Alice's desk drawer," he said. "She took her laptop, but she might have left some files lying around."

It annoyed her he didn't even ask Alice to turn anything in. What about the files on her computer? What about stories she might have been writing but never finished? All things that they might have used in this week's edition.

"Who's going to write the stories now?" October said.

Clive didn't answer.

"I guess I could write them," she said. It would mean more work but also more pay.

"We'll see."

October didn't have the reporting skills that Alice English had. She was responsible for sales and getting money to keep the paper going. It was a challenging job that was more difficult each week. She left his office and stood before the long mahogany desk that was all hers now. Did she have the skills to seize the role as a new Alice, pen in hand, gathering data, and asking pertinent questions?

The idea gave her energy. An opportunity like this might be good for her. She was up for the challenge. She felt her legs wobble a little but chalked it up to excitement. There might be a raise in her future, or an advance if she could prove she could take on more responsibility. Her dream of traveling to Italy would come a whole lot sooner.

October opened the drawer beneath the table where Alice had sat just last week. There were still a few things she didn't take with her. Some bright yellow sticky notes, blank; a couple of ballpoint pens; some paper clips; a peppermint; and a file folder that said Island Café on the tab.

She opened the folder, expecting to find all the information she'd need for the story Alice was working on, but there were just a few notes about the Island Café. In the folder's corner, she'd drawn a small heart, and underneath it, she'd written "Key West."

Alice was going somewhere too. Perhaps October had spoken so much about her plans to go abroad that Alice had made her own plans. Still, it was so sudden. Alice didn't appear to be a person who would leave for no good reason. But then again, she was a bit of a mystery.

October opened her laptop, created a blank file and named it "Island Café," then read through the pitiful notes Alice had left in the folder. It was a series of references but nothing valuable.

"Dim lighting, several round tables, a doorway, five chairs."

The word *window* was circled. October kept scanning the notes.

"After hours, hidden, set up, meeting time 11–4:30, add to Friday's edition."

October turned the paper over, but there was nothing more. No follow-ups with Bridgette or what spin Alice was taking. Just notes that made no sense.

She read the notes again, confused by it all. The café was anything but dimly lit. It was lively, with a vibrant style and flair. And there were way more than five chairs. What about the yellow ones at the bar? Had Alice gone somewhere else? Maybe these notes were for another story entirely.

She shoved the folder back in the drawer, then dialed the number for the Island Café.

Bridgette answered, and October felt the first twinge of nerves. This was it. She was a reporter.

"Hi, Bridgette," she said. "It's October Sinclair, from the *Honeycomb Beach Times*." She popped a pen behind her ear and leaned back in her seat. "Guess what? We can do your story!"

"Okay."

October gulped and sat upright again.

"Should I be there between eleven and four thirty?" October was happy she'd used Alice's info, thinking it would impress Bridgette.

"That's my busiest time. Can you come now?"

October took the ridiculous pen out from behind her ear and laid it on the desk.

"Now?"

"It's the only time I've got."

"Be right there."

She had gotten her first assignment. Alice may have stripped the desk of all her belongings, but she had left a gift of opportunity. And October wasn't going to blow it.

Chapter 5

First Assignment

O ctober hung up, excited about writing her first feature story. She didn't know the first thing about journalism, but as a customer herself, she had questions about the place. She'd start there.

"I'll be back later," she said to Clive, who didn't answer until she was halfway out the door.

"October?" His voice carried through the office.

She stopped and turned around, her heart racing with anticipation. Would he give her some words of encouragement? Say that they were a team now, that he was counting on her?

She stood in the doorway, holding her breath, waiting.

"Can you get me a coffee?" he finally said, his voice trailing off.

The words hit her like a cold splash of water. Her smile vanished, replaced by a tight knot of disappointment in her chest. She nodded, and the excitement evaporated, leaving her hollow and unappreciated.

As she stepped out into the street, she took a deep breath, determined not to let his indifference overshadow her potential.

She would prove she could take on this task, not for him, but for herself.

October rushed to the café with her notepaper in hand. This time, the place was packed and bustled with locals queuing up for their coffee. As she wedged her way inside, Bridgette recognized her in the doorway and came out from behind the bar, wiping her hands on her apron.

"Are you sure this is a good time?" October said. "Alice's notes said around eleven."

Bridgette pulled the strings on her apron and looked about the room.

"No, this is great."

Bridgette was a vibrant young woman taking on the world. She wore a cherry-red apron with the café motto Come in for a Jolt on the front, and her hair was tossed up in a large knot on top of her head. When she smiled, her eyes sparkled.

The interview was October's first chance at trying out a new position, one that could bump up her savings account to meet her goal even sooner, though Clive hadn't mentioned a raise. Yet. Her new opportunity was important, and she didn't want any missteps.

"I think we can chat back there. Is that okay?" Bridgette motioned to a space in the corner, farthest from the clanking of dishes, the sound of light jazz, and the voices carrying through the room that could easily make October's first interview difficult. When they sat down, October grabbed her notebook and a pen and got busy with the questions she'd thought about on her walk there.

"Tell me about this business," she said. "Why a café? What do you hope to give Honeycomb Beach that Glen's Bakery doesn't already have? Are you in competition?"

That was several questions, and October took a breath. She should take her time and not ask everything all at once. "Comparing and contrasting the two businesses would be helpful for residents," she said, wanting to appear professional.

"Competition?" Bridgette said. "Not at all. I'm also a wholesaler, and I've talked to Glenda about providing our coffee for her business. It's a win-win."

October scratched some notes on her pad. Bridgette continued the conversation. "I love coffee and have been to other countries, experimenting with the grounds, asking anyone who is in the industry to tell me about their coffee beans. When I first got into this business, I intended to serve coffee, but it's become more like a brewery, where we help customers find the coffee that's right for them. Sometimes, people just need to know what they enjoy. And I can provide that."

"Tell me more," she said, coaxing the conversation along organically, having decided to slow it down and allow Bridgette to do the talking but prepared to write it all down.

"We make our coffee in small batches. It's fresher that way, and our guests get to taste it the way it should be consumed. We have beans from all over. Costa Rica, Brazil, Ethiopia. We roast the coffee right here."

"So, is it a café or a roastery?"

"It's both."

Bridgette beamed with her love for her small business. Her passion for doing something she loved. October looked away for a moment, almost envious. She didn't know her interests; nothing was driving her except a poster of Italy and a number in her bank account. Many residents her age had figured out their purpose. Sarra Wilcox, the most obvious, became the singer-songwriter; Joannie Harper had started her boutique a few years back; Courtney and Eric had success with their bed and breakfast. Traveling had always been October's destiny, but Bridgette's love for her employment made October pause. Would her life have passion?

"Did you always dream of opening your own business?" October said.

"Yes. Always. You know what it's like to want something your entire life?"

She didn't know. Her dreams weren't big enough. Maybe she should want more in life. Traveling was great, but she would run out of money and need something tangible.

October looked down at her notes, stalling. She couldn't think of anything that she had wanted like that but hadn't already failed at. Bridgette was looking straight at October when she looked up from the page as if she were supposed to reveal her dream. Before she realized it, she said the first thing that came to mind.

"I've always dreamed of writing a novel. Like my mother did."

She could have choked on the sentence.

After all the rejection letters and all the time wasted writing poetry and submitting manuscripts with nothing to show for it, writing was not her dream. It was simply pulling a bunny out of a fake magic hat.

"Can you tell me anything else?" October asked, her pen poised over her notepad. "For the article?"

Bridgette smiled warmly. "We have plans to include more events, like tastings, and we plan to add places for people to sit outside and stay awhile, play games. We want to encourage people to relax, not rush out the door. We've already planned some group activities, and children's reading clubs so parents can enjoy their coffee while the kids are entertained. Maybe you could start a book club. Or writing group."

The last thing October needed was a critique group telling her she wasn't going to be a writer. "Maybe," she replied noncommittally.

They sat together while October finished her notes. "I think I have what I need," she said, tapping her pen against the notepad. "One more thing. Alice made some notes about the café, but her notes didn't match the ambiance. She listed five chairs, a window, a dim atmosphere."

Bridgette's expression tightened as she retied the apron around her neck but then relaxed again.

"Maybe it's some other place," she said.

"That's what I thought too. You said Alice was walking around one night as you were locking up. Do you know where she was coming from?"

"Out for a walk would be my guess," Bridgette said shaking her head. "And as far as her list, well, what she's describing isn't here." She motioned around the place: full of people, noise, and energy.

It didn't seem plausible. Alice would have been accurate. But Alice was gone, and she wasn't going to speculate further.

They shook hands and stood up from the table, with October following Bridgette back to the bar. "Do you need anything else?" Bridgette asked.

October remembered Clive's request.

"I do. A cup of coffee to go."

Chapter 6

Spilled Coffee

O ctober was waiting for Bridgette to pour the coffee when a woman standing near the doorway with jet-black hair down past her shoulders caught her eye. She wore an equally black jacket, not typical for someone staying in Florida for the summer, and a pair of dark sunglasses like Hailey Bieber, the socialite and model October followed on Instagram, would wear. She raised a hand to remove a strand of hair from her face, and a set of heavy gold bracelets fell halfway down her slender arm.

"Here you go," Bridgette said, handing the coffee across the bar. "It's the same one as you had this morning. From Peru."

"Thank you."

As October turned to leave, she once again caught sight of the woman, who'd left instead of buying coffee. Trying to see where she might be going, October slammed into the man behind her in line, pouring hot coffee down the front of his crisp white shirt and the Tolkien book he was carrying.

"I'm so sorry," she said, grabbing a fistful of napkins from the counter and patting them on his soaked shirt. The stains were too much for the fabric, and it made it a muddy mess.

"Can I have some ice?" he said over the top of October's head, and Bridgette handed him a cupful. His voice was deep and rich like chocolate lava cake.

"I wasn't paying attention," she said, applying more napkins as if she knew the man. As if it were helping. His eyes were dark, and his forehead held a crease from the pain she must have caused. "Are you burned?"

"I'm okay," he said while applying some ice to his chest. "The ice helps."

"I'm sorry," October said, saying it over and over. "And your book. I've ruined it."

He squeezed the book, and coffee ran between the pages and down onto the floor.

"I don't think I'll be finishing it," he said. "But I know how it ends."

She covered her mouth trying not to laugh about the book, which would have to be thrown away as the pages were glued together now. He smiled too, and she could barely take her eyes off him.

"I'm October Sinclair," she said.

He took a moment, smiled, then extended a hand.

"Dax."

"Are you new here?" she said.

"Visiting. Just here for the week."

"This isn't usually how I welcome people to town," she said.

"No. I'm sure it isn't."

"I usually spill the Ethiopian blend. Not the Peruvian." She smiled, hoping he would smile again. And he did.

"Let's try that again," he said, then ordered two coffees to go, and they moved away from the queue and stood awkwardly in silence, watching the line.

October wanted to talk to him but didn't know what else to say. They might chat about the weather, but that would be ordinary. She was curious why he would come to the beach during hurricane season when it was so hot and muggy. Fall was much more enjoyable, in her opinion. She could ask where he lived, but that might be rude. Did he travel? Maybe they would have that in common. He looked as if he would enjoy traveling, and since he was visiting, he certainly didn't stay home all the time. Except for the large brown stain on the front of his shirt, he looked nice in his slim-fitting chino shorts and casual loafers. She glanced down at his left hand. No ring. But he was only visiting for a week. She wasn't in a relationship, not that she wanted one. A relationship wasn't compatible with her goal.

This encounter made her nervous, so she started talking and kept talking even when she wanted to stop. "Maybe you and I could get together again. For coffee. I promise I won't spill any on you," she said and hoped she wasn't being too bold. She was willing to take that chance. He wasn't staying. As Bridgette had said, it's a win-win.

"I'd love to, but I'm only here for a few days."

"Of course," she said. What was one more rejection in the pile she'd accumulated? She couldn't write, and she wasn't worth seeing again. She forced a smile.

When the coffees were ready, Dax grabbed them and handed one to her, which she would take back to Clive and forgot about this terrible moment of embarrassment.

"Enjoy your visit," she said after he added some cream and popped the lid back on the top.

"Nice meeting you, October. Maybe we'll meet again."

It was a silly yet courteous goodbye. He'd already said he wasn't interested.

She watched him step outside, throw on a pair of sunglasses, and head down the road.

"Goodbye," she said in a whisper.

She waited a few minutes to ensure he had left and would not see her again. She wanted to avoid the possibility of waving at him as he drove past or discovering that they were heading in the same direction. When she stepped out of the café onto the front porch, he was gone.

With Clive's hot coffee in hand, she headed back to the newspaper, her mind spinning in several directions. She still had the jitters from spilling the coffee on the man named Dax, but she'd done a great job with the interview. She'd connected with Bridgette and found out more about the Island Café. In fact, she'd enjoyed the interview so much that the idea of another story filled her with initiative. A new idea came to her.

What if she pitched a story idea to Clive about tourists? Of course, she couldn't interview Dax—it would be too embarrassing to see him again—but maybe she could find the woman in the black coat. Other people were roaming around her town that came for the summer. It wasn't a life-altering concept for the newspaper by any means, but tourists did buy things and visit their beaches, and without them, the community would suffer.

She would have skipped back if it hadn't been for the coffee in her hand. Her job had some potential now. All she had to do was pitch it. And she'd be the next Alice for good.

Chapter 7

New Hire

W hen she got back to the office, loud chatter escaped Clive's side of the room. The walls were paper thin, and even though the door was closed, Clive's office was hardly private. His door was almost all glass, to allow a sliver of natural light into her side of the space. As October passed the door on her way to her workspace, she glanced inside.

A man sat in the metal chair opposite Clive, his frame so thin he barely filled it out. He pulled his shoulders back proudly, and his blond hair, like a mop, tumbled over his collar.

October was eager to pitch her tourist idea to Clive but decided to wait until his guest left.

As she set up her laptop and took a seat at her desk, laughter rumbled on the other side of the partition.

It made her suddenly feel like an outsider. Running the paper had been a group effort, and though Clive was in charge, he'd never made her feel as if she didn't belong. What was happening?

Perhaps the rejection from Dax had made her self-conscious. She'd made such a mess of everything and then got turned down besides.

It wasn't normal for her to care about what Clive did, but hearing the men laugh together in there made her curious. No one ever came into the office except Clive's wife, sometimes his kids, or a local who might have an obituary or an ad to run. But most of those were called in. Certainly, for Clive to shut the door, it must be important. He hadn't mentioned that he had an appointment today, and that was odd. They had worked together for two whole years, side by side. She knew almost everything.

I didn't know that Alice was quitting. Suddenly, she got a queasy feeling. Things felt different.

The two men in the other room made her question her fate. Of course, the meeting could have nothing to do with her. Her character weakness was her overly defensive nature and sensitivity to criticism. She shook these off.

It was time to put a stop to her silly feelings and insert herself into the discussion. If it was nothing, she'd simply leave. She grabbed Clive's coffee, went to the door, and knocked loud enough so that Clive would hear it over the banter.

"Enter," he said, sounding like a big boss. Clive was hardly a big boss.

When she stepped inside, the laughter stopped, and the man sitting in the chair turned. She had never seen him before. He didn't smile or even say hello.

"Clive," she said, "I got the story about the Island Café. I'll have that ready to go by this afternoon. I got you a coffee." She set it down on his desk and smiled at the man sitting there. He didn't smile back.

"Thanks," Clive said. "How are the ads coming along?"

She'd lost another account last week.

"Great," she said because she didn't want to say something bad in front of the man she didn't know. It might be bad for business.

"Good to hear it."

"I also have a great idea for a story that I'd love to run by you later," she said.

"We were just discussing that," Clive said.

October scrunched her nose. Why was he discussing it with a stranger? October planted her feet, waiting to be introduced, but could see that Clive wasn't going to do it.

"Hi. I'm October," she said. "I work in sales, but as of today, I also write the articles." She stood like a superhero with her fists on her hips, legs splayed wide. She quickly adjusted back to a normal stance and stuck out her hand.

The man stood and offered her a limp hand of all fingers. She did her best to give a firm handshake. "Philip Van Sloan," he said. "We're going to be working together for a bit."

Her eyes widened. Clive was rubbing his chin.

"I hadn't heard," she said.

"Philip just came to town, and we need someone to help out now that Alice is gone. I've told him you're one of my most trusted employees and that if he needs anything, you're the one he should talk to."

Clive should have talked to her about a new hire. No, he should have given her a chance to do the job first. Before he hired some stranger. She had no idea who Philip was, and now she'd be sharing the desk with him.

She forced a smile. "Well, it would be good to have another set of hands." She hated how agreeable she was being.

"Maybe Philip can look over your shoulder. Make sure everything looks good."

She raised an eyebrow, but Clive didn't see it. She had no say in the matter.

"Fine," October said, trying not to show her irritation. "But I'd like to talk to you in private later, about my idea."

She sped out the door and back to her seat at the desk, but before Philip could take over Alice's place, she took everything out of the drawer: the files, the sticky notes, and even the single paper clip. Then she put them in her drawer, shoving his chair as far away from her own as possible.

To shed her anger, she got to work doing the job she got paid to do and called her advertisers who needed to renew their contracts, praying that none of them would tell her they weren't renewing this time. In the past month, three had left.

As she went down her long list of contacts, Philip exited Clive's office and went out the front door.

October hoped he'd be gone for a while and would use that time to speak to Clive and get to the bottom of all these changes. She rushed to the doorway and knocked on the doorjamb. Clive looked up and immediately sat back in his chair.

"What's going on, Clive?"

"What do you mean?"

She could talk to him. He used to be one of the good guys. When her mother had died, he sat with her and let her cry. Today he'd acted out of character. Hiring someone he didn't even know on such short notice. Something was up.

"Why did you hire someone else? I can do ads and articles. Did you really need this guy? I was your new Alice. I could have handled it." She would have loved to ask for more pay too, but she wouldn't get it now.

Her nerves were rattling inside because Clive hadn't even considered her first.

"Well, the truth is," he said, "we've got trouble. And we've got it bad. Have a seat."

Chapter 8

Trouble

"Trouble? What do you mean?" she said.

He tilted his head and leaned in as if he were going to give her the code to his bank vault.

"I can't blame Alice for quitting," he said. "She was too good to be reporting on dog groomers and writing silly articles about where to get the best margarita in town. This paper is in jeopardy. Unless we can find a story that gets the public excited about us again, this paper is doomed. I needed to bring in someone who can find something gritty."

Advertisers weren't happy, so this shouldn't have been a shock. But gritty had never been the mission of the paper.

She did a mental tally of how much money she had and how much more she needed. If Clive was going in another direction with the paper, she didn't want any part of it. But if the paper was in jeopardy and she didn't have the money yet, what else was she going to find for work? Despite complaining about it sometimes, she rather liked her job.

"Wasn't Alice going to interview Sarra Wilcox again?"

Sarra Wilcox was a big name, and people loved to read more articles about her.

"She was. But Sarra canceled. Scheduling glitch."

"Oh."

"Besides," he said, "we can't use one name. We have to find something else that's interesting. Get curious."

It would be difficult to find a story to keep the paper afloat in a town where nothing happened except the occasional flea market, the barber shop getting an additional styling chair, or the grand opening of a business.

Clive started biting his nails.

"Then let me help find a story. I already have one, I think. About the tourists who come here in the summer. We could interview them and find out what they love, where they go, and what shops they enjoy. Really connect with the people. Make it a weekly piece. And we can link the business ads to the stories. I think the locals would eat it up."

He shook his head.

"Maybe. Larger publications are focusing on investigative stories, rather than the small-town stories we publish."

Clive, the unshaven boss of this morning, was suddenly concerned about larger publications?

"Is this something Philip said?"

"He's got ideas."

If Philip was there to find investigative stories, trusting him was out of the question. But if dirt was what he was after, he wouldn't find it in Honeycomb Beach. In fact, it was so clean it practically squeaked. That was part of its charm. It was also part of its misery.

"Are you sure about this, Clive?"

"Philip's a writer," Clive said. "He showed me some of his stuff on his Facebook page."

October couldn't stop the eye-rolling.

"I need you to work with me on this," Clive said. "If we don't find a story that has chops, then we're both out of a job. Just see if you can get us some leads."

She had no idea whether Philip had given Clive his résumé or how in this small amount of time Clive knew anything about

Philip's abilities, but there was nothing she could do. And when was the last time she'd heard anyone say the word *chops*? Clive was acting strange.

"Okay," she said but didn't sound convincing.

"Oh, and October?"

"Yes?"

"Can you get that café story to Philip by the end of the day? And if you want to find a story to keep the paper afloat, it can't be the usual stuff. And I'll need it soon."

Every Friday morning before the sun came up, Clive came in to print the paper and send it out to the local businesses, then to residents. She'd counted on having a few days. She'd planned to have her article about the Island Café written and submitted today, but for the next one, tourists would need to be located and interviewed—it would take her some time to produce that article, and now Clive also wanted her to find dirt and had added another layer with the new guy. If he was anything like she thought he would be, he'd want several rewrites, and she still had to do her normal job besides.

"I'll try," she said.

"October," he said. "Try hard. This might be our last chance."

October didn't have a clue of how to go about getting a juicy story in a town that didn't do anything bad. The weather looked clear, so they couldn't even use a hurricane as a story. Even when they'd done hurricane stories in the past, the articles were about the town coming together and helping one another. There were good people here, and unfortunately, that wasn't newsworthy. Certainly, people enjoyed hearing good news. Why did it all have to be bad? She was rather fond of the town's ability to be happy and not care about the bad things. But she understood Clive's issue. The newspaper, like Honeycomb Beach, needed news.

That's exactly why she wanted to leave.

Chapter 9

Café Article

The article about Bridgette's Island Café bloomed like a field of wildflowers over the blank page as October checked off all the whos, the whys, the whats, and the wheres, making her first article smart yet newsworthy. After proofreading it twice and checking it with free editing software, she relaxed. It was finished.

```
The Island Café and Roastery Will Give You a Jolt
              by October Sinclair.


HONEYCOMB BEACH - The Island Café has recently
joined Honeycomb Beach's business landscape.
Built in 2019 and doing business for some time,
the coffee beans and additional ideas purveyor
and entrepreneur Bridgette Hart has in mind
make it appear brand new. Sitting right between
Meghan's Pilates and the bridge entering town
stands a quaint, youthful building, with long
windows, a blue porch, and bright-turquoise
shutters.
```

Experience the pleasure of savoring a cup of coffee roasted to perfection by Bridgette and her skilled team, exclusively for your enjoyment. With a deep appreciation for the finest coffee varieties, Bridgette created the roastery to provide her customers with an opportunity to experience the best that the world of coffee has to offer.

"Not everyone can travel the world for perfect coffee," Bridgette stated. "Here, you can sit and enjoy sipping a cup of some special blends from another time and place."

You'll find a selection of well-balanced varieties, from mild to bold. As she explained, there's something for every connoisseur or beginner taster.

"We make our coffee in small batches," she explained. "It's fresher that way, and our guests get to taste it the way it should be consumed. We have new beans from Costa Rica, Brazil, and Ethiopia. We roast the coffee right here."

While the sun pours through the south-facing windows, acoustic lullabies from foreign lands softly enhance the mood. Coffee roasts in the back, and the aromas of nature waft through the small eight-hundred-square-foot space with big plans, designed for sipping and chatting and taking one's time.

Bridgette demonstrates a deep commitment to her coffee beans and customers. She takes pride in presenting her roasted blends to clients with joyful enthusiasm.

There is no rush at the Island Café. Enjoy your coffee and read a chapter of your next favorite book or sit on the yellow leather barstools and try a flight of coffee. The choice, like your roast, is yours.

October stared at the screen, proud of her work, tweaking a comma here, a phrase there. The story was not edgy or gritty but informative and good enough to make that week's edition.

There was only one thing missing.

A photo of the café.

She saved the article and sent it via text to Clive, ignoring his recommendation for Philip to read it.

After a few minutes, she checked her messages and cursed her impatience and self-doubt. Clive had yet to respond.

The rejection letters she'd received as a fresh young writer, a writer who so wanted to be like her mother, popped back in, her ego telling her that she was never going to be good enough. She promptly told it to keep quiet. It was then that Clive yelled to her from the other side of the partition.

"October," Clive said.

She went straight to his desk. Ready for his critique, already anticipating multiple rewrites.

"So," he said, his pen in between his teeth and his feet on his desk.

She braced for the bad news.

Clive took the pen from his teeth and began tapping it on the desk. "It's a tough business. The news. Figuring out how to make it interesting and giving all the facts at the same time. These days, it's hard to be competitive. Everybody's got a spin."

There was only one paper in town, so there wasn't any competition, but she nodded anyway as she wrung her sweaty hands.

He took his feet off the desk.

"Your article was good. We'll run it."

"That's . . . great. Thanks."

"But like I said, I want Philip to look it over."

Clive didn't have the confidence of someone who ran an entire paper; otherwise, he would have trusted his own judgment.

She sighed, but there was nothing she could do. "Of course."

"And dig a little deeper next time." He winked, and when did Clive ever wink at her like that? It was as if he was turning into someone else. A slick news guy who wanted stories with grit, not the nice person she had been working with for the past two years.

Philip, who had returned, apparently from trying out Clive's surfboard, shook his wet hair, splashing the floor, and bumped into October as she left Clive's office.

"Excuse me," she said.

He didn't seem to care or apologize for colliding with her. He slipped inside Clive's office and shut the door.

She disregarded Clive's instructions regarding Philip's critique. It wasn't that she believed she didn't need guidance—she did—but from Clive's clone?

Her eyes watered but not from tears. It must have been from the hibiscus she'd thrown in the trash near the table. She'd never enjoyed the high pollen season, and she was allergic to almost everything this time of year. Holding her nose with a finger to squelch the onset of a sneeze did the trick. She whipped out a Kleenex from the box on her desk just in case, but before she tucked it into her pocket, she dabbed a small tear from her eye.

She laid her head on her desk like a kindergarten kid who was in detention. It could have been the allergies, but she was more certain that Alice's notice and Philip's arrival were equally an issue. If Philip was going to stay there and Clive was at his mercy, then she would have to work hard to find a story so gritty that Clive would be impressed and leave Philip out of it.

Her eyes started to water again, and she blew her nose, cursing Florida plants of all kinds. In between blows, the mumble of conversation reached her from the other room. She tipped her chair to listen.

"October had a great idea about tourists," Clive said, explaining what she'd told him. His voice was easily heard through the wall. It helped that October had gotten up and was resting her ear on it.

"It's not interesting," Philip said.

"Could be though. With the right angle."

October smiled hearing some backbone in Clive's tone.

"Okay, then," Philip said. "How about we dig up the dirt? Make it a regular who's who of bad tourism."

October held her breath, waiting for Clive to answer.

"It would be bad for business, wouldn't it? I mean, we need the tourists."

"I have someone in mind," Philip said. "Someone with a past. We can send your helper out to get the story. Have her find the goods and rake this person through the coals. Your little town doesn't need that type coming here. Think of all the good it will do. Keeping the bad guys away. You'll be like newspaper cops."

October couldn't believe what she was hearing. Bad tourists? Was this some kind of joke? Her whole morning was bizarre. And she wasn't a helper. She oversaw all the ads. If it wasn't for her, there wouldn't be any money to run the paper.

"You already know someone?" Clive said. "Who is it?"

She championed her boss to ask the tough questions. To find out the truth about the new guy he had hired without any vetting.

The creak of a chair signaled that one of them had stood, the tap of a knuckle on the desk followed, then the squeaking heel of a shoe.

The swivel chair whined as she leaned forward and propelled herself back to her desk before being caught. She picked up her phone and started dialing at the first sign of Philip. The client answered on the first ring, an advertiser she had meant to reach out to before the day had gotten completely out of hand.

"October," the client said with such a pleasant voice that her shoulders lowered and her breathing returned to its natural rate.

"Hi, James."

James was her number-one client. He owned a bug-spraying business in town. He bought a quarter-page ad on the back page every month and had been a good client to the paper since he'd opened his business. The same year that October had started her job. They'd been acquaintances since, and she enjoyed it when they chatted to renew his monthly ad and collect his monthly check. The ad changed for the seasons, but not by much. So much of their conversation was about his family or his daughter's softball games.

"Can I put you down for another month?" she said.

Philip pulled out a chair next to her. She swiveled away.

"My ads used to generate business," said James. "Lately, when I ask my new clients how they found me, none of them mention your newspaper. I get my clients from my truck signs and word of mouth."

October hunched over her desk. She wanted to continue doing business with him. He paid a good amount of money, and though there was always a gamble in running ads, she knew that the paper wasn't doing a good job of keeping local interest at the top of its responsibilities. She didn't want to lose James the Bug Guy.

"We're working very hard to get better stories next month. And gain more interest. I'm working on something right now." Her words were for Philip's ears more than James's. Philip was taking over, and she needed to assert herself. She would show him what she was capable of. James remained silent—the echo of another client who was about to cancel.

She snapped her rubber band bracelet on her wrist, waiting for him to say what she knew he was going to say. That he was canceling too.

Snap, snap, snap. The last one hurt.

"Sign me up for this month. Then I'll have to see."

"Thanks, James," she said, her voice giving away her elation. "I promise we're doing everything possible to give the paper a new purpose. And we appreciate your business."

She hung up and swiveled back to the table. Philip was facing her, elbow on the desk, his cheek planted into his fist.

"I see you finished the story about tourists," he said. "Can I read it?"

"It's my piece about the Café, not the awful story you're looking for," she said.

"Do you always eavesdrop on private conversations?"

"It's not eavesdropping when you can hear through the wall."

She opened her QuickBooks account, ignoring him now, and generated an invoice for the Bug Guy's next order.

"We could work on it together," Philip said. "It will be fun."

"As fun as cleaning toilets."

Philip chuckled at this.

Her spreadsheet contained all the local businesses she worked with, information, names, numbers, and emails. She sent James a quick email with a link to his invoice, then scanned the list of her clients, determined to find a real story among them that would fit the bill for that week's edition and get her off the hook for the tourist piece Philip wanted to write. And proving to be busy might bore Philip into nonexistence.

Chief Jermain was an old friend of her father, so she picked him first. He'd always been concerned that her dad had abandoned her at sixteen to go to the West Coast without her. Along with Summer's parents, Kirt Jermain was a father figure. He answered on the first ring.

"Hi, Kirt," she said. The last time they'd talked was a couple of months ago. It made her feel secure talking to him now while Philip hung around like a bad smell. He didn't even have a pad of paper or a pen. She couldn't understand how he'd slithered into Clive's office.

"You okay?" Kirt said. The sound of his voice, like an old familiar song, made her melancholy.

"Just working. I'm looking for some ideas for a news story for the paper this week. Anything juicy on the scanner?"

"Juicy?" He chuckled at this. The only juice was that a few residents might have gotten caught in a riptide but were safe and a few of the elders from the Oaks were taken by ambulance to the hospital. "Well, Jeb Howard, the man who lives down by the golf course, lost his key and locked himself out. He missed his tee time."

She laughed at the joke.

"What about tourists? Have any of the new people in town been causing trouble? Shady dealings, that sort of thing?" she said, knowing full well the answer.

Philip shifted forward in his chair.

"Tourists?" the chief said. "No. Not a thing. What kinds of stories are you looking for? It seems extreme."

"I'm just asking, that's all. Glad things are all good."

"I have the most boring job of them all," he said. "But I'm glad about it."

October would have to disagree with him as her life proved to have little going on, at least until today. Her smile faded when no story was available, but she could honestly tell both Clive and Philip there was no story. Not about bad tourists anyway.

"Let me know if anything might be of interest," she said.

"We'll do."

They hung up, and she called the fire department, but other than the ordinary drills, there was nothing to report, except an invite for dinner, because she was single, and it might be nice for the guys to mingle. They were throwing a fish on the grill. And could she bring some of her friends?

"Another time maybe," she said.

She scratched out the police and the fire departments. There was nothing bad to report. She could rest easy. But she still needed a story. There was one more person she could call. Someone that knew everything that was going on.

"I have someone you might interview," Philip said while she was dialing, but she ignored him. She didn't want to have anything to do with him or his terrible ideas.

She dialed the number to the Seashells and Sandy Toes Salon which October and Summer frequented.

When Deanna, her hair stylist, answered, October got right to the gist of the call; otherwise, Deanna would keep her for hours with her small talk.

"It's October. And I'm looking for some new stories for the paper, and since you know everyone, maybe you could help."

Deanna took a moment before she spoke. "There's a good-looking guy that's just come to town. I saw him at the B and B while I was delivering our sunshine gift baskets. Courtney loves our trial-sized shampoos. I throw in some discount coupons and flyers. They're a big hit."

"What did he look like?" October said.

"He's got a thick head of glossy hair. Bet there's not a speck of dandruff. Great body too. I caught a glimpse of him running up the stairs. He was taking off his shirt. I think he's single. I'd love to get him in my chair if you know what I mean."

October kept quiet, thinking about Dax and the spilled coffee.

"That's not a news story, Deanna, but if you have anything else, then please let me know."

"Well, the tourists are getting much better looking."

She could entitle the series "Good Looking Tourists" instead.

It was clear. No one around town was shady. Philip was digging where there was no dirt.

"Thanks anyway," October said and then hung up. She should have booked an appointment. Her ends were splitting.

"You must see people come and go all the time, right?" Philip said. "I mean if you pay attention."

"I'm attentive," she said as she discovered a mint in the drawer, tore the crinkled paper away, and popped it into her mouth. She knew the town and who lived in it too well. Of course, she didn't know every single person. "I know enough."

But did she?

She had run into Dax and seen a woman dressed in black. Philip had arrived out of nowhere too. Not your average day at the beach.

39

Chapter 10

Bad Tourists

"Now are you convinced we should do the story?" Philip said.

She didn't understand why he had any clout.

"Bad tourists," she said. "No."

"I know you don't like it, but it's good for business. People love to hear bad news. They eat it up."

She saved all of the files on her computer, closed the laptop, and stuffed it into her backpack, along with paper and pens.

"I just don't think it's a very interesting story, Philip. I mean, locals don't care. And it's so slow this time of year. I doubt there are enough tourists to interview anyway. I think people would be more interested in what attracts people to our beach," she said. "Why they love it, what makes them come even when it's hurricane season."

"I beg to differ," he said. "And I know someone."

"Then maybe you should go find them." She threw the backpack over her shoulder. "And why don't I remember ever seeing you here before?"

He chuckled under his breath. "I guess you aren't as attentive as you think."

She ignored the comment as she walked to Clive's office door and poked her head inside.

"I'm going out," she said. "I need a photo for my story."

What she really needed was to get away from Philip, who sat at the empty desk doing nothing but analyzing his manicure. Clive was staring out the open window like a kid wishing he was somewhere else: in the sun, on the beach, a place far away. She wished he'd shut it because the humidity was thick in the room, but she said nothing.

"Did you hear me?" she said.

He gave her a thumbs-up, trusting her to do what needed to be done. She took off before another altercation with the new guy and breathed in the fresh air, hungry for peace and quiet.

When she arrived at the café again, she chose a table to set her backpack on and left it there. Bridgette was wiping down a table nearby.

"I forgot to get some photos of the place," October said. "Do you mind?"

"Sure."

"How about I get one of you in here and then a shot of the front of the building?"

Bridgette took off her apron and threw the cleaning cloth out of view, and October snapped a couple of nice shots. It was easy. Bridgette wasn't camera shy, and she was pretty and casual.

Next she went outside, crossed the street to get a broad view, and snapped a few photos. It was a cute two-story building with windows on the first floor. It had a peaked roof, and October wondered whether Bridgette lived on the second floor. The side of the building was covered with overgrown palm tree branches and a scraggly hedgerow that hadn't been pruned in years.

When she was done with the photos, October ordered a mug of coffee, and the barista recommended a new blend with notes of jasmine and berries and left room for cream and sugar. October sat down, took out her computer, and uploaded the photos to finish her article, even though she would still need to get Philip's approval, and sent a quick text to Clive with the photo and a note. When he received it, he shot back a text telling her that he was taking a break and going surfing.

She didn't want to go back in case Philip was still there, so she sipped her coffee, enjoying the quiet.

Bridgette was delivering a couple of coffees to a table nearby when October waved her over.

"I got the photos I needed," she said. "It's such a nice place. I was curious. Do you live upstairs?"

Bridgette grabbed some empty mugs from another table and wiped it clean with her cloth, then asked a woman at another table whether she needed anything else.

"What was that?" Bridgette said.

"It doesn't matter, I guess. But there is something." If October was going to get a story about a tourist, Bridgette was the one to ask. "There was a woman who came in this morning. She wore black and a lot of gold bracelets. Have you seen her again? I might like to interview her."

"So many people come in here, you know. I can't remember everyone."

"Of course. But would you remember if that hunky guy who I spilled coffee on this morning came in? His name was Dax."

Bridgette gave October a big smile. She remembered. "He hasn't come in again. Sorry."

Bridgette returned to her customers and left October there with her coffee. She wasn't about to order another. There were no story ideas, and she wouldn't see Dax again. Sitting there thinking about him was a waste of time.

Chapter 11

Bad Ideas

S logging back to the newspaper without any story ideas made her want to stop by Glen's Bakery and buy a cupcake even though she'd promised to avoid sugar that day. She ordered dark chocolate with dark chocolate buttercream frosting and ate it right there, on the spot.

Clive's surfboard was gone when she returned from enjoying the sinful decadence, but Philip was sitting at the table with nothing but his phone in front of him. It was a small weekly paper. Clive didn't need another employee to replace Alice. She knew she was capable.

"Find anything?" he said while he texted someone.

"I went to take photos."

"Of what?"

"Bridgette, and the Island Café. Why?"

"It baffles me to no end the things you are missing."

She squinted as if maybe looking at him this way would make him make sense.

"Like what?"

"It's your job to find out the things that happen within the confines of this town," Philip said. "Both day and night."

"The streets roll up at nine."

The bands at Jack's Tiki Bar were done around eleven, but she didn't bother with details.

"Let me read your article," he said.

She refused to show it to him.

"I gave it to Clive."

Philip appeared discouraged for someone who didn't have an investment in the paper or the town and kept saying things like "Pry into things," "Get some dirt," and "People aren't always who we think they are."

Thankfully, Clive appeared from the beach and said something about the waves not being any good. He took a seat on the edge of the desk near Philip.

"How's the digging going," he said. October didn't realize she needed to bring a shovel to work.

"Nothing yet," she said.

"Did Philip read your Island Café story?"

October gave in and took out her laptop to find the document.

"I don't care to read it anymore," Philip said. "It's just a puff piece."

"Puff piece?"

"Calm down," Clive said. "What else have we got?"

"You know," Philip said.

October huffed again. This was a disaster.

"Do you think a story about tourists is a good idea?" October said, pleading, hoping Clive would reconsider his terrible judgment.

The story idea was bad, and no one would want to read about the tourists who inhabited the beach in the summer months. Instead, Clive raised his thick caterpillar eyebrows and scratched his unshaven chin.

"It could work," he said.

"How about us—" she started, but Philip cut her off.

"I've been working on something," he said.

October glared as Clive read whatever it was that Philip had written and nodded.

"Interesting," Clive said.

"The case for keeping tourists out of town," Philip said.

"What?" October said. "That's a terrible idea. We have businesses that need them."

"It's edgy," said Clive. "Something we've never done before."

"Clive," October gasped, "you can't be serious."

October hated Philip for pushing this ridiculous story and even more because she didn't want to find dirt on Honeycomb Beach, not that there would be any. He was grasping at straws.

Clive appeared tired; his notable beach tan had faded, and his eyes had dark circles under them.

"I know it's not what we usually print, but let's give Philip some leeway. See what we come up with."

He left them and went into his office, but October wasn't going to let him off that easily. She sped from her desk to the door before he could shut it behind him.

"You want us to sink so low?" She stood in front of Clive while he sank into his office chair and let out a loud sigh.

"We've got no choice. So get to it."

October crossed her arms in protest, but it wasn't going to help.

"You know this isn't going to go over well, right?" she said.

"I have to find something. The paper is tanking. My father is coming after me. He says that I don't have a head for this business. He's always criticized me. Well, maybe he's right."

October knew a lot more about being criticized than she would admit. Her mother for one and the many rejection letters from publishers for another.

"And now my wife is upset with me," Clive said, "says I'm always surfing, and if I lose this paper, I'll have to move somewhere else if I want to work on another paper. Which I'm not even certain I do. My daughter goes to middle school here. She loves this place. They both do. This is our home. So yes, October, it's necessary to find something, anything that will keep us afloat. And it's got to be good."

"Or really bad," she said.

The paper was tanking. Even if they found a bad tourist or similar story, it was unlikely they could save it.

Chapter 12

Jack's Tiki Bar

After her lousy day and no luck finding any tourists or any-thing else worth writing about, October headed to Jack's Tiki Bar. She savored the sensations of a Honeycomb Beach summer evening: the sun; the salt air; the crashing waves; the sweet, newly sprouted plumeria blooms, which she loved even though her allergies were kicking up. It occurred to her that her town was a respite, a sanctuary. Before Philip had showed up, she hadn't needed anything to relax her after a day at work. And the after-hour cocktails and food with her roommate, Summer, were simply a way to finish the already boring day. The only thing that changed was the daily specials Jack added to the dinner menu.

As expected, Summer was waiting for her at their favorite spot near the bar, with a great view of the river. Sometimes, at the perfect time of year, they could watch dolphins jumping as the sun went down.

"Hey, cool girl," Summer said. Her roommate set down the Harlan Coben thriller she couldn't keep her nose out of and slung her long brown ponytail over one shoulder.

"Hey, hot girl," October said.

It had been their joke since childhood, teasing each other about the weather during their namesake time of year. Even though it was a joke, and Summer would always be the hot one, October didn't mind her thinking she was cool. Somehow, after all these years as friends, it had stuck. Summer Young and October Sinclair had been the best of friends since kindergarten. They'd grown up on the beach, and their two families knew one another. When October's mother had died and her father had drifted away to California, October moved in with the Youngs for the remainder of high school. The girls got into the same community college after graduation and got an apartment in Honeycomb Beach after that, but while Summer was happy to live in Honeycomb Beach forever, October couldn't help longing for more.

October threw down her backpack and hoisted herself onto the round barstool, tucking her feet under the railing. On the table were two tall curvy glasses of frothy pale amber garnished with a pink umbrella and a slice of banana. Their daily drink and dinner date was nice, but October would have preferred going straight home and crashing onto the old beat-up beanbag chair they'd had since college.

"I see you got the usual," October said, nodding to the banana daiquiris in front of them. Maybe she would have enjoyed some white wine or something different.

"You okay?"

She wasn't, and she had an unusual pit in her stomach.

"Just a long day," she said. "Alice quit."

"Didn't see that coming."

October hadn't either. But she'd seen firsthand the difficulties Alice had in coming up with new and interesting articles. She'd watch how Alice jotted down something on a pad of paper only to tear it up and throw it in the trash. Honeycomb Beach was a pretty boring town, aside from the occasional soda theft or fender bender, and October was bored with the way things were, but with the shakeup at the paper, she was also afraid of things being different. Alice was a few years older than October, and

Clive respected her. October wanted the chance to prove she could take on the new role and earn that respect too. But Clive's new approach . . . She was conflicted.

"What are you thinking about?" asked Summer. "You're shaking your head."

"I don't know what to do," October said and blew out a long breath. "The paper is in a jam."

"What kind of jam?"

"Clive gave me an assignment," October said. "I'm supposed to find a story. But not just any story. Something bad. Something awful."

"In Honeycomb Beach? That's never going to happen."

"That's what I said. And he gave Alice's job to some guy named Philip, and now I'm supposed to do what he says. Clive says the paper is in jeopardy. And so is my job."

Summer stopped mid-sip and then put her glass on the table.

"Wait a second. He gave Alice's job to some outsider? What the hell? And what happened to Alice anyway?"

"I don't know. He didn't say." Alice would not have approved of Clive and Philip's new angle, and if October had any inkling as to where Alice was or where she even lived, she might call her up and tell her what was going on.

The two sipped their drinks, ordered their usual tropical chicken nachos, and were silent for a few minutes while they crunched on the chips.

"I'd like to try Alice's job. But now, I'm second fiddle to some guy from who knows where. I guess he's supposed to be some writer, but I didn't see a résumé. He could be lying."

October sipped her drink and allowed the familiar smooth, fruity, and slightly alcoholic taste to relax her.

"Well, too bad about Alice," Summer said, "but at least you get to help with the stories. That's a big step from ads."

"I know. But I have to find a new story. Then I really will be the cool girl."

"October saves the newspaper."

49

October laughed at this. She hardly had the know-how to save the paper, but she might look good in a red cape. She could contact some locals, drum up new stories that Alice had missed, and turn things around. Her energy lifted.

Alice had interviewed a lot of locals. When Sarra Wilcox had come back to her hometown from Nashville, Alice had written the story from the viewpoint of a young girl. When the Surf Kings, the town's beach band, announced their retirement, Alice had written every detail of the lives of four middle-aged men and how their lives had created their love for music. The only story that she hadn't written that October knew of was the piece about the new chef at the B and B. She'd been sick. But if it was newsworthy, Alice got the job. Those stories were not plentiful though.

"Where do you think I can find tourists to interview for the story Philip and Clive want?" October said. They weren't halfway through with their drinks, and October wanted to leave. To get busy working out her plan on paper. Instead, she stayed because she always did.

"Tourists?" Summer said, staring curiously at October, as if she didn't get it.

"I'm supposed to find tourists to interview. Philip wants to call them 'bad tourists.' I hate the idea. And I don't think anyone wants to read about tourists, especially if there are bad ones. I mean, wouldn't that just scare people?"

"I don't like it either," Summer said. "And people want to read about themselves in their town, not strangers. Maybe you could do a piece about the best places to get a summer cocktail on the beach?"

"It's been done," October said.

"Or maybe a story about the Tiki Bar and how Jack started it," Summer said. "That might be cool, right?"

"Yeah, cool, but it's been done."

October sipped the last of her daiquiri until the straw sucked up nothing but bubbles. "How about," she said, "I could write a spread about Harper Originals and what the top trends for fall are on the beach?" But then she remembered that Alice had just interviewed Joannie Harper a few months ago.

"Done and done." They both said it at the same time.

"It's all been done," October said. She didn't say out loud what she was thinking. That Honeycomb Beach was a boring place to live and nothing ever happened there. It was like a broken record. *She* was a broken record. And was tired of it. And tomorrow, she would have no choice but to go and interview the tourists. And find someone who wasn't nice. She hated the idea.

"Another drink?" Summer said.

Drinks ran six-fifty apiece, and the nachos were twelve, though they split them. Every night, her bank account grew further from her goal.

"No, I think I'm going home."

"But the Summer Boys are playing here tonight. We could stay. They're pretty good."

The Summer Boys were another local band who did their best to fill the Surf Kings' void. They played every week at Jack's Tiki Bar. They were one of Summer's favorites, and October didn't think the band was all that great, but the name was what Summer loved the most. And the cute bass player. October had had no male relationships since a breakup with a college boyfriend years ago.

She'd had little interest in meeting people since her mother passed away, but it lessened further when her father left for California. Any relationship didn't feel complete. Summer had encouraged her to talk with someone about it.

"I don't need to talk to anyone. I just don't want a boyfriend," she had told her. "I want to travel. See things."

"And we're too young to have those commitments," Summer had said. They both knew she had many prospects, but over cocktails, she'd kindly agreed with October's current situation.

"Someday we'll want them, won't we?" October had said.

"Maybe. But for now, we have each other. And that's way better."

Even back then, they'd laughed and eaten from a huge plate of Jack's special tropical nachos made with coconut chicken, lime, and pineapple salsa. Just like they were doing right then. It was always the same.

October pulled herself out of the memory. "I think I should go."

"Please? Just for the first few songs. Then we'll leave. I promise."

"Sure. Okay. Just a few songs. And then I need to go home and figure out a plan for tomorrow."

It was after ten thirty when October slid off the barstool. She kissed her friend on the head, but she hardly noticed. The bass player was riffing, and the locals were going wild.

"You stay. I'll go. Have fun."

Summer probably couldn't hear October over the noise. Besides, she was busy giving the bass player take-me-home eyes like the groupie she was. And had always been.

October walked home in the dark, with the stars above to light her way. It wasn't that far, only a few blocks, and the Summer Boys played in the distance, keeping her company. The front light was on, but a shadow in the corner of the deck startled her. She crept up the stairs, and before she could make it to the last riser, a cat ran out from behind one of the chairs.

"Oreo? What are you doing here?"

She picked up the cat, who had become the town mascot ever since Courtney, the owner of the B and B, re-adopted him. He was a great mouser and catcher of the occasional grass snake. She scratched him under the chin and was rewarded with a loud purr.

"I don't have any food for you, but how about I take you home?" She set him down, tossed her backpack inside, and shut the door behind her. "Come here, buddy."

She picked him up again and started toward the Wild Honey B and B where she would deposit him on the front porch near his food and water. He didn't stir the entire way but allowed her to cuddle him and nuzzle her face into his soft black-and-white fur. She arrived at the small parking lot full of cars. Cars owned by tourists, who would use the Townie bikes, lined up next to the front steps, to enjoy the beach and the unique shops her town had to offer. A light glowed from the inside entry.

"What do you think, Oreo?" she said. "Should I take you inside, see if there are any tourists I could interview?"

The cat meowed and jumped out of her arms. He clearly disagreed with the notion of interrupting Courtney and Eric this late, even though there was a light on inside. He rushed up the stairs and began eating the food Courtney had left for him as if he hadn't caught a mouse in days. As she turned to leave, a thud came from the side of the house.

"Hello?" she said, rubbing her arms.

A figure, who must have exited the side door, turned away and headed up the path toward the riverbank, hands in pockets, head down. October strained to see who it was, but the lack of light made it impossible. Her inability to make out the details of the person in question led to frustration, so she had no choice but to follow them.

Chapter 13

Followed

The band would be wrapping up by eleven, and the perpetrator, whom October decided was a man, wasn't going south toward Jack's Tiki Bar anyway. He turned north and started toward the main road instead. To avoid being seen, she instinctively positioned herself behind a tall palm tree, a park bench, or some other object along the way to stay out of sight. The man continued on, apparently unaware of being followed.

Was this a bad tourist? It was a silly idea that made her pause, but she refused to give in to Philip's belief that her town had secrets. The town was safe. She believed with all her heart that no one would be out doing anything bad. Especially someone who was staying at the B and B. It was a quaint little respite for out-of-town guests, those who loved it here and would never come for shady dealings.

Her interest was piqued when the man walked beneath a streetlight that illuminated him briefly before he strolled into the shadow again. He was tall, maybe six feet, slim, and was wearing mid-thigh shorts, a long-sleeve shirt, and carrying a small satchel over one shoulder. One of his shoes might have been too big or too small, as a squeak penetrated the quiet night air with every other step he took. Other than the mysterious satchel, she doubted this man was in the midst of some caper. Whatever he was carrying, he appeared to drop, so she stumbled back behind a tree.

What *was* he doing? Nothing in town was open. Maybe he was one of those people who liked to do their walking at night. October didn't know any of those people.

She continued stalking him in her catlike way, eyes glued, keeping low, avoiding sudden moves that might make him aware of her presence. She remained in the darkness. When he reached the Island Café, he checked his watch and turned his head. Was that his destination?

She recognized him now. He was the handsome man from that morning.

Dax.

October contemplated possible scenarios. The obvious one was that he was meeting someone, which made her surprisingly jealous. The other less appealing choice was that he was there to break in and rob the store, take the coffee beans and all of Bridgette's hard-earned money. Clearly, Clive and Philip had put those images there, and she shook them off. Dax must have left something at the Island Café that he wouldn't be able to live without until Bridgette came, unlocked the door, and allowed him in to retrieve it.

As she stood near the Welcome to Honeycomb Beach sign, holding her breath, October watched Dax turn his head from south to north, from east to west. He appeared unaware of her, and before she could breathe out, he disappeared into the thick hibiscus bushes to the side of the café, the side of the building that could not be seen from the road.

She rushed from her spot by the sign to the corner of the building, her heart slamming into her chest at the potential danger of it all. It was surprisingly energizing.

Without thinking twice, she slid between the hibiscus bushes and bit her tongue to silence a remark when a branch tore at her arm. Dax had disappeared.

When muffled voices startled her, she moved back into the hedges even more to avoid being seen. The bushes rustled as she wedged herself away like a child playing hide and seek, crouching down beneath the shrubs, her bare legs prickly from the thick branches. She stayed there but forced a branch out of the way, hoping to gain sight of who was coming. The night didn't scare her, only the creepy crawlies that might be inside the brush with her. Her arm throbbed from a scratch, but it was no match for her beating heart and heavy breath that she concealed with her hand.

"Did anyone see you?" It was a man's voice coming from somewhere far above October's head as she crouched, frozen in the hibiscus.

"No." A woman's voice said. It was hushed and barely audible, and October leaned through the bushes enough to make out a pair of thick calves on bare legs. The flashlight that the woman carried aimed down, and the light swung around her feet so that October could make out her shoes. The woman's calves grew even larger as she raised on tiptoes, and then there was a rattle of a ladder.

Shadows danced on the ground while the pair of feet stepped onto the first rung. The ladder tapped against the siding, and October imagined the woman climbing to the top. Curious to see whether her instincts were correct, she thrust her head between more branches and looked up just as the woman made it to the top, straddled the window ledge, and disappeared inside.

She checked her Apple watch, hiding the face with one hand so the light could only be seen within her cupped palm. It was just shy of eleven o'clock.

Her interest shifted to the time. Eleven o'clock. One of the strange notations in Alice's file was the time. Finally, October understood. The times Alice had recorded weren't the café's hours or the time Bridgette was available. The time was now. Alice must have witnessed something like this. But she hadn't given October any more clues. Something strange was going on in the attic. And October was going to find out what it was.

56

Chapter 14

The Ladder

S he stepped between the branches and found the ladder that had been lowered for the woman to ascend. Dax must have been the man at the top, but someone must have gotten up there to begin with. Through the front door?

Her head was spinning. It was exhilarating. Something mysterious was taking place in her boring hometown, and she was witnessing it. It almost made her forget about her terrible day.

Adrenaline poured through her body, a wave of excitement she hadn't felt in ages. This was dangerous. A good reporter would get to the bottom of this. Two people, maybe more, were secretly meeting in the tiny attic of Bridgette's coffee shop. She supposed that answered the question of whether Bridgette lived up there. Obviously not.

She took a deep breath and gathered her thoughts. Tomorrow night, October would return and collect more data for her article. Photos would be necessary; dark clothing would be essential.

If she brought this to Clive, he would tell Philip. And she didn't want him to know anything. Not yet. He would take the story for himself. For now, she would keep it to herself.

Before she could get away from the side of the building and head out to the street by way of the bushes, something overcame her so readily that she stopped and held her nose with her fingers. She placed the tip of her tongue on the roof of her mouth and squeezed her eyes shut. The force that was trying to expel the pollen from the hibiscus blossoms was more than she could withhold. She made one more attempt, but the sneeze was imminent, and before she had time to reach into her pocket and remove her Kleenex, it was too late.

"Ahhhhchooooo!"

The window above her opened.

"You're late." It was pitch dark, and she couldn't see the person above her head, only darkness. "Hurry up."

October had two choices. One was to run away. They didn't know who she was. The other choice was to climb the ladder and see what happened.

What would life look like if she took this chance? What if something new and exciting was about to happen? October grabbed a rung of the ladder firmly with both hands and pulled herself up, climbing slowly, not knowing what she would face at the top. When she got to the last rung, she peered in the window. The man she'd met that morning was staring back at her.

"Dax?" she said.

He looked different. His hair was untamed, giving him a creative appearance, a far cry from his perfect locks from the coffee shop meeting. He wore a dark-blue satin shirt with onyx buttons, and the tapered sleeves showcased his slender frame, the cufflinks shaped like dragon heads glinting at his wrists. He wore a large ring with a symbol that she didn't recognize.

Without a word, he helped her inside the window ledge, steadying her as she stepped across it and planted both feet on the floor. They stood in a tiny alcove, with a shred of light coming through the window from a faraway streetlight. The old driftwood floor creaked from their weight, and the walls echoed the sound. Overwhelmed by Dax's stare, she lowered her eyes, noticing floorboards that hinted at a trapdoor from the café beneath.

They stood close, and the warmth of his skin against hers sent tingles along her arms. A tangible aura surrounded her.

"What is this place?" she said.

Without a word, Dax turned toward a wooden door and knocked three times as she watched and waited for a secret to be revealed. When the door opened, they were met by a large man with a shiny bald head, wearing star-shaped glasses and a feather boa around his neck.

"This is not Natalia," he said.

"No. But she's the one I told you about."

What did he know about her? October hesitated, revisiting her decision to be there, though it was far too late to make a run for it.

"Tell me your mother's name," the bald man said.

She gulped air, confused as to what this all meant. What did he need to know about her mother? Her pulse leaped, and she drew a hand to her throat to catch her breath.

"Why?"

"It's all right," Dax said. "You can tell him."

She trusted him for some reason.

"Lillian Sinclair."

"And what is the name of the book she wrote?"

"*When the Night Leaves You*," she said, and he nodded, her answer correct.

"Has Natalia turned up?" he said to Dax as if he'd forgotten that October was there.

"Not yet."

"You go. I'll stay by the window," said the man.

Dax guided October through the doorway into a room bathed in a soft, golden glow from flickering candles and small table lamps. She counted three small round tables, each with a thick pad of paper and pens at every seat.

A tranquil melody of wind chimes and flutes floated through-out the room, a soothing element that might have calmed her had she not been so nervous. October attempted to get her bearings and met eyes with a woman wearing a celestial-inspired wrap along with dangling earrings in the shape of planets. Dax stood nearby and placed a hand on her shoulder.

"This is October Sinclair," he said to the woman. "Our newest member."

"Member?" October said. She was having regrets about climbing up that ladder now. She should have run instead. What was this place? And a member of what?

October prided herself on knowing every inch of her town. The mundane landscape, almost always sunny, humid, and seasonally hot. The beautiful blue-green ocean was ever present, never changing except from one tide to the next. The slow roll of crashing waves onto silky smooth sand that might be bogged with sargassum in the winters. But even that was normal. Expected. And the businesses were popping up, certainly giving way to a new future for the town, but the people were the same. Kind and friendly, and other than a few events taking place year after year, the town remained unchanged. Nothing she wouldn't recognize on any given day. But at that moment, she sensed urgency inside her. To start paying better attention.

"Welcome," the woman in the wrap said. "I'm Korta."

October nodded.

"There are four of us," Dax said. "You make five."

"What do you do here?" she finally asked.

Dax stared at the woman with the planetary earrings and crossed his arms, revealing his cufflinks.

"You don't know?" he said.

She didn't. It was late at night, and she wished she had minded her own business and was back at the house with Summer watching a movie.

"No, I don't know. But I'm certain you're about to tell me."

She closed her eyes and waited for her fate.

Chapter 15

Fate

The man named Dodge came back into the room and stepped toward her, pushed his glasses onto his bald head, and told her the answer.

"We're the members of the Secret Scribes. An author's group. We all come here at night to focus on our books."

October relaxed, shedding the fear. They weren't going to harm her. They were writers.

"Couldn't you just write at the library?" October said.

"We like to keep it hush-hush," Korta said, and October recognized her voice as the woman who'd climbed the ladder while she watched from the hibiscus. She glanced at her calves.

"It's a tradition that started years ago," a man named Dodge said. "We come here for one week. Every year. And we have an extra chair open. And we want you to have it."

The woman with the celestial wrap moved in closer. "We adored Lillian. So sorry for your loss."

"Thank you," she said, her gut wrenching at the words she'd hoped never to hear again. The old wounds were opening once more. October's loss was of a mother who didn't think her daughter had any talent as a writer.

"You knew my mother?"

They nodded.

October gazed at the strangers, trying to envision her mother being here with them.

"I don't remember seeing any of you before," she said. She racked her memory to position them somewhere she would have frequented, like Glen's Bakery or the Tiki Bar. That morning appeared to be the first time she'd caught sight of them.

"She's finally here," Dodge said.

October turned and recognized the woman she'd seen that morning. In the café. Her dark hair and cloak were elegant yet frightening. The gold bracelets clacked together as she walked through the door.

"I see you didn't start without me," the woman said.

"This is Natalia," Dax said.

"Notoriously late as usual," Dodge added.

The woman they called Natalia was poised but remained cool. As if the dark wardrobe had sucked any lightness out of her.

"Hi." October offered a weak smile, but instead of returning pleasantries, Natalia walked past her to her seat at the far end of the room.

"We come for one week every year," Dodge said, ignoring Natalia's poor manners. "To finish our books. We write for hours every night until we finish our manuscripts. Then, we go home, and it's as if we were never here."

"Poof," the woman in the wrap said.

She was an older woman, maybe in her sixties, and October gave her credit for climbing the ladder and hiking herself over the window.

The woman smiled with stern eyes. "Were you in the hibiscus bushes?"

"No. I— No."

She didn't dare tell the truth.

"I like your, uh, costume," October said.

"It's all part of the charm."

The man named Dodge whipped the feather boa around his neck and took a bow. "We get into costume because it helps us write."

October couldn't imagine her mother wearing a costume to write, but her mother was more mysterious than she realized.

"And my mother. She was part of all of this?"

"Every year," Dodge said. "We adored Lillian. And her romantic novels were to die for." Immediately, he stopped short, using the inappropriate term. "Sorry, we just loved her writing so much. It was well received."

Her mother was proud of her achievement and based on the twenty thousand dollars she'd left October, there must have been substantial royalties, but October had been too young to understand the details of publishing. Lillian's accolades had made the mother-daughter relationship more distant, and the relationship her parents had had was shaky at best.

"My mother wrote one book," October said, shrugging as if it was no big deal. "But her novel was a one-hit wonder."

The others laughed.

"She was much more than one hit," Dax said.

October stood quiet, trying to process all that was transpiring there before her. It was like an obscure dream that needed dissecting the next morning to figure out exactly what it meant.

"It appears that she doesn't understand," Dodge said.

"It appears so," said Korta.

"Okay, what's happening?" October said.

Natalia appeared from her table and joined her fellow writers. The velvet fabric created a soft sound, her bangles colliding as she walked.

"Your seat is coveted," Natalia said. "Others would gladly accept the challenge and privilege of being here. Your mother wanted you to have it. Are you good enough?"

October swallowed hard. She didn't believe that she was.

"You kept it empty? For me?"

Dodge cleared his throat.

"Before Lillian passed away all those years ago," Dodge said, "she left strict instructions, that if ever you came to us, we'd allow you in the group. We've been keeping the seat open."

October shook her head. It wasn't true. Her mother hated her writing. She criticized it, and because of that, along with a heaping pile of rejection letters, October had stopped writing novels altogether.

"I'm not a writer," she said. "My mother was the creative one, but I was never good enough."

"See, I told you," Natalia said, waving her hands. Her dramatic nature suited her.

"Great writing takes time," said Dax. "And your mother clocked thousands of hours. You can learn. We'll teach you."

October could hardly digest this new information. Lillian Sinclair didn't need to come to a place like this late at night to write. She had a beautiful study at home, under large windows, overlooking the ocean. She was very introverted. October had put aside her desire to follow in her mother's footsteps long ago. And what about the newspaper? It wasn't the best job, but she didn't want it to fail either.

"There must be a mistake," October said. "She wasn't like . . ."

"Us?"

October had to admit that they were all slightly eclectic. It appeared they had all come to a Halloween party rather than an author's club. She was underdressed in her normal clothes.

"Your mother came to us because she wanted to write in private. Under a pseudonym."

"She used another name?"

"It was A. J. White," Dodge said. "She was a brilliant writer. We were all thrilled when she became successful with *When the Night Leaves You*, but her true passion was romance."

October slid back into her teens. Her mother was standing in the kitchen, staring out the window, pondering something there, her eyes focused on the space before her, in a trance. Her father slipped next to her and gave her a peck on the cheek, which her mother sidestepped. Her parents did not share a love like that.

They appeared to be more like roommates. And October always hoped that they would show affection in some way. Hold hands, sit next to one another on the sofa in front of the fire, or share an embrace. Things that make most children shudder. But she would have given anything to know whether they'd ever loved one another.

"I can't imagine my mother writing romance," she finally said, almost to herself.

"Well, she did. You can read her e-books at several online bookstores. You'll love them."

"She wrote more than one?"

"Twenty, I'd say. Maybe more."

The group of authors chatted about the facts of October's mother's books, leaving her outcast, wishing she had known more about her.

When they finished, Dax led October to a chair and pulled it out. With a bit of trepidation, she sat, slowly, cautiously, not thoroughly committed to the idea of staying. Taking a seat meant consequences. A terminal writing career, like an illness. Lillian Sinclair may have been a published author, but she didn't have a life. It was devoid of love and friendship. She wrote all the time. She barely had time to do her hair and makeup each morning. The other consequence was more severe. It meant bowing to her mother and not taking charge of her own life. Her mother had the last word. Saying "Sit in this chair and write." Was that the future October wanted?

After taking the seat, she grabbed her phone out of her bag and began searching for A. J. White online, not ready to believe this new truth.

"What are you doing?" Dodge said. He grabbed the phone out of her hand. "Not here. We do not use phones, take pictures, post to social media, search for ideas, use a thesaurus app, or check text messages. This space is to write. And that's it."

October shrank at the reprimand.

"Sorry."

He handed her back her phone, and she slipped it in her bag, eyes burning.

"Don't worry about it," Dax said. "Dodge is like this the first night. He'll relax."

To avoid the senseless old man, she searched the room. It was a good way to collect the data that she needed for her article. Small table lamps, three tables, five chairs. A coffee pot in the back corner, with five mugs and a carton of half and half. Sugar packets. Was that a radio? For an unfinished space that must have been used for storage, it was comfortable, though a bit cramped for five people, and would probably get hot by the end of the night. A faded green sofa, with sagging cushions, looked out of place on the opposite wall. Maybe Bridgette had intended to put it in the café but ran out of room.

"How did I not know about any of this?" she said.

"We keep our heads down," Dodge said, still standing too close, appearing to have relaxed already. "It's much more fun that way."

October didn't think he looked like a person who could have fun. The boa feathers were a costume maybe, but she didn't buy the lightheartedness of this man.

Dax sat opposite her at the small table, but their pads of paper were almost touching. She would be staring across the table at him all night. Good reason to keep her head down and write something.

"Where do you stay? To keep a low profile?" she said, wanting more information for the story she was bound to write about them.

"Airbnbs and the Wild Honey B and B," Dax said. "They keep it under wraps."

October knew where Dax was staying, having followed him there. Clive had mentioned seeing tourists around. And this morning, she'd seen Dax and the woman with the black coat and the gold bracelets getting coffee, but it hadn't sent signals about anything like this.

"Where are you from?" October said.

"That's none of your business," Natalia piped up from the back. "We need to write."

"I'm from Washington state," Dax said. He looked at the others, but no one else offered her more.

"Why only a few then? You could have a larger group."

"It's a select club," Dodge said. "You have to be invited."

"We write to get our books finished," Natalia said. "I think we've talked enough."

"But how—" October started.

"We just need everyone to be quiet about this," Dodge said with a glance at Natalia. "Like Natalia said, we are here to write. And we all must be diligent. We must produce the work. Everyone is responsible for a very high word count. We review each other's work when we're through and to high standards. Many writers want in, but most of us have been here from the beginning, and unless we decide not to write anymore, no one else gets to join."

Natalia made a sound from her table. Coughing into her hand.

"Your mother said you were talented," Dodge said.

This caught at October's throat.

"She never said that to me." October held her emotions tight. Of the years she'd spent trying to please her mother, she never had.

"Maybe it's because you weren't writing what you love. You can always tell when an author writes to please others and not to please themself," Dodge said.

October had submitted her novellas and even an entire manuscript to an agent, and she had been proud of her work. The novel was a literary piece about war and family fortune. They didn't want it. It was the last thing she ever wrote.

Assuming she did want to be a member of this secret author's club, it would mean hard work. And she had a job besides. And Alice had quit. Her responsibilities were building. As the authors took their seats, she had moments to object. She was torn. Here was an opportunity. To write. And it was only for a week.

Dodge stood at his table only an arm's length away.

"Do you take the oath to keep us a secret?" he said.

She stared at the feathers around his neck.

"Do you pledge to come every single night for the next week and pour your heart and your soul into your writing?"

She stood up straight, shoulders back, and imagined holding up her right hand.

This was it. She could stand up and say no. That she didn't have the energy. Which was a lie. She had plenty. She was young. But would she want to spend the rest of her life committing a week every single year? What about travel? What if her itinerary happened to conflict with the group? Or what if she moved? Would she travel back to Honeycomb Beach every single year for the rest of her life for the club? If one decided not to be a member, what happened?

"I don't know if I can."

Dax and the rest of the authors were silent.

"Someone else will gladly take your place," Natalia said.

"Oh, she'll come around," Dodge said.

"She must decide now," Korta said. "We have to get writing."

Her head was spinning. She wanted to join, but the real reason for her hesitancy was that she didn't know whether she could keep a secret. Alice had already started to find the pieces of a story. And now, with the shakiness of the paper and Clive insisting that she get a story, this story about the secret club might save the paper.

This was the story Alice had intended to tell. Her notes described the round tables, the low lighting, and the window. Alice knew. But why hadn't she said so before she left? October was the new Alice. Didn't the town have a right to know? She'd be a superstar. Advertisers would love it. "The Secret Scribes Society Revealed by October Sinclair" would save the day. Her desire to tell this story kicked in. Best of all, Philip would be fired. It was all the perfect solution.

Then why did she suddenly feel sick inside?

"We're waiting," Dodge said.

She could hear her heart pounding.

"I'll do it," she said with a wince. This decision should have been a happy one. But it wasn't.

Dax reached over the table and patted her hand. "Now can we finally begin?" he said.

October avoided his gaze, ashamed for wanting to use the opportunity for a story, but it was what reporters must do. Get the facts at all costs. They were only going to be there for one week. What harm would it do? By the next year, the locals would have forgotten all about it. There would be another news story to tell.

Dodge stood behind his chair. Like a master of ceremonies.

"Writers," Dodge said, "prepare to write your stories. We will write for fifty-five minutes and a five-minute break, then continue to write that way until four thirty. Write with your heart and your soul. The world is counting on you to tell your stories. We are all important. No story is too trivial."

While Dodge sank into his chair, the rustling of pads of paper and pens being clicked dispersed through the small quiet room. The low ambient music was there, but not overly annoying. October didn't like to listen to anything while she wrote.

"I don't have a story idea," October said to Dax, who held his pen in waiting like a sprinter in position to run, waiting for the gun to go off.

"Write what comes to you," he said.

"But—"

"Begin."

When Dodge said the word, the authors began like a classroom of students being instructed to start a test. The noise got a little louder now. Toes tapped, paper shuffled, fingers snapped, and bodies shifted in their seats as the authors scratched out their stories onto their pads of paper. The light music was necessary; otherwise, she would have been too distracted to write anything at all.

October picked up the pen and held it in her right hand. She twirled the smooth tool, feeling its weight, a nice pen, not the cheap plastic kind she had in her desk at the newspaper.

She pondered scenarios and story ideas while tapping the pen on a tooth.

Dax glanced away from his work, nudging her to start something.

She scratched out her name and doodled a little while watching him churn out his story in the dimly lit room, simply instructing his pen to write a fully fleshed-out story from his thoughts. She remembered how easily it had come when she was young, before she had been rejected. Criticized. The stress of the new club, of learning about her mother, of being among talented authors made it difficult to collect her thoughts. If only she'd had time to prepare. If Dax had told her that morning about this.

There was no clock, and she didn't dare fetch her phone, but she imagined the time was going as slowly as a sea turtle struggling up the beach in the sand. Hours remained.

"The Author's Society." She wrote the title of the article she would submit to Clive. That was her story. It wasn't fiction, it was fact.

Dax was concentrating on his writing, but she placed her hand over the page to ensure he wouldn't see it if he happened to look her way.

The Secret Scribes Society, by October Sinclair.

She began the first sentence, and a pang of guilt churned in her stomach.

The second story of the Island Café in Honeycomb Beach is more than an empty attic; it is a sanctum for four writers bound not by convention but by the unspoken unity of their craft. In their hands, fully fleshed stories are born. Here, amidst the coffee cups, scents of jasmine and spice, and the scratch of pens, stories come alive, waiting for the world to read them.

They dress in costumes appropriate to their stories. Dax, the handsome one, whose fingers are long and slender, dresses in a sumptuous purple satin shirt, adorned with dragon cufflinks with fiery eyes. He writes with an aura of mystique, and as fluid as the shirt he wears, each stroke of his pen is effortless, like a wizard weaving spells into narratives.

Dax tipped his head as he wrote, and his eyes caught hers. She sucked in her breath, but he simply smiled and got back to his work. She studied the table nearby and continued.

Korta the Greek and the oldest woman in the group, is draped in a celestial cape and planetary earrings. She writes with a desire that could only be inspired by the cosmos. Now and then, she hums to herself, appearing both otherworldly and grounded, while spinning tales that transcend earthly bounds.

At the helm of the group is Dodge, the self-proclaimed master of ceremonies. His feather boa and commanding presence set the stage for their gatherings. With a sharp tongue and an even sharper mind, Dodge orchestrates the flow of creativity, ensuring order and production.

Dodge noticed her staring at him as she wrote the description. His eyes were serious, like a father. Head down, she continued, her hand shaking as she wrote for fear of him reading what she had written. Would they share their writing at the end? Her face was warm to the touch, and her palms started to perspire. Her mission was to gather the details of the evening. She would jot down one more detail before switching to fiction, in case they asked what she was writing about.

Natalia.

October turned her attention to the woman in the back of the room, summing her up as a recluse, who cloaked herself in a long black cape, bracelets clinking on the page.

"Five minutes," Dodge said.

The last author writes with dark introspection, a character within her own story, whose fiction would keep any reader on edge, pulling them into her shadowy tales as she wrote under the flickering light.

"Time for our first break." Dodge stretched his arms above his head and shook out his wrists.

October rolled the pages of her article over, revealing a fresh blank page.

The authors leaned back from their work, stretching, groaning.

Dax stood and adjusted his belt, then walked around the small table and stood behind her.

"How'd it go?" he said.

"I got something written."

"How many words?"

She didn't know she was supposed to count or even how many words in fifty-five minutes would be acceptable.

"Not enough, I imagine. How many did you write?"

"We strive for a thousand every fifteen minutes."

That would be impossible, even for a seasoned writer. His pad was page after page of writing, and he would be onto the second pad of paper before the next break. She had only a couple of pages written.

"That's not human," she said.

He laughed.

"You'll get in the groove."

She got up for coffee, but Dodge blocked her.

"What's your story about?" he said, coming so close that she could feel a feather tickle her arm.

She had to think fast. Or be caught.

"The Pirate Princess."

"Ah, we have an adventure writer among us. Is it a historical recounting?"

Her nerves made her mute. Dodge waited, but she couldn't answer. She had written nothing yet. This is what she had been afraid of. The questioning, the ridicule.

"Coffee?" Dax said, pulling her away from Dodge.

Dax yanked her from the conversation. When Dodge started to chat with Korta, she breathed again.

"Thanks for saving me," she said.

"He just enjoys talking about fiction. It wasn't a test."

"Felt like one."

The authors congregated around the coffee pot, each with a mug. There were so many questions. Did Bridgette supply the coffee? How did the first to arrive get in? Who supplied all the pens and paper? Who cleaned up afterward?

October didn't dare to ask or be found out.

"How do you know what to write?" she said. The question was for Dax, but the others turned when she spoke.

"I write what I love," Korta said. "Planets, other worlds, science. I was a teacher before I became a full-time writer. It's in my veins."

"We all have our interests," Dax said. "You have a passion for adventure."

For the first time that night, she felt authentic.

"Yes," she said. "I do."

"Then write all about it," Dodge said. "Your pirate adventure will be a hit. Get it down fast. Don't hold back."

"Write what you love," Korta said.

Dodge finished his coffee and made his way to his table, and the others finished up and followed suit.

When he gave the signal, they all started again.

And October had a new sense of energy that she hadn't had the first hour. She would start a novel. Something she loved and had permission to write with abandon. All her reservations about her ability melted when her pen hit the page.

Chapter 16

Pirate Princess

When October was just a girl, her father would take her to the beach to collect shells. While he skipped stones into the ocean, he told her tales about long-ago relics resting on the seabed, some of them discovered just off the coast. About pirates, and how gold had been buried out at sea when fleets of ships went missing in the hurricanes.

October closed her eyes and imagined her character. A spunky young woman, privileged, but suppressed by the times she lived in, who would abandon her town to go to America, where adventure awaited her, leaving her old life behind. An Italian village appeared, as did the sounds and smells of the seacoast.

With the first word, October immersed herself in that world and delved into the story of a character she called . . .

Rose.

Denovelli, the small, picturesque village of rolling hills and ocean, bursts with color in June. The Italian stone walls stand in sharp contrast to the cascade of hot-pink bougainvillea draping the tall buildings. Men rush toward the docks to prepare the sailing vessels. My husband, Captain Daniel Montagna, can be heard barking orders at the crew. I scratch the high collar of my cotton dress and hold the parasol above my head to block the sun, though I doubt its rays could penetrate my gloved, hatted, and gowned figure. Every inch of me squirms, yearning to strip off my attire and dive into the clear, cerulean ocean to swim to freedom.

Freedom.

"Captain!" a young man sings at the top of his lungs. "We are almost ready."

I watch my husband, so full of himself, his dark features, fitted trousers, and crisp white shirt with a high collar making him stand out among the ranks. He is clean-shaven and fit, towering above them, proudly ruling over the others as he motions to them with his cap in hand.

He nods, and the young men scatter as he boards his ship. I walk toward the edges of the pier, driven more by boredom than interest. Already, I know this ship by heart. Daniel is also there more for show than substance, but he commands their respect. And he has it.

I used to respect my husband, but he has shown nothing but contempt for me, and now I'm tired. If only I could get on that ship and sail away.

My husband will be wanting children soon, and I've done my best to stave off his appetite by pretending to be sick or giving him too much drink so that he drifts off to sleep before he might have me. But he will demand an heir, and even though I desire a family of my own, I would never subject my children to him. This is my vow.

A forceful gust of wind catches my parasol, tugging me toward land. I step on a thick rope and tumble backward. A hand cups my back.

"There," he says.

I peer into the depths of his eyes, deep green like the emeralds on my grandmother's necklace, and imagine I'm swimming in his soul.

"Thank you."

I regain my balance, watching him go, curious as to who he is. He boards the ship and gives me a stare from the deck. I glance away, as I must be notably blushing. The breeze dies down, but I can still feel the darkness of the strong wind, begging it to take me away.

I've traveled down to the docks this morning, not to watch Daniel work—I have no interest in that, though it's a good ruse—but to learn the last details about the ship, the sailing schedule, and the layout, because tonight I plan on boarding that ship at midnight and stowing away until it reaches America.

By 4:25 a.m., October had written more pages than she thought possible, as Rose continued her journey. Several cups of strong coffee helped propel her to the end of a scene, and now she had a place to end. Rose would be ready to take that journey in the next chapter.

"See everyone tomorrow," Dodge said. The authors left their stories there, but October slipped hers into her backpack, leaving the new pad of paper on the table. There was evidence she didn't want Dodge to see. She was prepared to stand up for herself, but he didn't question her motive.

She followed Dax and Korta back to the window, and Dax lowered the ladder. Dodge remained, the first one there and the last to leave.

Another detail to add to her new story.

Chapter 17

Late

October tucked herself into bed at four forty-five in the morning and drifted off to sleep. Her dreams churned up images of her mother, writing, planets and dragons, feathers and gold. She dreamed of a woman named Rose, who was escaping her terrible husband by boarding a ship and stowing away under an old blanket full of holes. Rose could see a man on the ship, his tall lanky body walking across the bow, ordering the men around. There was gunfire now, loud banging in the distance, and Rose took cover once again, under the blanket.

"Wake up."

Rose tucked herself even more tightly beneath the blanket as the sound of pounding became more and more apparent.

"October."

The banging continued, and finally, Rose dissolved and was replaced by the sun pouring into the room. October groaned and turned over and pulled the covers up to her ears.

"Go away."

"Fine. Be late."

October opened one eye and then the other. The sun was shining into her eyes.

"What time is it?" she said.

"It's after eight."

"What?"

October shot up out of bed and checked the clock again. Summer was right. She had overslept and was late for work. In the last two years of working full-time at the newspaper, she had never once been late. Clive had entrusted her with the key because she was always on time. Always. He was never going to give her Alice's job and get rid of Philip if she couldn't handle it. She promised herself that she would never oversleep again. Even if that meant going directly from the Secret Scribes' Society to shower, change, and consume an entire pot of coffee after that. When she opened the door to her bedroom, Summer was on the other side in full makeup, a blowout, and wearing a hot-pink maxi dress with flip-flops.

"Here," Summer said, stuffing a hot cup of coffee into October's hand.

The thought of more coffee made her feel ill.

"Are you sick?"

"No. I just got to bed late." October couldn't give Summer the details of her evening, and she wished they could sit and have their morning coffee and talk about it, but they couldn't. One, there was no time to waste, and two, she had been sworn to secrecy. For now.

Summer left her there. No questions asked. She was glad there wasn't time for an inquiry.

October rushed to get ready, skipped the shower, but layered some deodorant under her arms, dry shampooed her blond hair, and threw on the first items that went together, no time to dress like a tourist in Italy. She grabbed a wrapped tuna sandwich she'd prepared several days before and headed out the door. By the time she got to the paper, her top was wet with sweat and her lungs were burning.

Philip was waiting outside, smoking a cigarette, the smoke curling from his fingertips.

"It's about time," he said. "Late night?"

Captain Daniel Montagne. But not as handsome.

Maybe she should thank Philip for giving her the idea for her antagonist, Rose's tyrant of a husband. She smiled at him, throwing him off. He smashed out his cigarette and followed her inside.

October unlocked the door, turned on the lights, and continued with her morning routine, opening the paper blinds and the door to Clive's office to allow some light to flow in. She took out her sandwich and popped it into the little refrigerator.

Philip sat down in his chair and took out his phone.

She worked around him without acknowledgment, sliding into her chair, opening her spreadsheets, and listing clients to contact. She, unlike him, had a job to do.

When Clive arrived, he went directly to his office without saying good morning to either of them.

October, happy to see that Clive had shown up rather than taken another half day off, clicked on an email from one of her reputable advertisers, ready to start doing the job she had been hired for. If advertisers kept quitting, it wouldn't matter what kinds of stories they wrote. She sighed when she read another email that was too familiar.

"We regret that we are canceling all our ads for lack of interest in the newspaper. It's been our pleasure . . ." She read the rest, but it was bad news. She had close connections with her clients. She remembered their birthdays and how old their children were. And she would miss them.

The paper was in serious trouble. Would her article about the Secret Scribes' Society be enough to save it?

Philip sat at his side of the table, thumbing a text while October buried her Secret Scribes idea in the folder labeled "Island Café" and shoved it in the drawer.

"October, would you come here for a moment?"

Clive stood near his office door and waved her in. "You too, Philip."

The two followed him to his office, and he motioned for them to take a seat. October did as he instructed and sat in the chair opposite his desk, but Philip hung back and leaned against the doorframe.

"I've given this serious thought, and I want you to work together on the tourist story."

"But I—" she started until Philip sliced through her sentence.

"I agree," Philip said. "I've read the past few issues. They were boring. News is supposed to bleed."

"Bleed?" October said.

Clive nodded and clicked his pen. Other than it being an aid for a nervous twitch, October had barely seen him use it to write anything.

"I saw someone this morning," Clive said. "I'd just gotten back from my early run as someone entered the door right next to mine. Dark coat, sunglasses. I was about to say hello, but she slipped inside before I got the chance.

"What did she look like?" Philip said, coming into the room now where October could see him.

"Hard to say," Clive said. "It was pretty dark."

It was most likely Natalia.

"Maybe she'd like to be left alone," October said. "She might have just moved in."

"Let's check it out," said Philip.

"Clive," said October in exasperation. "I don't think—"

"Glad you agree. Now go and find this tourist."

October knew where Clive lived. Philip didn't.

So when he followed her out the door, ready to divide and conquer, she acted uncertain of her whereabouts, even though she'd grown up there and knew every inch of the beach.

"I think it's this way," she lied, traveling west inside of east.

"I thought he lived on the beach."

"Oh, he used to, but now he lives inland. Down toward the Oaks."

Philip followed her on foot but began to lose interest.

"Is it far?" he said.

"Oh, about a mile. Maybe more."

80

He scuffed and stopped in the middle of the sidewalk. He was a thin man, but he didn't appear to exercise, as his chest heaved from the short walk they'd already taken, and beads of sweat dripped down his forehead. He took off his backpack and placed it on the ground.

"Do you want me to just go?" she said.

He didn't. She knew that he was dying to get this story, even though she didn't know why he was so interested.

"I want to read your notes," Philip said.

"Of course."

Philip grabbed his overstuffed backpack; its zipper was about to break. He walked a while, then waved down a local car for a ride back to the newspaper.

Her plan had worked. October turned, walked up one of the side streets, and then crossed to the beach where Clive lived. Whatever Philip thought he needed; she was not going to get. But she told Clive she would cover the story, and she would report something, even if it meant going against his wishes.

Clive's idea about tourists had gotten to her, and she cursed his name more than once while she walked back to the condos. The *Honeycomb Beach Times* was once a professional tribute to the town, full of events and interesting stories. Clive had let it go when his father retired. When her parents were around, they'd looked forward to the newspaper, as had many of the residents of the small beach town. But now, locals were more interested in Facebook and podcasts than they were in a newspaper. Maybe it was time for them to quit now that Alice was gone. Clive had attempted to keep his father's dream alive, but it was never Clive's dream.

October compared Clive's dream with her own and how her mother wanted October to be a writer, even keeping a seat open at the table. Did she want it? Or would she end up like Clive? Frustrated and struggling to find his calling and a future he enjoyed.

The paper was swimming in bills; they were using ancient software to write and publish their stories; and they continued to use inkjet printers when digital would have been far more cost-effective. It wasn't working.

And now this.

Creating terrible stories just to keep the locals' attention.

Chapter 18

The Tourist

October walked across the street, down the stairs between the dunes, and took off her sneakers. She passed the tackle shop, prominent beach homes, and a stretch of oat grass. She soaked up her surroundings. Philip's awful voice told her to pay attention.

She didn't want to listen, but the more she looked, the more she saw changes. The sand was wet from where the tide had come in, appearing much higher than it had been several years ago. The jagged dunes, sliced from the high waves, were eroding as the environmentalists had said they would. Yesterday, she hadn't thought twice about her town, but today, she made an effort to see it through the eyes of someone with more curiosity. The Beachside Grille sparkled, and the sand-caked windows were finally cleaned. A bright-green umbrella stood on the deck, a replacement for the faded one. She continued her walk down the beach, getting a seagull's view, a witness to small changes but changes nevertheless everywhere she looked.

When the stark white concrete buildings appeared, they reached up toward the clear blue sky. There were flowers on the balconies, and a bird perched on the peak of one of the flagpoles. The doors were painted in fruit-flavored colors: peach, mango, papaya. Clive's door, which she remembered as yellow, made her think of a honeydew melon.

The door next to Clive's was red. Strawberry. Or Blood.

Natalia would be sleeping and might not answer at all.

October didn't want to disturb her. She was there to write. She stood in front of the red door and waited, internally rehearsing what she might say and why she was there. A few important questions she might ask. She'd scrap Clive's tourist idea and get another story instead.

She knocked three times, the code from last night, and waited.

When the lock clicked, Natalia peered through a narrow crack.

"What do you want?"

"Hi," October said, her voice cracking.

Natalia's eyes stared without a blink.

"I'm October, from last night." She blushed at the awkward introduction.

"I know who you are, October. Why are you here?" Natalia's voice remained cold behind the door.

October shifted uneasily, staring at the pair of glaring eyes. This was no way to have a real conversation.

"Could I come in? I know you're busy, but I have something to ask."

"I owe you no favors."

"Of course you don't. But I need your input about being an author and coming here every year." She clasped her hands together, her eyes pleading. "It would be a great help."

"You're rambling," Natalia said as she closed the door.

October's hand pushed it open.

"Wait," she said. It was her last attempt at a story. Lying wasn't going to cut it. "I work for the newspaper. My boss is breathing down my neck for a story about tourists. I know it's a long shot, but maybe you could pretend to be one and I could interview you. It would help me out. I'm sort of in a bind."

"The newspaper?" Natalia scoffed. "Go away."
And she slammed the door.

Chapter 19

Philip?

October walked back to the newspaper without the story Clive wanted for that week's edition. Not only had she blown the interview, she'd disclosed her position at the newspaper. Overwhelmed and unable to focus, she reflected on her unprofessional, incoherent, and inept performance in front of a skilled writer.

Natalia had intimidated her.

She arrived back to work and overheard Clive grumbling over an issue in his office. Philip appeared to be away, and if she was lucky, he wouldn't be coming back anytime soon.

"I cannot get this formatting right," Clive said. She heard a slam, so she rushed into his office just as a computer mouse flew by and hit the wall. Clive's face was red.

"What's wrong?"

"Nothing. Did you get the interview?"

She snatched the mouse off the floor and placed it on his desk.

"No one was home."

He pushed himself from his chair, walked to the window, and peered out as if dreaming of the next big wave. She could see how much he hated being trapped in the office when the sun shone and the ocean beckoned.

"Can I help?" she said. She stepped around the desk and peered at the computer screen.

"I hate this software. Alice showed me, but I can't format the damn thing."

October navigated through the pages. The masthead appeared at the top, and a few articles filled the columns, but there were blank sections for the content she and Philip had yet to deliver.

"See," she said. "You just have to click this, and then it will take you to this drop-down box. Then you'll see the formatting window here. You can change the layout, add the jump lines, and cut lines. You can change the gutter sizes here."

She'd never used it, but it appeared straightforward.

Clive stared at the screen, shaking his head.

"You make it look easy."

She was enabling him, but she needed the job. Italy beckoned her like the waves beckoned Clive. His incompetence was everywhere. Small red flags she shouldn't have ignored. He wasn't punctual, giving her the key and making her responsible. And now Philip.

They only had a few days before the deadline. And they weren't even close.

Clive sat down and allowed her to do the work. He cradled his head in his hands, leaning back, staring at the ceiling, enjoying the break.

"How did you and Philip meet?" she said casually, offering him a chance to explain how Philip, who didn't do anything, had come to "work" there.

"We were both at the Beachside Grille having a beer. He bought me a drink. I told him I ran the newspaper."

October clicked around the screen, hoping he'd explain further.

"He said he'd seen one of my employees at the Island Café. Had a hunch she was going to quit."

"How would he know that?" October asked, her curiosity etched on her face.

"He overheard Alice talking to Bridgette, I guess," Clive said.

Bridgette had mentioned running into Alice while she was locking up, but she didn't mention anyone else being there. Her interest was piqued.

"When she texted me right there at the bar and said she was quitting, I thought, man this guy is psychic."

She stopped clicking. She wanted to hear every word.

"I told him she'd never do that to me. She knew how much I needed her."

Clive was using Alice too.

"So you just hired a stranger? Because you thought he was psychic?"

"I was out of a good reporter and needed to fill the slot, okay? Philip told me he'd done some writing. So I took a chance."

October could have thrown the mouse at his head. They didn't need Philip. He was bad news *and* there was something he wanted. She knew it; she just couldn't put a finger on it. And now she was a fool for falling into this trap of going above and beyond to help Clive, just as Alice had.

"Why didn't you consider me for the job?" she said, her voice steady despite the storm brewing inside her.

"You have a job. In ads. And you don't think I realize it, but I know they're canceling."

"That's hardly my fault."

"I had a tough decision to make. And I made it. Let it go."

"Where is Philip now, Clive? When we need him. We have to get this paper ready. And he just comes in here, takes something, and leaves? You're out of your mind."

It was unprofessional to speak to him that way, and a good writer would have rephrased it better.

"He says he's got a story he's working on. Think you can handle the formatting for tomorrow?"

October's blood boiled.

"Sure, Clive. No problem."

Chapter 20

Tourists in Our Town

C live left and grabbed his surfboard, leaving October alone in the office. Her nerves rattled, knowing that Philip had slipped into Alice's role just because they'd had some drinks and Philip's psychic abilities had impressed Clive.

She'd had a terrible day so far, with Natalia slamming the door in her face, Clive wanting more work from her while he surfed, and Philip having some kind of story he was working on that Clive would use no matter how relevant the copy was.

Clive had lost touch, not that he'd ever really had it. When he'd started two years before, the newspaper was still flourishing, and he'd still had a staff. Two journalists and a photographer. At her interview, October had handed him her résumé, printed on linen thirty-two-pound paper, nicer than the average twenty-four-pound. She strove to be more professional. Résumés were out of date, but she'd made one anyway to have something to hold rather than twiddling her thumbs. There was little on it aside from a degree in liberal arts from the community college, some coursework in accounting, computer management, editing, and publishing, and some small jobs that she'd done. She'd included an excerpt of a short story that was accepted into a minor magazine called *Ocean Views*. He'd laughed at her lack of experience back then. Philip, on the other hand, got the job with a beer and a vision.

She would make this edition work without their help. She typed the copy onto a clean Google document on Clive's computer and would format it later for publication. If Clive was going to be so cavalier about the paper, then she was taking over.

Tourists in Our Town

By October Sinclair

HONEYCOMB BEACH – June through November marks the height of hurricane season in Florida, a fact that most are aware of. However, despite the looming threat of storms, visitors continue to make their way to the Sunshine State. These travelers, who could visit more interesting destinations like Disneyland, the Grand Canyon, or New York City, settle among us in our sleepy seaside town.

Honeycomb Beach offers more than just picturesque sunsets and sandy shores. It offers a respite from the chaos of everyday life, a sanctuary where the sound of crashing waves drowns out the cacophony of city noise. Here, the salty breeze carries away the worries of the world, replacing them with the soothing lull of the ocean.

Our mission at the *Honeycomb Beach Times* is to uncover the stories of these visitors. What compels them to return year after year? Is it the quaint charm of the local cafés, the friendly faces of the town's residents, or perhaps the sense of belonging they find here? These stories have remained untold, and it's time we gave them a voice.

We invite tourists and snowbirds alike to our newsroom on Main Street. Come share your story and your reasons for choosing Honeycomb Beach over any other destination. Let's celebrate the allure of our town through the eyes of those who love it.

October saved the file and then sent it to Clive.

She clicked out of the document and went back to her desk to make some phone calls. The front door opened, and Philip appeared.

"Did you get the story on the tourist?" he said and tossed his large backpack on the desk.

"Do you live out of that?" she said, eyeing the bulging seams.

"I might. So did you?"

She hoped he'd have forgotten the question.

"No one was available," she said.

"You said you had another story."

As if she was going to tell him.

"Clive said you're working on something," she said.

"Is he out?"

She nodded.

Philip grabbed a folder out of his bag, headed to Clive's office, and slammed the door.

That man was bad news, and if Clive didn't see it, she'd get to the bottom of this. His presence was more than a stroke of luck. Had he known Clive would be at the bar? It all appeared too coincidental for her liking.

Chapter 21

Jack's Tiki Bar

October was heading out for the night when Philip appeared from Clive's office, stretching like a cat with a proud smirk on his face. She was sick of him, and confrontation was useless.

"Lock up, will you?" she said, closing the door behind her before he had a chance to answer.

Jack's Tiki Bar used to be a lovely place to go after work. Now, it was too familiar. The same locals there every night, the same boats moored on the pier, the same sunset, even the same drinks and conversation.

Summer would have a banana daiquiri waiting and nachos would follow. She loved her friend and wanted to spend time with her, yet she would have appreciated a shower to wash off the terrible day and the sand that still stuck to her feet.

Today, her regular table was empty. October took her seat, and the waitress appeared.

"Banana daiquiri?" the waitress said, knowing their routine so well she rarely told them the specials anymore.

"How much is a glass of chardonnay? Do you have any from Italy?"

"Just the house brand. It's five dollars because it's still happy hour."

"I'll try it. But no nachos."

The waitress returned momentarily with a nice pour of wine.

The honey-colored liquid glimmered in the sun. October didn't know much about wine but swirled the glass and took a sniff before sipping it. The buttery liquid sat thick on her tongue. She swallowed and allowed her mind to drift away to an Italian café.

She sipped and waited. Anxious something might have happened. When a chime on her phone pierced her thoughts, she read the text.

> I have a date. With the bass player. Sorry.

October forced a laugh. It would have been nice if her roommate had mentioned it before. October could have saved her money. But she was there now, so why not enjoy it? She observed new pink blossoms trailing out of fat wine barrels that were only green buds the night before. She inhaled a new spice coming from the kitchen, lifted her face toward the sun, and enjoyed a quick relief from the cool breeze on her cheeks. And pretended to be somewhere else.

"Can I join you?"

She was shocked at the voice and turned. Dax was standing behind her. He appeared casual without the dragon cufflinks and satin shirt.

"Of course."

He sat down opposite her and ordered a vodka tonic.

"Aren't you supposed to be hiding?" she said.

His eyes were hidden by dark sunglasses.

"We don't hide. We blend."

The waitress came back with his drink and set it down, none the wiser.

"She's much too young to know who I am," he said, and they both laughed.

She took in his features, now that she had time, now that they weren't waiting for coffee in stained shirts or sitting next to one another in a dark room writing novels. He was nice. And she was happy he was there.

"Are you looking forward to another night of writing?" he said.

She sipped her wine and smiled.

"I don't know if I can write that many words every night," she said. "I'm so tired by the end, and I'm out of ideas. It feels forced."

"It will get easier," he said.

She found herself staring at his face. The features were familiar now. She'd registered something about his face before she'd even spilled the coffee on him. And she gasped when it dawned on her who he was. She leaned in.

"Wait a minute, you're Dax Cooper."

He signaled to her to keep her voice down.

"You wrote *Ember's Reign*, didn't you? On Netflix. I love that series." Summer loved that show and had forced her to watch it nonstop last fall, but she had to admit she did enjoy it.

He grinned. "I'm busted. But the show is different from the books. The book is always better."

"How many have you written?"

"I think I'm up to forty now. I've lost count."

Dax was famous and prolific. October sipped her wine, thinking of what to say now that he wasn't just a writer anymore. The dragon cufflinks made sense to her now, drawing from his fantasy books.

"Do you ever get stuck with your writing?"

"I work through it. It's like anything. You must build muscle. And it gets easier."

She hoped that it would, but it would be like climbing a mountain without any training. The energy she felt last night surrounded by the newness of the secret club wouldn't last. And she would need to find her passion for the story. There was doubt, fear, and her past insecurities. Would she be able to write every night from eleven to four thirty at a sprinter's pace for seven days straight?

"You have to stay focused," Dax said. "We all go through periods of self-doubt, and the energy drops, but we are here for each other to keep going. That's how it's always been. That's why we choose our new authors wisely. We must remain lifted. Or it will fall apart."

October's mother was always lifted when it came to her writing. Susan Sinclair had gotten up every morning at five thirty, poured an enormous mug of coffee, and written all day in her pajamas. When October came home from school, there was no food on the table, and her father used to stop and get pizza, subs, hamburgers, and fries. October found the dinners at Summer's house more palatable.

"Tell me what happens next. In your pirate story," he said.

She didn't know. She hadn't written enough of her story the night before, and she hadn't had time to think it through, with all that was going on at the newspaper.

"I have no idea. I'm writing about a pirate ship and a woman who escapes from her husband."

"Sounds interesting."

She was happy to hear him say that, but she hardly knew how the story would unfold. But it was a subject she had positive associations with. Her father had loved to tell her stories about treasures and sailing ships, and she'd even dressed up as a pirate on Halloween one year. She had been obsessed.

"How about she escapes, and then hides herself away in a small town on the coast of America," October said, "but the townspeople come to accept her. She buries treasure on the beach. Or somewhere else. And it's never found."

"I like that," Dax said.

"And her husband will come for her later on, of course. To make her leave."

"But she kills him."

"With a sword. Right in the heart."

They sipped their drinks and talked for a while longer, and October continued to gain insights into what story she hoped to tell.

"Tell me about your story," she said.

"It's called *Veil of Draconis*. About a girl who wants to go to another world, another time. She makes friends with a talking Dragon who has promised to take her there. But when her friends find out that she is with the dragon, they try and keep her away from it. Because they are afraid that she will leave them."

October's skin prickled. How she wanted to leave Honeycomb Beach one day soon. Maybe leave Summer behind. But Summer was always going to be supportive.

"I think she would be willing to leave. Even if her friends didn't want her to."

"But the dragon is a human. And she is tricked."

"Oh," she said feeling let down. She didn't like that kind of story. She needed things to work out.

"You aren't interested in that kind of story?" he said eyes gleaming.

"It depends," she said. "If it's a happy ending, I would be."

He took another sip of his vodka, which was nothing more than ice in the glass now. Then he slipped off the barstool and left money on the table.

"Thank you for the drinks," he said even though he was the one who paid. "I look forward to seeing you tonight."

Before she could say a word, he walked away and vanished out of sight.

Chapter 22

Secret Scribes 2

October got back to the apartment, rinsed the sand off her feet, and hopped into her bed for a few hours of sleep to prepare for the long writing sprints that evening. Her alarm went off at ten thirty.

It would be an important night. Intensive work and a chance to blend among the others. She dug out an old bandana from her closet, found a white blouse with billowy sleeves, and made a patch for her eye.

October stuck a note on the refrigerator: "Going out. Be home late. Don't wait up."

Waves rumbled in the distance, and the night air warmed her as she strolled through the empty streets. Before she got to the side of the building where the ladder accepted authors, a set of headlights appeared, so she turned, shielding her eyes as the car slowed and pulled into the Pilates studio. She stood frozen in the dark and focused on the car with its engine purring like a happy cat.

It was almost eleven. The Pilates studio had been closed for hours.

The car's engine hummed, and her gaze remained fixed on the dark vehicle, unable to make out the color or the type. The streetlight was further down the road, making it difficult to get any details. She watched to see whether Meghan, the owner, would step out the studio door, a logical reason for someone being there to meet her.

After several minutes, no one appeared, and the car remained there. Her skin tingled. She was being watched.

None of the scribes drove to the Island Café to write. Everyone stayed locally and walked. She slid behind one of the hibiscus bushes, all the while keeping her sights on the car, hoping that all the writers were up the ladder and safe inside.

This surprised October. Before she had wanted to expose the story, but now, she wanted to protect them.

Her phone was turned off, so she couldn't see the time. If she was late, Dodge wouldn't let her inside. Dax would notice she wasn't there, but would Korta or Natalia?

The hibiscus pollen made her eyes fill with tears, and she held her nose to keep a sneeze at bay.

She cursed the driver of the car for making her late for fear of giving up the secret of the group if she was spotted clambering up the ladder. Instead of staying hidden in the bushes, she came out of hiding and strutted toward the car, ready to give whoever was in it a piece of her mind.

As she gained proximity, tires squealed, and the car sped out of the lot and around the curve. October stood on the grassy lawn of the café in her pirate costume, dazed. The night went back to quiet, but it didn't go back to peaceful. The car and whoever it was had stolen it.

There was nothing to be done, and if she didn't get upstairs, she wouldn't be allowed.

When she got up to the window, Dodge was waiting.

"You had thirty seconds to go. I'm serious when I say you must be on time."

She decided not to mention the car. It might have been there for another reason, and she dismissed the unsettling thought of someone watching her. She didn't need it right now. After the day she'd had with Philip and being snubbed by Natalia.

"Sorry."

Dodge gave her a grin and a little pat on the back.

"Come take your seat."

Dax sat at the same table as the night before, so October took her seat and opened her pages to where she'd left Rose.

"She's late again," Dodge said right before they all heard the loud knock from the door.

Natalia strolled in as if she were right on time and didn't receive a reprimand from Dodge.

"October," Dodge said. "You haven't been formally introduced to Natalia Murrow, horror author."

Natalia glared at October.

"It's nice to meet you," October said, holding her breath, waiting for Natalia to disclose the details about the morning and where October worked.

"The pleasure is all yours," Natalia said and then brushed by the table and found her own in the corner.

October sighed at the brush-off, but guilt washed over her. She had lied about the newspaper and the details she'd been collecting about the author's group. All October wanted was for Dodge to tell them to begin so Rose could take over the conversation for a while.

"Dax is going to be your mentor for the next week," Dodge said. "Be on your guard. He looks pretty, but he's tough on young writers."

October looked across the table at Dax, now seeing that his appearance for drinks was nothing more than a mentorship.

"Mentor, huh?" she said.

"Every new member has one," Dax said, still standing close enough to hear. "Dodge took me under his wing ages ago. He got me to where I am today."

Dax put a hand on hers, and her heart slowed to a moderate tempo. *Thump, thump, thump.*

"It's a rigorous week of writing. It's easier with someone to guide you through it. Writing for five hours straight seven days in a row is hard work, but you'll have a manuscript finished when we all leave. We all will. And someday, it will be published."

"I'll finish a manuscript in one week? How will I be published? I don't have—"

"You leave that to us. This is how this works. We have connections."

Connections. She was intrigued by the information and made a mental note to add it to her folder at work. Tonight, she would focus on her story. She'd let the newspaper go for now and delve into her character's next quest.

"We can meet at Jack's tomorrow," Dax said with a wink. This would mean she'd have to tell Summer she couldn't meet her for drinks after work for the next several days.

Last night, when she first learned of the club, she was shocked by the secrecy. Tonight, it was apparent that she would be part of this for as long as she wanted to remain a writer. Is that what she wanted? She was good at writing ads for the paper, but writing a novel was a different experience, filled with the five senses, dialogue, conflict, and character arcs. She had some ability, but her mother had been hard on her, even declaring once that she would never find what she loved to do if she didn't stick to something.

"Who did my mother critique?" she asked Dax, who was looking over his words from the night before.

Dax pointed to the woman with the bracelets. The one who had slammed the door in October's face that morning. Natalia practically sneered at October from her seat.

October quickly looked away.

"Did my mother and Natalia like each other?"

"Natalia respected her," Dax said. "There was a spot open, many years ago. Your mother knew of her work. There was also a brother, but Natalia got the spot. Natalia is the most prolific and successful author here. She writes under two pseudonyms but is also traditionally published as Natalia Murrow, her real name."

"We have a five-minute break every hour," Dodge said even though he'd said it the night before, but October assumed it was for her benefit, "but that's it. We have a finely ground Ethiopian blend tonight. Load up. It's going to be another long night."

"Does Bridgette know about this?" October said to Dax. "Who brings the coffee?"

He smiled with his pen ready. "Did you think about your story after we talked about it?"

She nodded.

She wouldn't tell him that she went to sleep instead.

"Then write as fast as you can."

"Shouldn't I plan it out in some way?"

"We are all pantsers here. You don't need an outline, just write. It will come."

October was a planner. She organized her desk at work, her files at home, her bills, her journals, and her books alphabetically or by subject. She liked things clean and tidy. She did her laundry by colors, not throwing it all together as Summer often did. This wasn't her style.

She and Dax might have discussed it vaguely, but she had no idea what should happen next. Up until now, she'd been looking forward to the night of writing. The ideas she had stashed in her brain had vanished. Writing without purpose was like driving without a map. How would she know where she was going?

When Dodge said to start, she would have nothing to write again. This time, she didn't dare to write about the authors. She had more details now, especially about Natalia, and would file that information tomorrow at work. Tonight, she needed to get words on the page, or she would be miles behind the others.

"Maybe I should write romance or something else," she said to Dax. Changing direction might be the right approach. Romance was what her mother had written.

"Do you like to read romance?" Dax said.

"Maybe."

She didn't, but Rose might enjoy a little love interest.

October reread the pages she had written to regain the excitement she'd had before. She might not know which road to take, but she certainly knew where Rose would end up. She closed her eyes and allowed Rose to speak to her. To tell her what she wanted to happen next. The goal was to write as fast as she could.

The others were preparing for Dodge's signal. Natalia lit a candle, Korta shifted her chair closer to the table, Dodge set his funny glasses beside his coffee mug, and Dax held his pen, ready to get to work.

October slipped her pirate patch onto her eye and stretched out her arms, clasping her fingers together to wake them up.

"Begin," Dodge said, and her heart pumped, racing the best track stars, wanting to keep up.

I must run for my life.

I flee in the middle of the night, the time when Daniel sleeps most deeply, but I must have made a noise, for he's behind me now, aware that I'm escaping. He knows every inch of this town and the docks, but so do I, having studied them for months while planning my getaway.

No lights guide me as I retrace my steps to the docks, a path I've walked hundreds of times in the daylight. Clutching a small trunk holding my life's possessions—just a few articles of clothing, my favorite jewels, and small gold candlesticks—I hurry forward. My long skirt with too much embellishment, catches on something sharp, and a rending sound fills the air as the hem tears. I fall hard, wet muck splattering around me. I push myself up and continue toward the shipyard, my skirt now dragging more mud. My body aches as the trunk grows heavier with every step.

The path to the shipyard is simple, yet in the dark, it is treacherous. For weeks, I've studied my husband's movements, secretly following him to the shipyard. I know every move he makes, every ship he boards, and every person he praises or berates. I know his enemies and those who would die for him.

He's still following me. I must outrun him. I'm thankful for my head start but terrified that he'll catch me and make me pay for my disobedience. I crush myself between narrow walls, slipping into the dark spaces where he cannot follow.

Each step is a battle, but I push forward, my heart pounding in my chest. I must reach the shipyard and find my freedom. Every second counts.

October wrote as many words as she could in the first hour, but something was bothering her. What if someone was following her to the café that night? Who would be aware of the secret club? Did Alice receive an anonymous tip? If the driver of the car was just a random person who was lost or had pulled over to text someone, then why had they sped away?

She shook her head, jogging the idea of being followed from her mind, and got back to her story and allowed Rose to guide the plot.

Daniel's footsteps grow softer as I edge farther along the path toward the ship—the one I found that morning, the easiest to hide on. The man who helped me when I lost my balance was still on board when I left, but that would be a concern for later. I have a plan and will not be swayed.

When I reach the docks, I quickly board the ship and head for the first set of large barrels I see, then hide and listen for the sound of my husband's footsteps, the sharp clunk of his boots hitting the old boards. A few men pass by, but it's so dark they are unaware of my presence. Other than the low hum of their voices and the breeze off the coast, there is no other sound and no sign of Daniel. I might just make it after all.

This flight through the night is terrifying, but I am determined to escape my marriage. The ship creaks gently beneath me, and I find solace in the shadows, hoping they will keep me hidden. My heart pounds as I brace for my husband's arrival, every second feeling like an eternity. I cling to the hope that the ship will sail before he finds me, that I can reach freedom before it's too late.

"Five-minute break if you need it," Dodge said.

October had reached a decent place to stop and had gotten a cramp in her fingers. She removed her eyepatch, which wasn't the best idea. She would keep it off for the remainder of the evening.

Her back ached from hunching over the table, so she stretched as she stood, then went to get her first cup of coffee of many she would drink that night.

Dodge stood in front of her, pouring a large cup of the Ethiopian blend that smelled like a mixture of oranges and jasmine. When Dodge's feather scarf came close to the coffee, October tossed the scarf over his shoulder to save it.

"How's the pirate story going?" he said.

"All right. I don't know who I am as an author yet."

He let out a loud laugh that made her blush. The roar woke everyone up from their break.

"You have to have been here more than a day to know who you are as an author, my dear." Dodge threw the feather scarf around his neck and pushed up his star-shaped glasses. "But someday, maybe in a few years, maybe more, you'll know."

"Did my mother know?" she said.

"Lillian was a rare bird. We loved her."

Natalia was still writing in the corner, not taking a break.

"She rarely comes for the coffee," Dodge said as if seeing October's interest in the woman in the cloak. "You'll get to know most of us, but her, well, she keeps a low profile."

October grabbed her coffee and left Dodge, who had already picked up a conversation with someone else. She would approach Natalia gently, keeping calm. Going to her condo like that had been wrong, and she needed to apologize.

"Can I talk to you?" October said.

"I'm working," Natalia said, continuing to write, bracelets jangling together.

"I just wanted to apologize. It was wrong of me to knock on your door. I know you were probably sleeping, and it's just that my boss—"

"You're rambling again. Is that how you write as well?"

October stepped back. She was only trying to be nice. This woman had an issue and didn't want anything to do with her.

"Never mind. Happy writing."

She walked back to the table and placed the coffee next to her pad of paper but refused to look over at Natalia again. She'd tried to explain. It was no use.

"How's the writing coming along?" Dax said, jolting October out of her head and back to reality. She wanted to tell him that it was going great, but she had no idea how to make the words in her head translate onto the page.

"Terrible. My mother wrote all day long. And now I see that she wrote even more at night. I feel like a failure already."

Dax patted her on the shoulder, and her skin tingled.

"Don't give up," he said.

She had no intention of it. Rose was hiding behind an old barrel on a ship in the middle of the night. If she could continue, October could too. And when Dodge said to start again, she wrote more about Rose, and her story grew. And the night of writing continued.

Chapter 23

A Bit of Control

October flopped down on her bed after her night of writing, hoping to get some sleep before another day of work. The caffeine buzzing in her system and her mind still racing from hours spent writing was too much for her body to handle. Sleep was out of the question. She removed her pirate costume and whipped the silly eye patch across her bed, then slipped on her robe before gathering her journal. She sat down at her mother's desk and closed her eyes, waiting for her mother's words of wisdom.

There had been so much animosity between them, some of it October's own teenage angst, but also, now having learned about her mother's secretive writing and her love for writing romance, she wished she'd known all along, that Lillian Sinclair felt that October had talent and wanted her to be part of the group. October traced her fingers over the carved wooden legs of the desk and over the smooth writing surface where her mother had penned thousands upon thousands of words.

Am I a writer? she said without speaking the words. She waited to hear Lillian Sinclair tell her that yes, she was. Go forth and write.

When no sign or encouragement came, October determined that even in death, her mother was still criticizing her choices. Maybe those in the group were just being nice.

The merger of her job at the newspaper and her new membership in the Secret Scribes' Society was hard for her brain to untangle. She enjoyed the paper when it ran well, but the future was uncertain. Taking on the role of author was inspiring and a bit scary. And the future as a writer was shaky at best. But then, nothing in life would be certain until one tried it out. The question was, could she do both?

October did not know. And for a planner, a journal aficionado, and someone who enjoyed mapping out her destiny, this was disconcerting.

She sighed when she couldn't find an answer.

The idea that she would ever be a success at anything felt far- fetched, so she moved her journal aside and skipped her daily mantra.

One thing she could decide upon was that getting an early start at her job would mean having the place all to herself. As she walked the streets, the story of Rose crept up, surprising her with bits and pieces of a story idea that she could use on the next night of writing. She took out her phone and opened a recorder to dictate her thoughts, some half-formed sentences, an obstacle, and vivid description of what Rose looked like. The ideas percolated until she inserted her key and found the door already open. She stepped inside. A light in Clive's office shone through the glass door.

Whether it was because a car had appeared to be watching her last night or because Philip was now on staff, she picked up a large pink-and-white umbrella she had earned as a gift for getting her yearly mammogram and grasped it in both hands.

"Who's here?" she said.

A shadow grew larger as it cast upon the glass door. October lifted the giant umbrella over her head, ready to crush the skull of whoever had broken in.

"What are you doing?" Clive said. He stood in the doorway in his shorts and wrinkled button-down shirt with the palm trees, the one that he'd been wearing the day before.

"I should ask you the same question," she said. "You never get here this early."

"I own the paper, you know. I don't have to answer to you."

She lowered the umbrella to her side. "You scared me."

"I was working late."

"You slept here?" October said.

He shrugged.

"I read your story about tourists in our town," he said. "It's not what I wanted."

She shrugged back. It was a game of who would give in first. She wouldn't.

"We needed something," she said.

"I told you to give it to Philip." He turned and walked back into his office.

Whether it was her lack of sleep or the ample amounts of Ethiopian blend running through her veins, October followed Clive into his office. He had a coffee mug on his desk and piles of paper strewn all over it.

"Did Philip write a story?"

"No. Not yet, though he told me that he had something. He'd better hurry up. The deadline is in two days.

She was tired of hearing about a bad tourist story that wouldn't be good for the newspaper no matter how they told it. Both of them knew better than this.

He rubbed his eyes like a child still half asleep and then ran both hands through his hair, his fingers getting lost in the thick strands. "Did you even try to interview the woman in my building?"

Clive looked ashen and pasty, not like the surfer he was, who always glowed with a perfect tan. Today he looked sad; his eyes were no longer the beautiful, piercing blue ones of a year or more ago. Back then, he'd only had to stare at her once to make her smile; he'd had a fun, fresh attitude that had brought life to the paper. More than ever, she believed he'd never really wanted this job. He was doing it for his father.

She assessed the desk and the tools that he was using, and after he explained his frustrations, she understood. The software he'd inherited from his father was professional, but because it was so expensive, Clive had let his first designer go. It was cut and paste for a while, but now that advertisers were bowing out and article lengths were getting slimmer, there was a steep learning curve to adjust. And Clive was not tech-savvy and had been using Alice to get by. October was willing to step in, but she wasn't going to do a bad story just to make Philip happy. Clive had hired the wrong guy.

"The woman in your building isn't a tourist," she said, hoping it would suffice.

"Really? Damn it. I thought she was. I guess I don't know my neighbors very well."

Clive was not a good businessman. She should have noticed this before. His father was, but Clive didn't know the first thing about the newspaper. When she'd started, it had all run seamlessly, simply because the people in town didn't consider that things were changing, but after a while, the articles dried up, the advertisers started to notice, and now, here they were. October knew that Clive was desperate, but Philip was bad news. The paper needed direction, not grit.

"I have a story," she said after considering whether she would tell the secret about the authors' club. She might not have a choice, though she would hold off until the last minute and find something else if she could. "And I'm not going to tell Philip about it either."

She looked over his shoulder at the newspaper on the screen.

"I'm going back to the archives," she said. "We'll have to run some of the old stories. If they're old enough, maybe no one will notice. We can pair the rerun stories with new related content, approach old stories from another angle, find some social media comments, that type of thing."

"Old stories?" Clive said. "That's not news."

She was certain that Clive had no idea what he wanted. She was going to have to save the weekly edition on her own. At the least, she could buy them time.

"One story is not going to save us," she said. "We have to do some fiddling."

There were stories they had run about the beach, about the history of the town, about things she could rework. She would give James the Bug Guy and some of her loyal customers even bigger ads without them having to pay extra. She'd give another call to Kirt, the chief of police, and find Jeb Howard, the man who missed his tee time when he lost his key and locked himself out. It would be a fun story, and she would run the article next to the golf club's ad, which thankfully, they hadn't canceled, and pray they might have something to share, like the names of those who hit holes in one that week, or any events she could report on. She kicked herself for not thinking of it before.

She left Clive to fumble around with the formatting while she made some calls. Ezra Howard, Jeb's wife, was more than happy to have her stop by for an interview and didn't mind the early phone call, as Jeb had an early tee time. She would also like to talk about the women's golf league. It was music to October's ears.

"I'll be there after lunch," October said. The story would be brief, a follow-up with details of Jeb missing his tee time because he lost his keys and had to call the police. She could write it as a personal interest story, something that maybe the town would like to know about Jeb and his wife.

She moved on to more important matters and drafted a quick outline about the Secret Scribes' Society with the notes she'd been keeping in her files. How were the four famous authors able to visit the town, year after year, without anyone noticing? Was Bridgette involved? Why was Natalia always late, suggesting that perhaps the horror author had something to hide? She also noted their first unpleasant encounter at her condo. All the pieces were there, but something made her wonder whether she was missing something, something that if she were a decent reporter, she would identify and find out.

October churned one sentence out after another until her article was complete, though there were still questions. But she had the gist of what she'd learned about the group. It occurred to her once again that someone knew about the secret society and had given Alice a tip. But who? It was all so mysterious.

Reporters dealt with more than being followed. She decided to take her new reporting role more seriously. Weren't the locals entitled to know what was going on in their town?

But aren't people also allowed to have their privacy?

She struggled between fact and fiction. Who would she let down? The authors who wished to remain anonymous? Or her suffering newspaper?

It was already one o'clock when October looked up from her computer. She had been working all morning and had received several emails about clients who had bailed.

Her phone chimed, and she smiled when she saw a text from Summer.

See you at Jack's after work.

October didn't have the heart to tell her she was set to meet Dax instead, so she decided she'd go to the library to tell Summer in person. After that, she'd head down to the Oaks and meet with the Howards, write a quick story, and be back to work in time to add it to the empty pages on Clive's computer.

She popped her head into Clive's office to tell him where she was going. He was slouched in his chair fast asleep.

Chapter 24

Library

The Honeycomb Beach library was one of October's favorite places. When she entered, she inhaled all the smells of newly delivered books mixed with those of dusty old covers.

Summer was speaking to another woman at the front desk, so October headed through the stacks and perused the books as she'd done in her youth, glancing at the rows and rows of novels, running her fingers over their colorful spines. She admired the tall bookcases, filled with every kind of book, having read so many of the authors there. She scanned the numbers on the shelves and remembered her mother showing her how to use the Dewey decimal system to find things.

"What do you want to read?" Lillian Sinclair had said after she'd given ten-year-old October a chance to browse the isles alone and find the perfect book to keep her company through the hours alone in her room while her mother wrote.

"This one," she said.

October smiled now, remembering the book she had chosen that day. It was *The Hundred Dresses*, by Eleanor Estes. She still had the book today. It was a classic.

Her mother had taken her to the library every week, and they would leave with arms full of books. October was to select one and read it thoroughly before they returned the following week.

October came back to the present as she strolled down the fiction aisle until she reached the *M*'s.

There were several books by Natalia Murrow. October selected *Fingers of the Fallen*, published in 2010. She read the inside jacket of the hardcover. The story was about a piano teacher who lived in a lighthouse, trusted to keep the glow of the light at all costs. Then the keeper disappears, and the town can't figure out what happened. When the eerie tinkling of piano keys haunts the town, the locals start to disappear. After the town mayor finds a journal entry by the piano teacher about the force within her that was going to kill her, the hunt is on to figure out how to stop the killings.

"I didn't think you enjoyed horror," Summer said. October jumped at Summer's voice. "Scaredy cat."

The two giggled, and October relaxed.

"Research," October said.

October followed Summer back to the front desk but paused when they got to a table with used books for sale. There was a copy of *The Hobbit*, still in good condition. It was the book Dax had been reading the day they first met. The one she'd ruined. She grabbed it and handed both books to Summer to check out.

"I can't make it to our usual dinner tonight," October said.

"This one's two dollars," Summer said, and October handed her the cash.

"And I can't make it the rest of the week either," October said.

Summer smiled. "Who is he?" she said, leaning over the desk, ready for some juicy details.

October bowed her head as if she'd been caught by her mother.

"Just someone I met at the Island Café. I'll tell you everything soon."

Summer would die when she finally got to tell her that Dax was the author who wrote the TV series *Ember's Reign*.

October wanted to tell her everything about him. How his eyes made her skin tingle, how he knew everything about writing, and had a way with words, and was both smart and funny. She wanted to break down all the things she'd seen at the Island Café after hours. About the secret knock and how they all wore strange costumes. And especially about the mysterious Natalia. The one whose book she was about to read.

Summer handed her the books, and October left the library and found a small bench on the side of the building. She read the jacket and flipped to the acknowledgments.

Thanks to my author friends and those who stay up late through the night to read my stories.

To Charles. Don't lose your soul.

She tried to conjure up an image of this Charles. He could have been a husband, son, any number of acquaintances.

Maybe Natalia had lost someone, and that's why she was so bitter. October had such an interest in this and would have loved to find out more, but Natalia didn't want to talk to her. It appeared to be a dead end.

Chapter 25

The Oaks

October headed back to her apartment and threw her things into the basket of her bicycle, a pale-yellow Townie that she'd purchased when everyone else she'd known from college was buying a car. She could fit everything she and Summer needed for groceries into the basket, and everywhere that she needed to go was within riding or walking distance. If there was a party out of town, Summer would drive anyway. She would get a car someday, but for now, her bank account thanked her.

As she pedaled down the road, she enjoyed the cool breeze that whipped through her hair but held her nose in parts to keep the drifting scent of sargassum from spoiling it. Her legs flexed at every stroke of the pedal, and her breathing was easy from all the biking. She knew of the Oaks but had never been there. It was a hoity-toity retirement community on prime real estate, with the best view of the ocean. She sped down the road and reached the large iron gates of the Oaks in exactly ten minutes.

She pressed a button outside the gated community and waited.

"Yes?"

"It's October Sinclair. From the newspaper? I'm here for the interview?"

She waited for the buzzer but got a voice instead.

"Don't know a thing about it."

In the background, another voice said, "Jeb, I told you. It's the paper coming."

"The paper?"

The gate finally opened, and October pedaled down a winding road that wrapped around a very large oak tree, one of the largest she'd ever seen.

After she stowed her bike in the bike rack, she headed inside, with a pen and paper ready. The lobby was decorated with a fresh young vibe, one she didn't expect for an over fifty-five community. The thick aroma of fresh paint made the inside of her nose sting as she walked across a clean beige carpet.

Opposite the elevators stood a grayish sideboard con-structed of driftwood topped with a vase full of bird-of-par-adise. October checked herself in a large mirror, adjusting pieces of hair that had become scattered in the wind.

The Oaks was home to the rich and retired. A place she imagined held aqua aerobics classes, reading clubs, and square dances. When she arrived on the proper floor, she exited the elevator and walked down the long hallway to apartment thirty-eight, the number Ezra Howard had given her over the phone.

October knocked and waited.

When the door opened, a man who appeared to be in his mid-seventies stared back at her with a confused expression. He was wearing nothing but a towel.

"Oh. Is Ezra here?"

She averted her eyes.

He shrugged, agitated, then motioned her inside.

"What's this about?" he said.

"I'm October Sinclair. From the *Honeycomb Beach Times*."

"Don't know anything about it."

This was not going as planned, but she needed a story, as weak as it was.

"I was promised an interview."

"Well, come in then. *Ezra!*"

She waited in the entry while he rushed back to another room. The apartment was small and crowded, full of large family photos. She looked at a few, five children possibly, based on the eight-by-tens decorating the table in the entry. In the living room, dusty books and other old things, like cuckoo clocks, statues, pewter vases, and shells covered every table, and even some of the chairs.

She didn't sit, because there wasn't a place, so she stood and waited for someone to come out from the other room, hopefully fully clothed.

When Jeb Howard returned, she was glad to see him in trousers and a golf shirt. Ezra, his wife, followed.

"Can I get you some coffee? Water?" Ezra said.

She shook her head and took out her pad and paper. Time to get the story she was after and then back to the paper to write it and add it to Clive's computer.

"Sit, sit," Ezra said, who sat herself after moving a pile of trinkets.

"That's an interesting button," October said, noticing the small round piece of silver near an old map of some kind.

"I found it on the beach," Jeb said, finally participating, handing it to her. "We deal in antiques, I'm always adding to our collection."

October examined the button as if she knew something about old things.

"Very pretty," she said as she handed it back. "Is it old?" She had never been that interested in old things, but the place was full of old stuff, and if it meant they would eventually get to the story at hand, she would play along.

"Could be," he said. "It's silver and was badly tarnished, but I rubbed a little polish over it and got it to shine."

She took a closer look.

"Is that a—"

"It's a rose," Ezra chimed in.

"I doubt it's going to be worth much. Maybe twenty-five bucks, give or take. Still, it's an interesting item. Years ago, a ship ran into the island after a hurricane. Had some stuff on it. My wife and I have looked there for treasure many times over the years, after the big storms, but other than some old pieces of wood from the ship, I don't think there was any treasure. Hard to say."

This might make a news story. Maybe a series on interesting items found on the beach. She noted the idea in her notebook.

"So, tell me how you locked yourself out of the house and missed your tee time?" she said.

While Jeb Howard traced his footsteps from his house to his car and back, golf clubs in the car ready for his eight o'clock tee time, she smiled and took some notes. But while being attentive, nodding, and laughing along with Mr. and Mrs. Howard about the unfortunate event, October was filing away the information about the silver button and how the pirate ship her character Rose stowed away on crashed into the east coast of Florida in the late seventeen hundreds, leaving shards of the mast and bow on the beach.

She sped back on her bike to the newspaper, excited about the information she'd obtained, both for the paper as well as for her manuscript.

She placed her notes along with Natalia's book on her desk next to her computer.

Philip, who had been in Clive's office again, returned to his desk and leaned over her chair, his body too close for her comfort.

"I know what you're going to say," she said, "but I've already spoken to Clive about it. There isn't a tourist story."

"He told me. But I think you're hiding something," he said. "I know that you are."

She let out a small nervous laugh.

"Clive thinks you're psychic."

"Maybe I am."

She shrugged and got back to her job.

"What kind of car do you drive?" she said, proud of the question, but she cursed herself for not paying attention to any details. Her inability to remember anything about the car made her self-conscious about her abilities as a reporter. There was so much to learn. How would she allow her curiosity to delve into the nuances of her surroundings—the subtle shifts in light, the murmur of voices, and the physical details of certain vehicles?

"That's an odd question," he said.

"Just wondering if you like to drive around late at night, that's all."

He stared with no expression on his face for her to judge.

"I like to walk," he said.

She didn't believe him.

She scooched her chair closer to her laptop, grabbed the mouse, and began Jeb's article.

"I know something is happening in this town," Philip said, a hint of challenge in his tone.

She shifted in her seat.

"Why would you think that? It's as boring as they come."

She glanced at the drawer in her desk. Had he seen the contents of the folder? The details about the authors' secret?

"I can tell when someone is lying," he said. If only she had the same superpower. "Whatever story you're hiding, I want it by the end of the day."

She made a fist and considered using it. "You mean, Clive wants it."

Philip had no authority there, and she would push back at all costs. And though she'd told Clive she had a story, she wasn't going to give up the secret author's club unless she had to.

"As you say."

Philip reached over October's arms and picked up Natalia Murrow's book. He held his thumb on the pages and flipped through it like a speed reader trying for a Guinness World Record before tossing it back onto the desk, unimpressed.

Without another word, he slid the oversized backpack over his shoulders and exited the office with a slam of the door.

October picked up Natalia's book as if he'd given her a clue. But she had no idea what it might be. And how on earth would she give Clive what he needed for the newspaper while keeping the authors' secret? The facts might keep the paper going, but fiction offered her an escape from her mundane existence. And she'd been sworn to secrecy.

Chapter 26

Drinks with Dax

October was excited to finish work and meet Dax at the Tiki Bar. She'd gone home to run a comb through her tousled hair and change, putting on a pretty blue-and-white floral maxi dress with sandals, and some fresh makeup.

Jack's Tiki bar was lit up with twinkle lights, and today even more flowers poured out of the wine barrels along the pier's boardwalk, welcoming guests. Dax waved when she arrived. There were drinks on the table.

"I hope you don't mind my ordering."

She beamed as she sat opposite him, noting his vodka tonic and her new usual, chardonnay.

"I'm glad you came," he said. As if she wouldn't. "I'm looking forward to hearing about your story. Who's the main character?"

He got right to it, barely giving October a chance to brush off her day at work, something she and Summer did each night, discussing the negative and then getting into a more positive mood after that. She would have told Summer all about her Philip problem, and she would have helped her solve it, but Dax was there only to hear about her fiction and nothing else. October placed her shaking hands on her lap.

"This is hard," she said.

"Do it anyway," he said.

"Okay."

She took a small sip of chardonnay for courage. "My character is Rose Adaline. She lives in an Italian home. Far greater than her friend's homes, in the coastland of Denovelli, part of the Italian Riviera."

"Denovelli?" Dax said.

"It's a fictional town."

He nodded.

"Rose was abused by her husband, and at that time, no one listened to a woman who was under the brutal power of a man like him, so she stowed away on one of his boats in the shipyard. She was prepared to work like a man if she had to and had learned about sailing from her husband's books, taking them secretly to her sewing room and poring over the text, learning how to tie ropes while her husband slept, learning about maps and how to chart her course to a better place. That being America." The silver button came to mind, and she considered telling him about it, but she was already going on and on.

She wasn't explaining it very well. Not like the pitches that her mother used. Always simple and to the point. She was rambling like Natalia had said.

He smiled, but as she spoke, his eyes darted around the place, and then he took a drink of his vodka tonic and shook the ice around in the glass.

"It's terrible, isn't it?" she said, prepared for the worst. She heard Lillian Sinclair's voice tell her "This isn't very good."

"I like it, I do," he said.

"I don't have a knack for writing," she said. Her confidence was lacking, and once she gained sight of it, she uncrossed her leg and sat up straight in the chair. She swallowed some wine and brushed herself off. "I have a lot to learn."

Her mother's wish to include her in the club was a mistake. She shouldn't have agreed to stay. It was all because the newspaper was failing that she accepted.

"What do you love about this story?" Dax said.

She thought for a moment. Rose was her hero.

"I love Rose. She's a woman who is capable of anything if only she could get in the right place and time. Away from someone who doesn't want her to dream."

"What do you dream about?"

The way he said it made her melt, or was it the wine? His eyes were dark and dreamy, and his voice was smooth like the buttery chardonnay.

Before October could answer, he reached out across the table with a hand. As if he knew what she was thinking. How handsome he was. Her fingers shook, and she allowed them to linger at the wineglass before she extended her hand out for him to hold. It made the skin warm, and blood rushed up her arms, across her chest.

"Do you have a pen?" he said.

A rush of warmth ran up her cheeks.

"Yes, of course." She pulled her sweating fingers away, reached into her purse, and fumbled around until she found an old beat-up pen under a stick of gum. She handed it to him with trembling hands.

He took it from her and grabbed a napkin from the napkin holder that resembled a thick pineapple slice.

"That's why stories are wonderful," he said, jotting something down. "In the story, we can have all of those things."

But not in real life, she wanted to say.

"Keep working on your story. Don't quit. Too many authors quit."

October faked a smile but was sad deep down. Quitting was the likely thing to do.

He handed her the napkin.

"I've got to go," he said, and his eyes searched the place again.

She'd bored him.

He stood quickly and stepped over to her side of the table. "I'll see you tonight."

"See you," she said as he rushed away from their table and out the front door of the Tiki Bar as fast as he could.

October finished her wine and set it on the table.

"Was that Dax Cooper?"

A woman whom October recognized from around town appeared by her side. October paused before speaking. What was she to say?

"No. I don't think— I mean, I think I'd know if it was him. Wouldn't that be something?" October said. "Dax Cooper having drinks with me."

"That would be something."

The woman chuckled and left her alone once again.

This was the reason the authors wanted to still be secretive. They would never get anything written if they were constantly interrupted by requests for selfies, book signings, or explanations of their last book. No wonder he was gazing around. He was easy prey.

After the woman had gone back to her table, October opened the napkin and read the curved penmanship.

He'd detailed a quick reference to story structure, something she'd seen before. Her mother was a planner, and this method of writing appealed to October as well. Always needing things to be tidy.

She gasped and tugged the napkin to her chest.

Dax had drawn a heart.

Chapter 27

Secret Scribes 3

October splurged and ordered one more glass of chardonnay, her lack of sleep energized by the note. The celebratory glass was even more so when the waitress kindly gave her the happy hour price. She lingered there by herself until the sun set over the river, watched boats sway on light ripples, and gazed longingly at couples taking a sunset walk. The Tiki Bar was getting ready to close as the pink cotton candy sky transformed into a shade of deep magenta, then a bit of gray.

She headed home and sank into the sofa. Rather than falling asleep she reread her story to prepare for the night of writing. She would follow Dax's structure if she could and try not to stare at him across the table. Dax might be there for only a few days, but it might be worth pursuing some sort of short-term relationship, love, or friendship.

For the third night of writing, October selected a pair of slim-fitting black pants and a long-sleeved black top to go with her red bandanna. If the unknown car arrived again, she'd blend with the night, and no one would see her. She strapped on the eyepatch and let out an "Argh" into the mirror, making herself laugh.

At just before eleven, she crept behind the hibiscus bushes, a ritual she now looked forward to. That night, there was no car, and she glided up the ladder with ease, ready to continue with Rose's story. She stepped over the frame of the tall window and closed it behind her without making a sound, then turned to face the door that only she, and the four authors, knew was there.

She rapped three times on the door and waited.

The door opened, and Dodge let her in. She smiled, enjoying the familiarity.

When October walked into the dim room, there was a waft of brown sugar. Every night so far, there had been a different aroma depending on the coffee. She was certain Bridgette was responsible but didn't ask again. When she took her seat, she smiled at Dax, and he smiled back. They shared a secret of their own. The heart.

She took out *The Hobbit* and laid it between them.

"I got you something. Found it at the library."

He picked it up, inspecting it.

"No coffee stains?"

She laughed. "I thought you might like to finish reading it."

"Thank you," he said.

Their eyes held, and her pulse leaped.

"I also got a copy of one of Natalia's books," she said in between the fluttering heartbeats. "I'm not sure if it's my style, but she is an interesting person. One that I would like to understand more."

She wanted to dig into Natalia's work to see what she might find. To figure out the person behind the mysterious façade.

"You should read one of Dodge's books," Dax said. "He wrote a traditionally published novel of literary fiction, about a man trapped in a silo, who died there. The whole book was about his disillusionment with his life, his wife, and his son, and how being isolated in a small space made him understand his vitality. Even Dodge admitted that the book was quite dark."

"Think I'll pass," she said.

"Dodge has a fascinating writing life. Not even his publisher knows his real name."

She leaned closer to get the scoop.

"He goes by Richard J. Osburn," Dax said, "a name he uses at writers' conferences, signings, and publishing events. He writes his self-published fantasies as Vail Stillbreaker. It's a fantasy-generated name he almost used for one of his characters in his first book, but he didn't. Instead, he took the name Vail as his pseudonym."

"Why do you think he has so many pseudonyms?"

He shrugged.

"He's also a lawyer. I think he likes to keep it all separate."

October was beginning to understand the necessity of the Secret Scribes' Society. Some wrote under different names and didn't want their publishers or their fans to find out. If they wrote out in the open, they'd never get any work done. It was such a shame that the newspaper needed a story this badly. She'd have to find something else to save the paper. She wanted to do what was right for them both but didn't know how to do it.

"Are you ready?" Dax said, flipping through his notebook and then flexing his fingertips.

She yawned. "Yes."

She sat up straight in her chair like a thoroughbred waiting for the starting gate to open at the Kentucky Derby.

"On your mark, get set, write," Dodge said.

October stared at the page where she'd left off, then quickly got to writing. She would attempt to write four thousand words by the time the first break began. Rose dictated her story. Hearing the character speak was exciting, and October's words flowed easily on the page. She'd learned from the first night of writing not to sit back and think too much. Rose told the story while October transferred it onto the page.

Daniel Montagna is a Captain in the Navy and the owner of a shipyard. He is my husband in marriage, but he has never been my lover. Not in the way I hoped he would be the day we married. Daniel provides me with the money he made from his business. His abuse is harsh and terrible, but his guilt from it provides lavish dresses and jewels, to show that he is better than others, parading me around as his trophy wife.

In the past, he inherited a great number of antiquities from his parents, who are still alive, but do not live nearby. My mother-in-law noticed I was carrying around some bruises one time when they visited and gave me a piece of motherly advice.

"Love your husband. Respect him and you will be safe for now. And then, when the night is darkest, escape."

I crouch behind the barrels of whisky, whale oil, salted meat, and grain, tucking the end of my long skirt under myself and away from view. A dress with less frill would be more practical, but I couldn't fit everything I needed in the small trunk I lugged halfway across the village. The dress was a gift from Daniel and a reminder of a time when maybe he was kind. The lace and brocade are the finest made, and the silver buttons shine like stars on deep-blue satin.

I watch as the men bring aboard horses and cattle, followed by several men who long for a better life, like I do.

The rain comes down hard.

Daniel forecasted this storm the other morning, warning of a difficult departure. It pours from the heavens, and the dirt on my shoes slowly turns to mud. I can't catch my breath, as the cold water flows over my body, my hair drenched, sticking to my face.

My heart beats hard, reminding me I must be cautious and alert or lose everything. My heart also reminds me I'm still alive.

Daniel will not be on this ship but another following it the next day. If we land first, I will have a head start.

The ship leaves at dawn.

I've studied the details of Daniel's logs and will hide for now but seek out a better hiding spot once I know I won't be caught. When the sun rises above the horizon, I will hide in one of the old chests and hope that I'll be able to breathe. I have barely been able to take a breath in the last five years. This should be no different. And if I die, I'll die trying.

"Time."

October stopped her flow of writing and stretched her arms over her head, yawning again. The room was warm, and the cinnamon made her drowsy. Like a Thanksgiving afternoon. She headed to the coffee pot, along with the others, and waited for her turn, Dax standing close behind her. Natalia clucked from her dark corner table, appearing frustrated. October smiled. Even someone as talented as Natalia got stuck occasionally.

"So much of our truth comes out in our fiction," Dodge was saying to them. "We authors write what we know, but more so, we work out our struggles on the page."

They all nodded, and she agreed.

Rose was escaping her bully of a husband, and October was escaping her small town and the awful Philip. Was fiction just people's lives told through a different lens?

It was a quick break as they all went back to the tables before the five minutes were up. They only had a few more days to complete their manuscripts. October had hoped she and Dax would have more time to talk, but time slipped away, and the writing continued.

After the horses are brought aboard, there is a lull in the rain, and I lean back, happy it's over for now. A commotion on the deck startles me, so I poke my head around the large barrel. Daniel is only a few steps away, his jaw tense, his arms crossed, and the large cross around his neck dangles from the gold chain.

I gasp at the sight of him, and my body trembles.

The cry of a young woman pierces the light fog. She appears in shackles while presented before him. Her face is obscured almost entirely by a white scarf. She's half my size, though I do have my father's height. I strain to see her, but the only detail is her pale hands.

The poor girl.

If he hurts her . . .

I grab hold of a stick of wood nearby, ready to protect us both. I knew all too well the wrath Daniel is capable of. And what will take place if she doesn't do as he says?

"Tell me where she is," Daniel says. He rips the scarf from her neck.

Her voice is that of my husband's cousin, who had been staying at the house. I had seen her in the hall, but she ignored me. Why would he put his poor cousin in shackles? He is a beast.

I clench my fingers more tightly around the stick and push myself up until I can see over the barrel, but my shoe kicks the wood and creates a loud sound. Daniel turns, and I dip down again and muffle my breath by pinching my lips together.

I wait.

"Again," he says. "I command you. Where is my wife?"

"I don't know," she says with an added whimper. "I didn't see her last night."

"You saw," he says, and I imagine him lifting a hand to her because I've seen it firsthand.

I cannot allow him to hurt her, but my body betrays my morality and stays idle.

"I didn't, sir. I swear."

I press myself up, peering over the barrel, but am too afraid to give myself away. He might kill us both.

He raises a hand, and the girl shrieks, but instead of hitting her, Daniel unties her wrists.

"Get out of my sight."

The girl runs so fast I barely see her go, and I sigh in relief.

Someone grabs my arm. I gasp a silent plea. He stares down from above, and our eyes lock onto one another.

The man is the same one who propped me up that morning on the docks when the wind practically turned my parasol inside out. I stare into his green eyes, pleading with him not to give me away. He shoves me down behind the barrel, and my knees punch me in the chest.

"Find my wife," Daniel yells in the distance. "She couldn't have gone far."

The man leaves me there, and my gut tells me that I might be safe.

"Time for another break," Dodge said.

October reread her last few paragraphs, happy with the course her story was taking but uncertain where to go with it next.

They had three hours to go, and it was hard work. She wanted to go home and crawl into bed. She'd been running on nothing but coffee, a cupcake, a few nachos, and wine for two days, and it wasn't likely she would keep up this pace with only a few hours of sleep. Everyone looked tired too, but she had a job to go to in the morning. October pressed herself to remember the summers. Had her mother found sleep that one week a year? She couldn't remember.

She grabbed another cup of coffee, sat down on the green sofa, and took a couple of sips before placing the cup on a table nearby. Her hands jittered from the writing and the caffeine, but her body felt numb and fatigued. She leaned back and closed her eyes for a moment. And the comfortable pillows engulfed her.

And then she fell asleep.

Chapter 28

The Next Morning

"Wake up," a voice said.

"You're handsome," she said.

She snuggled her arms around herself and didn't want to leave the story of Rose and the man who would become her lover in the end.

"October."

There was a light nudge and a gentle tug on her arm, but October had come out of her dream, and the man with the green eyes had vanished. She blinked, preparing for the blinding sun, yet the room was lit only by the small amber glow of a table lamp. Her dream was replaced by the horrible reality of the events. She had fallen asleep on the sofa. And Dax was witness to it.

"No," she said.

He tugged her arm and raised her to a seated position.

"It's quarter of five," he said. "We need to go."

She looked around the empty room; only Dax remained. She'd slept as the real authors wrote around her.

"I can't believe you didn't wake me up hours ago."

"I tried. You are a hard sleeper."

There was a light shawl around her shoulders, with celestial embellishments. Korta must have covered her during the night.

"They must all think—" She flushed thinking about them staring down at her while she snored.

"Don't worry about it," Dax said.

Of course she would worry. She might never recover from this. How would she come back tonight? Her mother would never have allowed this to happen. And Natalia Murrow? She probably had a good laugh.

"You didn't have to stay here," she said. "I could have found my way out."

"Dodge locks up behind us. But he gave me the key." Dax held it up as evidence. "Luckily, it's still dark, and we can get out of here before anyone on the beach notices."

At least he'd woken her before dawn. She still had time to go home and make some breakfast to absorb all of the coffee that hadn't worked.

"I'm so sorry you had to stay. I didn't realize I was this tired."

"It's fine," Dax said. "Really. I enjoyed watching you sleep."

This was not the proper way to get to know someone.

"Let's have dinner tonight," he said as he dusted remnants of the old boards off his trousers. "We can talk more about your story if you like, but we can also just talk. Get to know one another."

"After this?"

He was kind, and she relaxed a bit but was still embarrassed by her situation.

He took her hand and gently pulled her off the sofa. They locked eyes, and his fingers were tangled in hers. For a split second, she imagined kissing him. Instead, he let her go, and she followed him to their table where they grabbed their things and headed to the doorway and the little entry near the window. She waited while he locked the door behind them. Their bodies were close because the room was so small. The window was at her back, so when Dax leaned around her to open it, he grazed his cheek against hers, and she tingled at the rasp of his unshaven face.

"Dax," she said.

She caught his attention, wrapped her arms around him, and then she kissed him.

He kissed her deeply as the wind blew through the window, and she enjoyed a moment she might never experience again.

She let him go and stepped away, smiling.

"That was unexpected," he said.

"Was it?"

He smiled, and she did too. Then, the two descended the ladder, jumped down to the grassy landing, and returned to reality.

She followed him out of the shrubs, searching for anyone who might be passing by. The coast was clear. He took her hand as they walked down the path toward the river.

"I didn't write enough words," she said. "My story will never get done now."

"We can talk it through at the Tiki Bar."

She looked forward to seeing him again, especially now, but she didn't want him to be recognized there. It would be safer somewhere else.

"Let's go to the Beachside Grille," she said. "It's quiet, and you won't be noticed."

He nodded. "That's a good idea," he said. "We'll get a nice table in the shadows. Somewhere private." Her body tingled. "Meet me at the beach tonight. Around seven."

Wanting to be with Dax as long as she could, she walked with him to the bed and breakfast and left him there as the first light appeared on the horizon.

"I'll see you tonight," he said. "Just head down to the beach. I'll be there."

She waved, then headed through the parking lot and past the kite store and took the back way down to her apartment building. She wanted to sing out loud and to skip all the way home like a child without a care in the world.

October was wide awake now, smiling brightly to herself. Her big travel plans to Italy were the last thing on her mind. Dax was wonderful. Smart, funny. And a gentleman too. She, on the other hand, had never been so bold. Maybe Rose was rubbing off.

Before she arrived at her apartment, a rustle came from the other side of the street, like a large animal coming out from the dunes.

"I knew I'd find you."

The voice wasn't directed at her but at someone else. Thanks to her all-black pirate costume, she blended into the scenery.

"What do you want? I have nothing to say to you."

The two people stood in the shadows, one much taller than the other, the second voice, a woman's. They appeared as one-dimensional silhouettes.

"Not happy to see me?" the man said.

The man, she could only tell this from his size, stepped closer to the smaller woman, who held out a hand, forcing distance between them, convincing October the woman was in danger. She grabbed her phone out of her backpack and prepared to dial, but her eyes caught on the woman, who had moved closer to the lamppost. Her long black coat floated in the ocean air.

Natalia.

"Leave me alone," Natalia said. "We have nothing to say to one another. Not anymore."

Before October could dial the police chief, Natalia lunged at the man. He staggered to his right, hitting his head on a palm tree, and fell to the ground with a grunt.

"You've ruined me," he yelled from the ground. Natalia left him there and made a mad dash toward the dunes, her long coat flapping like a broken bird's wing.

The man cursed her and crawled onto his knees, shaking his head, holding it with a hand. It was too dark to get a good look, but the stranger appeared dazed and moved slowly up to his feet and walked erratically, zigzagging on the sidewalk.

This was like nothing October had ever seen on her beach, and for the first time, she was afraid. For herself, for Natalia, who wasn't October's favorite person by any stretch of the imagination, but she was worried about her now and the possibility of danger.

She darted inside her apartment, slammed the door, and turned the lock.

Summer staggered out of her bedroom with a sleeping mask on top of her head.

"What's the matter?"

October peeked out between the curtains.

"I'm not sure," October said.

She shut the curtains and sat down in the old yellow beanbag chair, her heart pounding. Something was going on in this town. Things were changing more than she had realized.

"A man and woman were fighting across the street."

"Should we call the cops?" Summer said.

October didn't want to make this one of the Honeycomb Beach news stories. Natalia would be furious with her if she turned up in the newspaper like this. It might hurt her reputation.

"She got away. She pushed him backward."

Summer fell onto the large beanbag chair and put an arm around her friend. The two sat together for a moment.

"I can't believe you locked the door," Summer said.

October nodded, and the two sat smushed together in the chair, but neither of them moved. Their bodies touching was comforting. Summer could have asked October why she was just getting home, and October could have told her the truth, but she kept it inside. They stayed silent for a moment, each quietly processing it all.

"Maybe I'm seeing things," October said. "Nothing ever happens here, and I hate to think we aren't safe anymore."

"I'll put on some coffee," Summer said. "I'll make some pancakes."

October peeked between the curtains once more, but there was no one there. Her life in Honeycomb Beach had gone from boring to frightening. And she didn't like it. She didn't like it at all. A few unexpected drops of rain tapped the window as she shut the curtains and turned back to her tranquil living room, and to Summer, who clanked utensils in the kitchen. The locked door brought safety once again, the dark vision of the man and Natalia slipped away, and the tranquility of the old Honeycomb Beach she knew returned for the time being.

October leaned on the refrigerator while Summer collected her measuring cups, wooden spoons, and metal mixing bowls.

"I have a date tonight," October said. Their friendship was meaningful, and she was so interested in sharing things with her but had to edit out the important parts.

"Isn't that what you've been doing?"

Summer measured the dry ingredients in the bowl, smiling as if she knew all about October's secret rendezvous.

October wanted to tell Summer about the Secret Scribes' Society too, but she couldn't.

"Thanks. For being a great friend," October said. "I love watching you make pancakes." She also enjoyed watching Summer make a mess in the kitchen, creating her breakfasts and packing lunches for them. If she didn't have a great job at the library, Summer might have rivaled Glen's or even the Wild Honey B and B with her recipes.

"We need to get back to our routine at Jack's," Summer said.

"Could we take a break from Jack's after work for a while?"

Summer stopped stirring the pancake mix. "Okay."

"I just thought it might be fun to stay home sometimes."

"Tonight, we've both got plans anyway."

"We both do?" October said.

"Tonight," Summer said, "I'm cooking for the bass player."

Chapter 29

Threat

The trickle of rain became a downpour.

October, full of pancakes, left her apartment and tucked herself beneath her raincoat hood, wishing she had remembered to bring home the pink-and-white umbrella. Her sneakers were unable to repel the water on the sidewalk. There was little traffic, but she stepped back once to avoid the spray from tires passing through deep puddles. The early morning episode of two people fighting across the street from her apartment was still on her mind, and she checked behind her to see whether she was being followed.

Waves crashed hard on the shore, churning over and over like a washing machine with a load of rocks in it, and the rain pounded on the road. It was a far cry from her normal morning routine, a slow pace, sun on her skin, and smelling the aromas of the flora on the island. She glanced behind her once again before she entered the building, her key ready in her hand.

Darkness surrounded her like Natalia's long black coat. She cursed herself for being suspicious. Perhaps it was simply that her routine had shifted. She had slid on her daily mantra and hadn't checked her bank account as often as she should. Plus, she was sleep deprived. She promised herself she would attend to her needs as soon as this strange week was over.

She found the light switch and flicked it on, breathing easy at the routine she was used to. She poked her head around the partition as if checking for the boogie man. Whatever had happened early that morning had nothing to do with her. Just a spat between Natalia and someone else. It was none of her business.

"Clive?"

No one was there.

She shook out her wet raincoat and placed it on a hook by the door. The room was gray and gloomy. The glimpse of the first light only lasted a moment and was replaced by darkness and a continued heavy downpour.

Today, she would do her job and fill in the gaps so that Clive could get the paper out tomorrow without a hitch. He appeared incapable of managing this week's edition without someone doing it for him, but if she was going to keep her job, she would make certain the paper was ready with the information she had.

The altercation that morning would have been news, and considering this, she should have reported it. The battle of words between the man and Natalia replayed in her head. She was still frightened.

As a witness, she had a personal spin, and a story like that would be so much better than a golf story. But Natalia intimidated October. She had slammed the door in October's face and knew about her position at the paper. October thought about the consequences. The personal interest story about Jeb Howard would have to do.

By eight thirty, the rain still hadn't let up. She called the golf course and convinced them to do a half-page spread, including a coupon for a free basket of golf balls on the range. Another page was almost complete.

Clive still was a no-show.

When the front door opened, the mild aroma of the sea wafted through the room, but Philip entered with it.

After witnessing what had happened to Natalia that morning, she didn't want to be alone with a man she didn't know. Especially since her intuition had been telling her Philip was bad news since he'd arrived.

Clive, though flawed, was a good person, and she was comfortable with him, or she had been, up until the last few days. His disdain for his job and lack of interest concerned October that he might quit and leave it all in the hands of Philip.

Philip shook a bit of water from his shirt, his hair slicked back as if it was filled with grease. October shot up from her desk, headed to the microwave, and started cleaning it with the wipes she kept nearby. Philip slapped his wet coat over a chair and hoisted his backpack onto the desk with a loud *kerplunk*.

He headed to the coffee pot, and she stepped aside to make room.

"No coffee?" he said.

"Coffee grounds are right there."

He huffed while he added some coffee grounds to the paper liner and grabbed a pitcher of filtered water from the refrigerator. Philip selected a mug and stood there holding it until the coffee percolated. Any attempt to avoid him now was futile, as he had trapped her in the corner. She glanced at his face, which bore a large bleeding gash.

"What happened?" she said, cringing at the blood that dribbled down his temple.

His hand went to his face, touching the crusty red skin, only making it bleed more. He grabbed a tissue out of his pocket and dabbed the bloody mess.

"I hit my head. Damn palm trees." He winced as he said it.

October touched her lips with her fingers as she sucked in an alarmed breath.

You've ruined me.

It was Philip's voice. It was him. Her heart raced and her mind led her back to the early morning hours and how she needed to lock the door. Was she safe to be alone with him? She didn't have the courage to ask him about Natalia.

Philip dabbed his face and threw the blood-soaked tissue in the trash, leaving a bit of the paper on his cheek. He poured the hot coffee from the carafe and returned to his pompous self.

"Did you hear the news?" he said. "Clive's father is selling the paper." He sipped the coffee between his teeth, making a sucking noise.

Anger rushed through her, hot and jittery.

"That's not true."

"Oh, it is. Ask him when he arrives."

Philip chuckled under his breath, which made October think of the villain in one of Natalia's horror stories.

"I will," she said. Clive hadn't said anything about selling when she'd spoken with him before.

"Maybe I'll take a stab at the tourist article," he said.

"By all means," October said, calling his bluff. If she couldn't find anyone, how would he? "But if Clive's father is selling, then why go to the trouble?"

"I would think he would want to show the next buyer the paper's value. If the paper doesn't get finished, how would that look?"

Philip slurped more coffee and headed to the desk, giving her room to breathe.

"Let's just focus on our own things today, okay?" she said.

"I'm good with that," he said.

October sat in her chair but pushed it far away from his. Philip pulled a laptop from his large bag and set it on the desk.

She followed suit, not to be upstaged.

Philip stabbed at the keys using two index fingers, like a toddler learning chopsticks on the piano.

She smiled to herself, sat upright, and placed her left index finger on the *f* and the right index finger on the *j*.

Her fingers raced over the keys, leaving Philip's in the dust.

HONEYCOMB BEACH — A local man's Sunday golf routine took an unexpected detour yesterday morning, transforming his usual tee-time routine into a spectacle for the neighbors. Jeb Howard, 72, found himself locked out of his third-floor condo at 7:30 a.m., dressed in golf attire without his clubs.

"At seven o'clock, I was ready to go, in my lucky Izod shirt and my Payne Stewart checkered pants, with the pocket for my tees. I had my Callaway golf shoes in the black golf bag but walked right out the door, big as life, thinking about how today would be the day I beat my opponent. That's when I realized I'd left my clubs inside, along with my keys. When I tried the door, it was locked. I rarely lock up, because Ezra is home, but that day, she went to the store early."

For Jeb, winning was his primary concern, and he was going to be late.

"I was feeling pretty good about my swing," Howard recounted, "until I realized I'd left my keys on the kitchen counter." While his golf clubs sat propped against the hallway wall, he tried every pocket, turning out lint, a forgotten breath mint, and a divot tool.

Determined to keep his 8:00 a.m. tee time, Howard headed down the elevator and outside, then promptly climbed the fire escape up to his third-story window. "Let's just say, climbing in plaid golf pants and loafers isn't my finest moment," he mused. Howard's ascent was met with the perplexed stares of early morning joggers, one of whom offered to call emergency services—an offer Howard declined with a sheepish grin.

Things took a turn when his downstairs neighbor, Mrs. Peterson, appeared in her window with curlers in her hair. Known for her formidable pickleball skills and lack of patience, she agreed to let Thompson use her phone to contact a locksmith. "She wouldn't let me leave until I promised to be her pickleball partner the next weekend," Howard added. By the time the locksmith arrived and sprang the door, it was well past 9:00 a.m. His golfing buddies were already on hole number seven. Howard learned a valuable lesson. Always double-check for keys before closing the door. Jeb lost thirty dollars to his rival, Earl Grover.

October added a photo she'd taken of Jeb in plaid slacks and Izod polo, holding his putter, then saved the document.

Philip was still chopping at his keyboard when Clive finally arrived.

"Sorry I'm late," he said. "Nice to see you two working together this morning."

Philip ignored him.

"Clive could we—" October wanted to have a word with Clive about what Philip predicted but decided against it. "It can wait."

"Well, I'll leave you to it," Clive said and left them there. "I'll need those stories ASAP." He was growing more distant by the day.

October didn't have any other options except for the story about the authors. She didn't want to write it because, after the last few days, they were becoming her people. She'd felt something connecting them ever since Korta covered her with her wrap and they didn't kick her out when she fell asleep. She was having a nice dinner tonight with Dax. It was a terrible position to be in.

"The paper's failing," Philip said as if he knew what she was struggling with. "And you are responsible."

He'd gone too far. She was killing herself trying to do it all. What had he done besides have a few beers at the Beachside Grille?

"You don't know what you're talking about."

"Clive asked you for a story on tourists, and you've spent your morning writing a silly personal interest story. No wonder the paper's going bust."

She turned the computer from his view.

Every emotion wrestled inside her. All she wanted was to make enough money to travel, and now, she was knee-deep in a failing paper with a man who was connected to Natalia somehow.

"Why did you want to work here?" she said, steaming. She'd intended to keep quiet, but she couldn't. "Shouldn't you be working on your craft? What is it you write, anyway? Who is your publisher?"

Philip, for the first time, remained silent.

Which convinced her he wasn't a writer at all. That Clive was naïve.

October reveled in her win.

He was only right about one thing. She had been working on a filler story that had nothing to offer. She had a good story right under her nose, and she wasn't using it. Surely, if she published the story about the authors, Clive would find her more valuable. Possibly, she could convince him to fire Philip, and the two of them could make the paper succeed.

It was a risk she might have to take. Or find another story, which was unlikely.

There would be no harm in writing the story about the authors just in case. It would be a last resort. The article would be positive and show the authors in their best light. How they wrote as a way of producing the most words, not to shun their readers, but to create new stories for those who loved to read them. The keys clacked beneath her stumbling fingers, but her desire to get it out on the page dominated her moral judgment.

The Secret Scribes of Honeycomb Beach by October Sinclair

In the midnight hours between eleven p.m. and four thirty a.m., five prolific and well-known authors meet in the empty room above the Island Café. Each year for one week only, they enjoy the beauty of our town, a writer's paradise, and have been doing so for over a decade.

They maintain a rigorous schedule of writing their stories at a rate of one thousand words every fifteen minutes, taking five breaks throughout the night to get coffee and stretch their legs, after which they promptly resume work upon instruction from the master of ceremonies.

Dodge, the well-respected head of the group, holds the key to the writers' room, arriving before the rest, and locking up at the end. Known in publishing as Richard J. Osburn and Vail Stillbreaker, he is a prolific author of several series, writing both literary fiction and thrillers. Dodge is a full-time lawyer.

Dax Cooper, famous for the *Ember Reign* series, comes to our beaches from his hometown in Washington State. His hands craft stories with ease; his wit and charm command the room. His smile is magnetic. His long fingers press his favorite and only ballpoint pen between his fingers, able to keep writing without looking up once in all the fifty-five minutes of a sprint where most would need to release their pens to allow their hands to relax for a moment before starting once again.

Natalia Murrow, the most prolific of the authors, weaves best-selling tales of horror, including *Fingers of the Fallen*. She writes with a candle, her pen always moving over the page. She rarely takes a break but goes on without a breath, spinning tales of darkness and speaking to no one.

Lillian Sinclair, a well-known author among the local community, had been a member since the club's inception. It will come as a shock to those who only knew her as the *New York Times* bestseller of her

```
debut novel, When the Night Leaves You, she also
wrote as A. J. White, author of romance.
   Korta the Greek . . .
```

October didn't have much to write about Korta but her olive skin, large eyes and poised and likeable character made October think of her this way. And she didn't know as many details about the author as she needed to finish the piece. She'd come back to it.

October read what she'd written so far. The piece needed more information. And her fingers hovered over the keys as she determined whether adding her own name to the list was wise. She wasn't famous or prolific. After a little more consideration, she decided to leave herself out.

Her notes detailed the writers as clearly as she could remember them, having only been with them a few evenings. It was such a lovely group of writers who she would never hurt in any way. They only wanted to write in private, to keep people from asking for autographs and getting in the way of a ritual that had been going on for over a decade. October did not know how the group had begun, though her mother had been involved, and it was still a secret who had allowed the group to use the upstairs of the Island Café in the first place. In her opinion, Bridgette was suspect.

She jotted down the names and pseudonyms she was privy to, the sounds, the aromas, and the reason for writing as fast as they could to finish the manuscripts in one week. She described the outfits: the feather boa Dodge wore around his neck, Korta's planetary garb, and Dax's dragon-themed accessories, as well as Natalia's dark clothes and gold bracelets. It was outrageous that they cranked out material so quickly. October was only up to thirty thousand words of her story, but she had wasted her first night taking notes and then had fallen asleep.

She released a heavy sigh. There were gaps and questions she didn't have answers to. It wasn't a complete story.

She checked the time on her computer.

Tonight, she would meet Dax and needed time to go home and get ready. Her clothes were filthy from the mud she'd kicked up that morning, and her hair was kinky from the rain.

She saved the partial document as "Secret Scribes Story" and clicked off the screen to avoid Philip's wandering eyes. Philip tucked his own story away when she closed her laptop, and it appeared they were both finished. What Philip had written remained a mystery, but whatever it was, she would make sure it wasn't published, especially if it was about Natalia.

By the time she completed her normal job, called four more clients and convinced them to run their ads that week, it was time to leave. Clive barely came out of his office the entire afternoon, and she didn't go in. It was better to do her job the best she could and go home. By four, she was putting on her raincoat, as it hadn't let up the entire day, and grabbed her umbrella. Normally, she would take her laptop home with her, but since it was still pouring outside, she decided to leave it on her desk.

"Have a good night, Clive," she said.

"Did you send me any articles?" he said.

"Still working on them."

He gave her a small wave, but he appeared to be upset again. She was tired of his mood so avoided the offer of help. There was nothing more she could do for him.

Philip stayed in his chair. She was happy to walk out alone. He would probably go out for drinks with Clive after work again. She cringed at how they appeared to be best buds.

She sloshed through the puddles on the way home and arrived back at her apartment feeling sick inside. Tomorrow, she'd have to submit the article about the authors unless she found a better story that proved she was a capable journalist. One thing Philip was right about, and she cringed thinking that she agreed with him, was if Clive's father was really selling, the next buyer would want to see potential, and a complete issue. And she would surely lose her job, and her dreams of Italy would be even further away.

Chapter 30

Dax on the Beach

S ummer wasn't home when October arrived, and her hopes of chatting about her upcoming date with Dax were dashed. It was up to October to figure out what to wear and what topics she and Dax would discuss. A friend was always necessary for these moments, and Summer gave good advice. The lack of company, the gloomy rain, and the article looming on the horizon dampened her enthusiasm for the evening.

Changing her initial plan of wearing a skirt with a purple top, gold earrings, and platform shoes, she chose a denim jumpsuit and cute sneakers instead. A girl must be flexible. She grabbed a wrap from a drawer and threw it around her shoulders, thinking of the feather boa that Dodge wrapped around his neck. She checked herself in the mirror. With a swift toss, it landed perfectly.

October left a quick reminder about her date on a sticky note for Summer and left the apartment, locking the door behind her as both roommates had promised that they would continue to keep the door locked for now. As a precaution.

She headed down the sidewalk, looking forward to seeing Dax, her umbrella keeping her dry. The rain was lighter now, but the sidewalks were still wet, and the grassy areas squished when October stepped on them. She hadn't walked after dark on the beach in a long time and smiled anticipating a sea turtle nesting, a topic she was well versed about. Her father had taught her about the sea life where they lived, and October recited the names in her head in case Dax was interested.

Loggerheads, leatherbacks, and green turtles.

The moon hid behind thick clouds. Only on occasion did it peek out to guide the way. Hardly October's idea of a romantic evening stroll on the beach. Her imagination wandered to their momentary kiss as she skipped over small puddles. She planned out the conversations they might have, discussing their books and shared versions of their stories. There would be plenty to talk about. Their main common interests were the writers' club and their characters, but October wanted to know so much more about Dax. And not just for her files on the computer. She wanted to know where he liked to travel to, the food he enjoyed, what he'd done before becoming a famous author, or whether he had ever wanted anything else.

She'd told him about her lust for travel, but she wasn't certain what she wanted anymore. Writing had sparked something inside her that was unrecognizable, and her job was making her miserable, yet there was a dash of excitement at her impending deadline.

October arrived at the beach at seven thirty. The rain had finally let up, and the skies were turning a beautiful shade of pink and purple. Some of the best sunsets happened after a terrible storm, and this made her relax. Her life might be in shambles today, but there might be something beautiful in the end.

The parking lot was empty, and a flickering streetlight led the way to the stairs down to the beach. She crept down the stairs, careful of her footing, then removed her sneakers at the end and held them between her fingers. A soft light from the sky lit up the waves.

A flashlight glowed on the sand.

Dax stood on the beach, looking out at the ocean. Her breath caught, and she skipped to his side.

"Hi," she said before he'd even turned around. When he did, his face lit up.

"I'm glad you could make it," he said. "Ready to go?"

They walked slowly, each holding their shoes. The restaurant was half a mile away, but she didn't care. She loved long beach walks and hoped that he did too.

"Sorry about the weather," she said. "The sand is so wet."

She wanted him to see Honeycomb Beach in the best light. One week a year was hardly enough time to understand the kindness and the honest nature of the place.

"It's not your fault the weather turned. Besides, I don't mind it. It's cooler."

"Yes."

She struggled to find words as her heart raced in her chest, and her ideas of what to discuss washed away like the shells beneath the ocean waves. The night had already been more than she had dreamed. This summer would go down in the record books as the most interesting. None of it was making much sense, but it was a far cry from the boring summer she'd imagined. In a place where nothing ever happened, it appeared that everything was happening all at once.

They walked silently on the empty beach. The perfect place for a well-known author to be.

"Look," she said, pointing to the distant edge of pink clouds colliding with the edge of the ocean. "The storm brings pretty sunsets."

She memorized the colors. Rose would see this sunset too.

Dax rolled up his pant legs before the water washed up further on the shore. She waited for him, happy they could be together in private.

"Where do you live?" she said. "In Washington?"

"Orcas Island."

"I've never been to the West Coast. I've never been anywhere. My father lives in California, but I don't visit him."

"You should go. It's beautiful."

"Maybe someday."

"Your mother did a book signing in my town," Dax said. "That's how I learned about her."

"Is that how you got into the group?"

He nodded as they strolled.

"I had finished my third novel," he said, "and it was doing well. We struck up a conversation, and she told me that they were expanding the club to five. And I signed up. I've never looked back."

"What about Korta? What's her story? And how'd she get in?"

He laughed. "You make it sound like a college fraternity."

"Just curious. And who supplies the coffee? Does Bridgette know about you? How did you get the key?"

"Tell me more about your story instead."

She wanted more information about the club for her article, but she didn't want to force it, so she inhaled the ocean air and calmed herself. There was plenty of time for those details over dinner.

"After my character Rose found a hiding place on the ship, her husband, Captain Montagna, boarded, to her shock and horror, of course. And then he brought on a young girl and tried to intimidate her into disclosing where Rose had disappeared. Rose just watched. It turned out the poor girl was the man's cousin."

"Nice twist."

October didn't like her character Captain Montagna, but she enjoyed telling stories. Rose wasn't really a pirate princess but an inspiring female figure whose life would be changed after escaping from that monster. The scene of Philip and Natalia played out in her head, and she shivered.

"Are you getting cold?" Dax said.

She shrugged.

"I should have done something," October said and realized she'd spoken out loud while comparing Captain Montagna to Philip and his encounter with Natalia that morning.

"You?" Dax chuckled. "You're truly living your story out loud."

She blushed. Telling Dax about seeing Natalia was private. Maybe Natalia didn't want anyone to know. But there was something between Philip and Natalia that she needed to discover. Philip's outburst about her ruining him.

"Yes. I guess I am. It's like it's my own life happening and not my characters'." Rose was a new friend. And she couldn't wait to see where she would take the story next.

"I understand," he said, and she believed that he did.

As they got farther down the beach, some of the condos came into view. The lights were left off to avoid getting in the way of the sea turtles nesting at night. It made for a romantic walk after all, with only a few lights glowing inside the windows. When the sun sank into the ocean, they were entirely alone under a handful of stars.

"So, what's your favorite part of my little beach town?" she asked.

"The people." He gave her a wink. She wanted to melt right there on the sand. Was it too early in the evening for a kiss? She stared into his eyes and wanted him to pull her close. But a wave crashed at that moment on the sand, sending a long swell of water over their feet, soaking the bottoms of their legs.

"Oh," she said, laughing.

Dax held out a hand, and they ran from the water, kicking sand up on their backs, laughing like school kids. They jogged at a steady pace down the beach until they reached a place that had a couple of reclining chairs, next to a pile of charred wood.

"I didn't bring any towels to dry off before dinner," she said.

"I guess we arrive like this."

She was cold now and rubbed her hands over her arms.

Dax flicked away the water on her chair. She collapsed into it and relaxed while the waves rolled in and then out like a lullaby.

"Look," Dax said, pointing toward the waves.

A dark object rolled inside a large swell of the ocean. October scooched up in her seat to get a better angle and watched as it appeared, as if in slow motion. A creature surfed in and marooned on land. And the bit of moon shone on its gigantic shell.

"It's a leatherback," she said and smiled while she analyzed its shape and size.

Out of the corner of her eye, Dax looked on and stared at the great beast of a turtle, with its teardrop-shaped form, with seven ridges down its back.

"They are on the endangered species list," she said.

"Is that right?" Dax smiled at her and her knowledge of something that he probably didn't care a bit about, but he cared that she cared. "How do you know all of this?"

"My father."

Dax sat back against the chair once again and laced his fingers behind his head. October gathered her legs up beneath her and faced him, glad that he was interested in her.

"My dad told me all sorts of things about the sea. And he loved telling me pirate stories as a kid. We would put on silly skits sometimes, and my mother watched, and we'd make her laugh. I was the Pirate Princess."

"Bet you had a sword."

"Of course. And a stuffed parrot."

They continued to watch the turtle struggle through the thick wet sand, finally finding its nesting spot. The large flipper kicked sand as she dug the hole to deposit her eggs. They watched the turtle cover them, leave them there to fend for themselves, and head back to the ocean.

October's mind drifted to a time when her mother had left her alone with a neighbor to run to the store but hadn't come back for hours. October had felt abandoned. Had she told the neighbor she wasn't actually returning soon? She'd been writing most likely. She shuddered at the memory of that kind of abandonment. And then, she'd died leaving her to think that she had only written one book, never telling her about the author's club or that she thought October deserved to be among them.

Dax touched her lightly on the shoulder, bringing her back.

"Maybe I should extend my trip this time," he said. "Not go back to Washington quite so soon. You could tell me more about your adventures here."

His eyes held her gaze and sparkled in the night. He wanted to stay.

"I'd like that. If you stayed."

October could have stayed in that spot for the entire night, except that they had dinner reservations at the Grille, and then they were going to the Island Café for their evening of writing. The breeze was getting cool, and she rubbed her shoulders to keep warm.

"Dax?" she said staring at her toes now, hoping that this question wouldn't ruin the mood. "Can I ask you something?"

"Shoot."

"Do you think anyone inside the Secret Scribes' Society would tell someone about it?"

It was the first that she had mentioned something like this to Dax. About the club itself rather than simply about what they were writing.

"No. I don't think so. We all enjoy the freedom it gives us."

"I get that," she said. "But maybe one of you is envious or something. About how many books the others are selling? About money."

Dax sat up straight and leaned onto his elbows.

"What's this about?"

She didn't want him to know about the newspaper or Philip and Natalia, but she needed some answers.

"I think I was being followed the other night. But I'm not sure. Natalia was arguing with someone early this morning when I was walking home."

"Who?"

"The man I work with. Philip Van Sloan."

Dax shook his head, confused. "I don't recognize the name," he said.

"He told Natalia that she'd ruined him. And she's always late. Maybe she—"

Dax held up a hand, and she stopped.

"Natalia is a well-known author. We are colleagues who have sworn to secrecy. No one knows about the club."

"But could Natalia have told someone? Like Philip?"

"It's unlikely. Believe me, she doesn't want anyone to know she's here."

October believed Natalia could reveal the secret. And Philip had to be involved, she hadn't pieced it together yet.

"Did Natalia ever mention anyone who might dislike her?"

"No. She's not the kindest woman, but it's not our business. We come here to write."

"Yes, but maybe she had a publisher that doesn't like her. Or an ex-husband?"

"I don't know," he said. "She keeps to herself."

"What about me being followed?"

"No one has ever followed us to the Island Café. Until now."

He stared, and she realized what he meant. She was someone new. She was to blame if they were being followed. Not Natalia.

"I just think there's more to this," she said, unable to stop. Someone came up to me after you left the Tiki Bar, having recognized you. I think someone knows."

He sat back and drew in a deep breath.

"I'm happy that you took your mother's place in the Secret Scribes' Society, but I think from now on you should just write. Focus on your story. You don't have to know all about us. Only that our rules apply to everyone."

"Of course. I know that."

October didn't want to talk to him about this now and wished she'd never brought it up. She only wanted to enjoy the night and get to know him. His demeanor was different than it had been when they'd begun walking down the beach. Before, he'd appeared excited to spend time with her, but he was drifting away.

"Natalia told us, while you slept, that you came to see her and that you work for the newspaper."

A rush of heat pressed up through her chest to her face.

"I was just trying to get a stupid story. About tourists. I didn't have a choice."

The lie she'd been caught in was like a thick rope, taking her breath away.

She never submitted that story. And it was Clive and Philip's idea. She considered telling Dax that someone might have given Alice the information she needed to write the story but decided not to. This relationship could go somewhere if she didn't mess it up and tell him that she had the bones of an article about the Secret Scribes' Society on her laptop. And she didn't want to get kicked out of the club either.

"I need you to promise that our secret author club will remain secret," he said. "Please don't disclose the information about our whereabouts or anything about us to anyone."

She gulped. "I swear I won't tell anyone."

The article was written. And it would be so much better than the Jeb story.

Although Dax might have believed her, there was a new distance between them, and she sensed that she would always remain an outsider in the group.

She hated how clingy she was feeling. And wanted to undo her burst of feelings.

Dax had not mentioned whether he was in a relationship. Tonight was supposed to be a way of getting to know one another but she was messing it all up.

She hugged herself again, but it wasn't the cool air giving her a chill.

"Mind if we get to the Grille a little early?" she said and hoped they could get back on track. "It's getting cold out, and I think I felt a drop of rain."

Dax grabbed her hand and helped her off the chair, but when she took a step toward the restaurant, he stayed in place, tugging her back.

"What's wrong?" she said with a smile, but he didn't smile back. "Are you okay?"

"I think you're right. I shouldn't be seen out at the restaurant tonight. I would be wiser to keep a low profile and leave after the week is over."

Her heart sank in her chest. She wanted him to stay. They were supposed to have a romantic dinner, and she was already thinking about the plans they would make if he stayed after the authors all went home. Maybe they would even form a closer relationship.

"I'm sorry I didn't tell you the truth about working at the paper," she said. "But really, it's nothing. I only work in ads."

"Maybe we should go home and work on our stories," he said. "Get a head start before tonight. That way you won't be so far behind. It's cold, and you need a sweater."

All October wanted was for Dax to take her in his arms. That would keep her warm. But he was cooler now as he leaned back and stepped away.

He didn't look at her. Instead, he set his gaze on the sand, on the waves, and focused on the ocean. His distance made her heart ache.

Look at me, she wanted to say. His eyes drifted elsewhere. She squeezed his hand with both of hers to suggest her disappointment, that she needed him. He was to be her friend, her mentor, and maybe even more.

"I'd love to have dinner," she said. "We could talk more."

"Maybe another time."

She had said the wrong things, and it was too late to gain back his trust. She was sorry to have brought up the subject of the authors club at all. There were so many other things that she might have said to him. Asked of him. Instead, she'd blown her opportunity for a wonderful evening.

"Should I even come to the author's club tonight?" she said. It was childish, and she wanted to take it back. Still, having to sit next to Dax for the entire evening without him speaking to her would hurt her even worse. It would be torture.

"Maybe you think we are ridiculous to do this in secret," he said. "A bunch of big-name authors writing together in private.

You will never understand how difficult writing can be and that, without a community of peers, it can be a lonely existence. Your mother understood this. She needed us. And we needed her."

October had needed her too. But she didn't say so.

"You're right," she said letting go of his hand. "I should go."

She turned and walked as fast as she could without running. When she reached the parking lot, tears stung her eyes, but she kept walking. Tonight had been a chance to get to know Dax and find someone like her who enjoyed the same things.

But she had just failed miserably.

Chapter 31

Rose

By the time she got to her apartment, the rain poured down in buckets again, and she was drenched. Her hands shook as she inserted the key into the lock, missing it the first time, and she cursed under her breath.

She needed a friend.

"Summer? Are you home?"

October stripped down, changed into something dry, and then slipped into her bed under the comfortable blanket. She tucked her knees up and hugged them tight.

What had she done? She never should have asked Dax about Natalia. And writing the article about the author's club made her sick inside. Tomorrow, she would delete every word.

She wiped the last tear from her eye and grabbed a paper and pen out of her desk as her stomach growled. *Don't eat*, she said to herself. *Feed the fiction.*

October read through her last few pages of the *Pirate Princess*, making comments in the margins, then began writing where she had left off.

The old ship smells like dead fish, old men, and urine. Can I endure without food, without shelter, and live to see America?

I must survive.

My hiding is not foolproof. The man with the green eyes knows that I'm here, and there's no telling whether he'll turn out to be my ally or my enemy. Thinking of his strong hands on my back at the docks makes me quiver. For now, he leaves me alone, but his presence keeps me on guard.

As the Red Temptress sets sail, my journey begins. Living on this ship with strange men will not be easy. I know where we are headed; the trip will be arduous, but I will prevail as I know what I will no longer tolerate.

I reconstruct the diagrams of the deck and the rooms below from the nights I pored over the maps and books in my husband's study. As the men readied the sails, I rushed down to a new location below decks, near a niche in the starboard side.

As the ship rocks from side to side and the men carry out their duties, I think about my husband's mother. Did she have the same fate?

Escape.

My plan is in place. I will go to America and find freedom. As I lean my head back, my breathing slows. I will be safe.

I fall asleep; the time passes, and I drift in and out as the ship sails on. When I wake up, there's a fist clenching my wrist, and I choke on my breath. Calloused fingers scratch my skin. The man with the green eyes gazes upon me. I shudder.

"What are you doing here?" he says.

I want to be coy and spit out a nasty response. Knowing who my husband is, he should know the answer, but he's a man, and they're all the same. I bite my tongue.

He tightens his fist harder around my bony wrist, and I cringe in pain but don't let out a sound.

"Captain Montagna is my husband, you mongrel, and he runs this shipyard, so let go of me."

"Your husband, eh?" He lets go, and I massage the bones of my wrist, dirty from the mud. My lips are already parched from the salt air; my voice cracks when I speak.

"I'm leaving him."

The truth is all I have. If he turns me in, I'm dead, but there's also a chance he won't. I'm taking that gamble.

He towers above me and his nostrils flair. I hold my gaze. Stay strong. He steps aside, leaving me there squatting on the damp floor. When he returns, he shoves an old leather satchel at me.

"Take it. It belongs to him."

The thrust of the large bag forces me backward, crushing me against the wall.

His eyes twinkle, and my heart races. The bag is heavy, and I unzip it, staring shocked at the contents.

He steps away and peers around before speaking.

"You are safe on this ship. But if you get caught, it's your own damn fault."

He leaves me there, weighed down by the contents of the bag. I sift my fingers through piles of gold coins that shine through the dark niche, playing with them. I want to wash my face with them.

October sprawled out on the bed and reread the scene. What happened next? She jotted down a few notes, enjoying the thrill of the writing process.

As difficult as it would be to sit by Dax that night, October was eager to be among the group of successful authors working quietly throughout the night. The long hours of writing as fast as she could until the timer sounded would push her to get this story finished. It was also a way to get away from her troubles and sink into a story about someone she was beginning to enjoy writing about. Every move Rose made was her own doing.

With a lack of more ideas, she sat up, closed the pages, and set them aside.

Natalia Murrow's book sat on her desk, a thick book with a cover depicting a lighthouse beneath an eerie sky and a large hand coming out of the water, ready to engulf the beacon of light.

She picked up the book and opened it.

Chapter One.

The Steinway piano covered with a dusty film sat in the corner of the old music room. Hundreds of students had walked through the halls of Emma Jacob's lighthouse for decades, but now it was the faint, ghostly whisper of a once-familiar melody that sent icy shivers down Emma's spine as she realized she was not alone that night.

October continued to read the chapter and then couldn't stop. Natalia's writing was moving and chilling, and the skin on October's arms prickled as she read about the ghost demon that haunted the lighthouse after one of the students had died and appeared to be blaming the poor piano teacher.

She flipped through the pages, wanting to know more, Natalia's writing was so profound, moving, and emotional. Things that her own story lacked. As she read, she found herself so engrossed in the tale of the piano teacher who managed the lighthouse that she had almost forgotten about the time. She glanced at the clock, impressed by how Natalia had managed to keep October engaged.

The small lamp on her desk was the only light in the room. The event between Natalia and Philip had bothered her before, making her lock the door, and now, the story about the ghost demon sent a shiver up her spine and tingles across her skin.

It was just a story. She was being ridiculous for being scared. It was pitch dark outside her bedroom window, and the rain was still coming down. *Drip, drip, drip.* It was a creepy sound, and October turned on some music to drown out the noise. She drew the curtains and cursed to herself at worrying about a boogie man under her bed but took a glance underneath just to be safe.

Tap, tap, tap, tap.

October froze on the bed when the noise came from the window.

Tap, tap. Tap, tap, tap.

She peeled back the curtain, and someone stared in.

"*Eeeek!*"

October rushed to the bed, the novel falling from her hands. The pounding on the glass returned.

"October," Summer said, "you locked me out."

October opened the curtains again, and Summer stared back.

"I'm sorry."

"I forgot the key," Summer said. "Forgot we were being cautious."

She was drenched from standing outside but smiled at October anyway.

October ran to the front door, unlocked it, and Summer walked in soaking wet.

"Did I scare you?" Summer said.

"I'm reading *Fingers of the Fallen* and just got to the part where the demons take over the main character's mind."

"That man this morning really got to you. We should've called the cops."

Summer was right, and then October would have had a story for the paper as well.

Summer stripped off her coat, hung it on the hook, and headed to the kitchen, where she started emptying the refrigerator of ingredients the way she always did. Cooking was her specialty, and from the marinara and cheese on the shelf, it appeared that tonight's late-night meal would be lasagna. October wished she could join her.

"I think I have an idea who it was," October said, but by then, Summer was taking out her cookbooks and finding her next recipe.

She left Summer in the kitchen, returned to her room, and made sure she had marked the book so she could pick it back up later. It was a scary story, but looking at it now, from a writer's standpoint, it stirred more energy in her about writing a story for herself. She had gone from embarrassed and staying home that night to being excited to join the authors once again. Writing, when done well, could be so all-consuming that reality simply disappeared.

Though the story had frightened her, as it was intended to do, October wasn't going to allow Philip to do the same. She had locked her doors, something she had never done before he came to town. It was time to figure out who he was and what his intentions were.

If he was anyone in the writing world as he'd told Clive that he was, his name would be easily found using the search engine. She opened her laptop and typed Philip's name.

"Philip Van Sloan."

She pressed Search and waited.

Clive said he was a writer. If that was true, his name would be found somewhere at the top. At least, if he was any good.

Nothing.

His name didn't appear anywhere in the search.

She went to a prominent online bookstore and typed his name there. Surely, if he had written anything, it would appear with a list of his books. Nothing popped up on the first page, so she scrolled down, but by the time she'd reached the tenth page, she gave up.

She sat back and stared at the Search bar.

Then she typed the name that had been renting space in her head since she'd learned about her mother's pseudonym.

A. J. White.

Unlike Philip Van Sloan, A. J. White romances were on the top fifty on Amazon, the top twenty on Apple, and the top five on Barnes & Noble. October scrolled from one book to the next, finding over twenty-five books written by her mother. They were still making money. Either her mother never bothered to put the passive income of these books into her will, or she had, and October was never going to get any of it.

The money wasn't really the issue. It wasn't. Yes, she could use it to get out of Honeycomb Beach faster, but it was more the lie. Lillian Sinclair did give her daughter ample amounts of money, for any woman her age, it was a good amount, and October was grateful. But there was so much about her mother that she didn't understand. And never would. Her mother was gone. It was permanent, and she would never be able to ask her anything. Like how did she become a bestselling author? Did she truly love romance, or was it just a money maker? Did she love October's father? Did she ever love October unconditionally? And seeing this pseudonym, capturing the hearts of readers everywhere, left a hole in October's heart. Others knew of her mother and loved her, but her mother had never let her in.

She went back to the searches for Philip Van Sloan, simply to refocus and stop thinking about her mother.

An Edward Van Sloan kept surfacing, so she did a little background research and learned he was an actor famous for old horror movies. Not being a huge fan of horror movies herself, she didn't recognize his work, and it didn't have anything to do with Philip anyway. October clicked out of her laptop and slammed it shut. Philip, it appeared, was a mystery. Just like her mother.

There were only fifteen minutes before she needed to be at the Island Café to write, so she quickly dressed in normal attire. The pirate garb seemed as if she was trying to fit in, and she didn't have that many outfits to wear, and the pirate eye patch made it difficult to write. As Dodge had said, it would take more than a couple of days to find out who she was as a writer, and trying to act like the others only made her feel more of an amateur. She stuffed her pens and pad of paper inside her backpack along with some sticky notes, a highlighter, and a tube of lip gloss and headed out to the living room.

The food Summer was preparing in the kitchen smelled like an Italian restaurant, and October wished they could meet at home after work instead of going to Jack's every night. Summer loved cooking. October decided to address it later.

"I'm going out," October said.

"How was dinner with that guy?" Summer said.

She didn't want to talk about it.

"What are you making?"

"Lasagna."

"For the bass player?"

"Do you think he'll like it?"

It was funny to see her hot friend worried about her date.

"He's going to love it."

On her walk to the Island Café that night, she knew that Rose would befriend some of the crew and start making allies. She'd cook for them.

And the red bandannaed pirate would fall in love with her.

Chapter 32

Secret Scribes 4

October stood at the bottom of the ladder beside the Island Café, staring at the window. Her heart fluttered thinking of Dax sitting there next to her empty chair. Would he be happy to see her? Sorry that they'd had a squabble on the beach? His reaction to the evening shouldn't get in the way of her writing and creativity. Rose had been on her mind since she'd left the Italian aromas of Summer's kitchen, and her enthusiasm for the story ignited her drive to get to the top of the ladder and to her table to write. She checked her watch. Only a few minutes remained. As she reached for the ladder, the story that October wanted to tell set off running like a dog that broke away from its leash, ready to start without her.

She gave in to the ideas, stepped down, opened her back-pack and searched inside for something to write on. The idea wouldn't wait until she got upstairs. Her experience of recalling something later always ended in not remembering it. She wouldn't allow that to happen this time. Her pad of paper with the Pirate story wouldn't suffice because she didn't want to add the notes to her pad of paper. That was strictly for her first draft. She dug around some more, pulled out a new stack of loose pages full of notes, ideas, random journal entries, and placed them on the ground while she searched for a pen. Before she found it, a gust of wind picked up, scattering her pages everywhere.

Out of the shadows crept a woman, and Natalia appeared.

"You are going to be late," Natalia said.

"My pages."

The thick black wedges of Natalia's boots stood idle as October squatted down to retrieve some of the pages. Her hair whipped across her face, in her eyes, forcing her to use one hand to remove the stubborn strands while attempting to pick up the notes with the other.

Natalia knelt and began to help.

"It's all rubbish, you know," Natalia said, stabbing one of the notes into October's already full hand.

October hated to hear what she already knew. Especially from Natalia, whom she had begun to admire having spent her evening reading her novel without being able to breathe, the story had scared her so.

Natalia stood, and October assumed she'd leave her there, tired of helping an amateur who shouldn't have been in the club in the first place, but instead, she began to search the bushes for more pages, speaking as she went. "I wasn't implying that you are rubbish, silly girl. But it has been my experience that the first draft of a story is truly terrible."

"Oh." October forced a smile, not telling Natalia that the missing pages weren't the draft, though they were equally important.

October's hands trembled as she picked up some more of the pages, hoping she would find them all and nothing would be left for someone to find later. She looked up at the window. They might not make it.

"You should go," she said to Natalia. "Dodge won't let us in after eleven."

Natalia snickered.

"What?" October said.

"I didn't think you cared if they let you in."

October sat back on her heels, the pages she'd found crinkled in her lap. "I care."

"You care about yourself," Natalia said, still searching for pages even though October was prepared for her to abandon her at any moment. "You think you have big plans, am I right? To do something with your life. But are you doing anything right now? Here. At this moment. What are you doing for your town? Your community? This"—Natalia stretched her hands wide—"is life. Work hard, and pay your dues. The big dreams will come later."

Natalia pushed the pages she'd collected into October's hands before she crept up the ladder, but before she made it to the window, she looked down at October and said, "You coming or not?"

October shoved the pages into her backpack and crawled up the ladder to the window where Natalia was waiting. When she got to the entry, Natalia knocked three times.

"He's not going to let us in," October said. Her watch said 11:01.

"He will not let us stay out here."

Knock, knock, knock.

The tension advanced with every moment they waited. Finally, the door opened, but Dodge stood in front of the gap and stared at them.

"You're late. You can't keep doing this, Natalia. And October. You should know better."

Natalia clucked at Dodge and grabbed October's hand, and the two of them ducked past Dodge, shimmied through the gap, then entered the room where all the rest were waiting.

"Sorry for our tardiness," Natalia said. "We had some unforeseen complications. But we are here now."

They took their seats, Natalia at her small table in the back, and October opposite Dax. She smiled at him, and he smiled too but then looked away. She wanted to mend things and tell him how much he meant to her. How much the writing meant to her or at least what she hoped she would be able to say with her stories.

169

We are here now.

Natalia's words stuck in her head. She wasn't in Rome, Florence, or Tuscany. She was in Honeycomb Beach. And it was time to make the most of it.

She watched Natalia light the candle at her table, flick the match out with a flip of a wrist, the little puff of smoke traveling in a winding fashion up to the ceiling. A ritual that made her who she was. October pondered ideas for her own writing ritual and jotted them down on one of the many scattered pages that she had stuffed in her bag after having saved the scattering of notes in the bushes.

Natalia wouldn't have told Philip about the author clubs, October realized now as she shuffled her papers onto her desk, noting where she had left off the night before. Natalia wasn't the awful person she'd assumed she was. Scary maybe, but not awful. She'd been wrong to assume that one of them might betray the others. If anyone, she was the traitor or could be if she didn't delete the article she'd written. For now, the notes about the club and the authors were safely on her laptop at the office.

October grabbed the pad of paper that she'd been using to work on her story, read through the last few paragraphs to give her context once again, and grabbed her pen.

Dax had his pen ready, reading over his work from the previous night, not looking at her at all. She wanted to reach out and touch his hand but kept hers still.

Dodge sat down at his table, started the timer, and then said, "Make it count, people. Only three more nights to go."

It was challenging to write the one thousand words every fifteen minutes that was required to finish a novel in just a few days, but she wrote as fast as she could, her pen having to catch up with Rose's actions. The pens started scratching at the paper so fast that October could hardly hear Rose's voice in her head.

October wasn't sure what an appropriate meal to cook on a ship in the late seventeen hundreds would be, and she didn't know what food might have been furnished to them. Some would have been servants or even slaves, but she would make certain that before she finalized her novel, the facts would be straight. As for now, her creativity did the talking, and Rose had found some meat and spices aboard and was able to come up with a tasty meal for a few of the men.

For the first hour, the words came, but then after that, October's creativity waned. Could she do this full-time? Her mother was always at the computer, in her office by herself, only coming out for the occasional cup of tea and a store-bought muffin. When October had handed her mother her very first short story, Lillian Sinclair had ripped it to shreds.

"That's rubbish," she'd said. "Write something interesting."

Natalia also used the word *rubbish* to describe the first draft. Perhaps, the great Lillian Sinclair had also told Natalia that her own words were rubbish. October started to feel better. Her mind drifted off to a time when she was small, and had written her very first story about a little girl who loved dogs and wanted her parents to adopt one. It was a true story.

When she had handed her mother the story, colored with pictures of the dog she had wanted her parents to adopt, Lillian had read it, reading glasses on, as if she were an editor or agent at a famous publishing house. October sat on the sofa, waiting, knowing that her mother wasn't going to give her any input until she had read it through first. After she finished, she took off her glasses and gave October her harsh criticism of the story, that there was no middle, and the ending wasn't realistic.

Would the protagonist get the dog in the end? And if yes, then how would she convince her parents in the story that she deserved it?

This, of course, was an exercise for October to learn how to tell a more convincing story. In the end, with much work on her craft, the protagonist, and October both, were able to convince her parents that a dog would be a good fit for the family.

The dog, Bailey, came to be and was her best friend for ten years until he passed away.

October kept writing stories, and her mother kept critiquing them. Her father, who had read those stories, praised her, but her mother would say that he was only being nice. It made October a better writer, poring over books on how to write a sentence and how to structure a story, but even so, her mother was her harshest critic.

Her mother was not a harsh woman other than her writing. She was kind to October when she came home from school or at the dinner table—a dinner her mother didn't cook. And she was kind allowing her to get the dog in the end. But the writing. She challenged October with every submission. And October missed it now that she was gone.

"Time for coffee," Dodge said.

October stopped her fingers from moving, though the words were slow and the ideas weren't coming to her. She looked at Dax and smiled at him, pleading with her eyes that they make up.

He gave her a small smile. It was a crumb she would take.

"Can we talk?" she said.

They left the table and walked to the coffee pot. Natalia had gotten up herself that night and was chatting with Korta, the one who wrote about another realm. October watched while Natalia took an interest in the other author's work and appeared to be providing constructive feedback. The two even laughed, and October released any notion that Natalia was a bad person. She'd helped her find her missing pages, and for that October was grateful. Her armor of meanness was softer now, and October was even more curious about her relationship to Philip. But tonight, she only had two goals. One, to sprint to one thousand words in less than fifteen minutes, and two, to ask Dax for forgiveness. The first she'd almost done, but she was slow going from the start. Rose was still creating a dish for the men on the ship, and October had done her best to show the aromas to create an engaging experience for the reader and, hopefully, a salivatory reaction as well. Now, for Dax.

"I'm sorry about tonight. On the beach," she said. "I was looking forward to our dinner. To getting to know you better."

There wasn't any way around it. They only had a few minutes of break, and she couldn't ramble on. She had to get to the point.

Dax took her by the hand and led her to the corner of the room where it was more private.

"I'm sorry too," he said. "I guess I just want to protect the group. We are friends, all of us. And that includes you."

"I don't know why I said those things. I've been having a rough time at work. Maybe it's getting to me."

"It's all right. I guess I was on edge too. People are catching on that I'm in town. I hate ignoring my readers, but if they see one of us, it sabotages the rest. Do you understand? I shouldn't have snapped at you. Maybe another evening?"

They only had a couple of nights left before the writers' group would disband for another year. Would Dax stay on the beach as he'd said or go back to the West Coast?

"Will you stay?" she said.

Before he could answer, Dodge had come between them to discuss something private with Dax, and October turned away so she didn't pry. After only a few seconds, Dodge turned to her.

"How's the writing going?" Dodge said. "What's happening?"

She bit her lip. Telling Dax about her story was one thing, but Dodge? She wasn't certain how he'd respond. She took a breath and went for it.

"Right now, my character, Rose, is stowing away on a pirate ship called the *Red Temptress* and cooking dinner for some of the men that she's managed to befriend." The ship's name had occurred to her long ago when she was just a little girl, telling herself stories to pass the time.

"Ah. La *Tentatrice Rossa*," Dodge said, the name slipping off his tongue like silk.

He sipped his coffee again while she stared.

"You speak Italian?"

"Oh. A bit. I took a couple of semesters in college."

Something told October that Dodge was playing it down. He was probably fluent.

"I've always wanted to visit Italy," she said. "I have a poster of it over my desk at work."

"Lovely place," he said. "You *must go*." He enunciated the words like it was mandatory and that she should book a flight the moment she got home.

"It's on the list," she said.

"What else happens on la *Tentratrice Rossa?*" He smiled at her and waited patiently, though they hardly had the time. The five minutes would be up soon.

"The ship is carrying treasures from the Italian coast, and a hurricane is going to throw it off course, sinking it off the coast of Florida.

"Treasure. Intriguing."

This was the part of the story that October didn't know. Like a lot of things about the story she wanted to tell. It had been ages since she'd considered writing it and now, her desire to rekindle the story was powerful. She told the story as if it were happening in real time. The details were like a film in her mind.

"Nothing will ever be found," she said, waving her hand. "Just the hull and the mast of the ship. I got the idea when my father used to tell of that very thing happening on the beach. There was an excavation back then, but I guess they didn't have the money to continue it.

"I bet there's plenty of treasure on your beaches."

The Howards had devoted their time to looking and had found the silver button.

"I think I'll have her lose a button, and her husband might use it to find her when he comes looking."

He patted her on the shoulder.

"We've got to get back to work."

He set his coffee cup down on the table and took his seat while the others followed suit. It was good to discuss the details with him, and she smiled, ready to get back to the story where she'd left off.

Dax picked up his pen and stared at his work. She had wanted to ask him about his story, but there wasn't any time to talk to him now.

She hoped that he was pleased with his progress. She would make certain that she added his books to her reading list. "Let's get busy," Dodge said with his usual boisterous tone while he rubbed his palms together. "And nice of you to keep your eyes open this evening, Miss October."

The authors laughed, but it seemed they were laughing with her, not at her. She chuckled and allowed a satisfied smile to spread across her face, displaying her pride in being there. To think she almost hadn't come.

Eyes fully open, October got to the task of writing, and the words slipped off her pen onto the page.

After feeding a small group of hungry men, I believe I can hold out here until the end and keep to myself for most of the journey. They don't all like me here, and there's one man who stares at me as if he could kill me if I turn my back. The meal I served was barely edible, but they ate it anyway. I long for the days of eating outside, alfresco, hobnobbing with the neighbors and close friends while breathing in the clean air and taking in the picturesque view of the coast. Instead, I'm coated in salt from the sea and smell like dead fish and rotting manure from the large animals.

The ship rocks, and I close my eyes. And fall asleep.

When I wake up, there's commotion. The men are yelling, running.

"Get up," the man who has been kind to me says, pulling me by the elbow, but I am weak so can hardly stand. He leads me up to the deck. The sun is beating down hard, and I long for my parasol. I'm sick to my stomach and wretch over the ship's rail.

"Look," he says, not caring that I've vomited in front of him. He moves to the bow of the ship. A small island is jutting out from the horizon. We have made it.

Have I been hiding on this ship for months now? It seems more like years. I'm starving and tired.

"We're here?" I say, my voice is inaudible because I've barely spoken to anyone in weeks. I slopped food on plates without saying a word. There's a hidden glimmer of a smile on his face. He hasn't indicated any intention of turning me over to my husband when Daniel's ship arrives later. Maybe I will be okay after all. But there's a jump in the beating of my heart because I don't know where we are and what I might find in this new world. I'll have to make a home for myself in this new place. I have some of my things, and a bag full of coins, but I don't know whether I will survive. I'll be alone.

"Once we get to shallow waters, abandon ship," he says.

I nod, pulling my arms around myself, thinking about the chill of the water and how I will be able to take my things and swim with them.

"It will take a few more days, and we are heading for a storm. Take this."

He throws an old blanket at me, and I wrap it around me. If there is a storm, I'm not sure that this will help.

"Thank you."

He leaves me there, and when I look up at the sky, the clouds are becoming larger and darker. And then I feel a drop of rain.

It was clear to October that Rose would come to the island by hiding away on a ship in which the man with the green eyes might very well be a pirate. He allowed her to escape and promised that he wouldn't tell, except that she would owe him. Not sexual favors. October wanted to keep her story relatively clean, but later on, in the middle chapters, an obstacle would keep her from getting what she wanted. And she would owe him something then.

By the end of the evening, October had written thousands of words and several new scenes. She was excited by her progress in the few hours that she'd been with the group. She could understand now the importance of comradery, of having others to write with, to cheer for you, though she still didn't understand the secret-agent-level secrecy. They could have met at the café downstairs after closing or at someone's condo during the daylight hours and gotten just as much done.

The secrecy, though strange, had its appeal too. She looked forward to the evening, the quiet walk across town to the café, sneaking through the hedges, ascending the ladder, and crawling through the opened window. There was never a moment of writer's block. Of course, some nights were easier than others, but with the entire room writing at the same time and the smell of coffee brewing—a reward at the end of every fifty-five-minute sprint—she was getting her manuscript closer to the end.

Natalia's candles flickered in the room, and the glow of the lamps on the tables created an aura, like a cloak of ghosts from each writer's past. She no longer missed her laptop but enjoyed the velvety ink that glided over the pages each night.

"That's a wrap," Dodge said, and the authors stopped with their writing, some finished a sentence or two. He leaned back in his chair, clasped his fingers, and wrung the stiff joints out over his head.

"I'm getting too old for this," Dodge said. "And too heavy to climb this ladder."

Korta nodded in agreement.

They were the oldest, but neither was large from October's standpoint. Dodge might have joked but had the ability of a younger man.

"Can I walk you home?" Dax said, jumping down from the final rung.

She beamed at his invitation and accepted without hesitation. "That would be nice."

The group crept through the large hibiscus bushes, supplies in tow, which was the most difficult part of the entire evening, Natalia taking it slow to avoid catching her long cloak on her high heels. Somehow, they all disbanded in one piece, and all walked to their residences in the early morning, like spirits unseen.

"Could we try dinner again?" she said.

Dax smiled, and then he extended a hand, which she took, holding it tight.

"Let's just focus on getting through the rest of the week. I haven't made any plans to leave just yet."

It was what she'd hoped to hear him say. That he might stay a while longer after the writers had all left.

"Fair enough," she said.

This time, he walked her home. When they got to her door, they held hands, and Dax pulled her close. She could smell the coffee between them.

"I had a good night," she said.

"Me too."

Dax kissed her with soft, warm lips.

"Goodnight," he said.

The rush of caffeinated energy flowed through her body like an intense charge.

Their hands gently released, and Dax turned to go.

"Goodnight," she said.

She stepped inside and shut the door, locking it behind her, then separated the curtains a little to see him go, under the streetlight.

A zinging energy surged through her. And she couldn't wait until the next night to write to see him again.

She tiptoed through the living room to the kitchen to grab something to eat. The kitchen was clean, but October could still smell the heavy aromas of thyme and rosemary. She couldn't remember the last time she'd eaten.

She plucked a note off the refrigerator.

"Hope you had fun. I left you some lasagna."

October smiled. She had a wonderful life on this beach. A good friend, a newfound interest in writing, and even, if she was honest, a passion for the newspaper.

She heated the small piece of homemade lasagna in the microwave and ate it standing, thinking about Italy, Rose, and Dax.

When she was finished, she rinsed the dish in the sink, wiped it, and put it back where it belonged, leaving the tidy kitchen as she'd found it. She snuggled into her bed and closed her eyes, thinking about how Rose was falling in love.

Chapter 33

Overdue

B efore the alarm sounded, October woke up, ready for her day at the newspaper with plenty of time beforehand to go through the rituals she'd abandoned the last few days.

I deserve success. I am free to create the life that I desire, and my future is bright. And," she continued, *"I will not give away the secret.*

She jotted some notes in her journal too. About kissing Dax. About enjoying the secret authors' society and about the thirty-four thousand, seven hundred and ninety-three words she'd written.

She checked her bank account and prepared to write the new balance in her journal. It was payday.

As she read the numbers, her mood soured. The account balance was wrong. Sure, she had spent more money at the Tiki Bar, but her paycheck would have increased the sum. Instead, she was farther away from her goal.

It must be a mistake, and she would make certain that Clive fixed it when she got to work.

October had more than enough coffee in her system, so she drank some orange juice and crunched down a slice of toast with peanut butter before heading out the door. She was grateful the rain had vanished.

The sun poured onto the beach, the clouds having left with the rain. She let herself into the office and set her bag on her desk. She stared at the poster of the Italian countryside, the lush fields of gold and the old buildings dotting the landscape, but it didn't have the same uplifting effect it had earlier that week. It wasn't going to change things if she got away from her town. Her real goal was to get away from herself. Her boring self. And be the person she wanted to be. But what did that look like now? She wasn't sure.

She peered inside Clive's office to see whether he had fallen asleep there again.

"Clive?" she said softly. "Are you here?"

No one answered. She stepped inside the room, noting that Clive's chair was empty, and lifted the blinds to allow more light to enter, illuminating a thick pile of envelopes covering the top of his desk.

She glanced at the door to make certain she was alone and then picked up the stack of envelopes.

Bills. All overdue.

"Oh, Clive."

This confirmed what Philip had said, but she didn't want to admit it. The newspaper was in jeopardy of closing. Clive had wanted the foolish story about the tourist because he didn't care about the paper anymore.

She sat in his broken leather office chair and pulled it closer to the desk, tugging to get the one bad wheel to give way so she could get a better look. There were bills for the lights, the air conditioning, the cleaning, and the supplies he insisted they needed to get the paper out each week. Postage. Printing costs. Pens. October didn't understand how he'd let this go so long. If she were running the paper . . . Well, that didn't matter. She wasn't. She could barely keep her ad sales going.

There was an envelope in the pile different from the rest. Not a bill but something else. Clive had printed a name on the front: "Philip."

What's this?

She checked out the thick envelope under the light bulb, straining to see what was inside. Why would Clive be giving Philip an envelope? He had only been working on the paper for a few days. And he hadn't even been doing anything. Only yesterday, he decided to work on something at his desk while October worked on her laptop beside him. What type of agreement might they have made?

The contents might tell her why Philip was in town, and what the two of them had in common. She opened up the side drawer and searched for something sharp to open the envelope with. It would have to be very sharp for her to do it without a trace.

A steak knife, cleaned and lying near its partners, fork and spoon, gleamed up at her. As her curiosity overwhelmed her good judgment, she peeled back the edge of the envelope's flap with the knife's tip, lifting the edge until it flipped open.

Her breath caught as she pulled out a wad of bills. Hundreds. She counted them out loud, sliding each bill away from the stack.

"One hundred, two hundred, three hundred . . ."

Her bank account was going nowhere, but Philip, who had done nothing since the day he'd arrived, was receiving a load of cash.

At the end of the pile, she stared at the thick wad and pretended for a moment it was hers.

"One thousand dollars?" she said, envisioning Philip counting the hundreds, licking his thumb each time he counted them out.

She stuffed the bills back into the envelope and closed it, not caring that she hadn't sealed it properly. Philip had done nothing, and Clive was throwing money at him. The money the paper didn't have. Then she had one tiny moment of celebration. He was not on the payroll. This was cash, and that meant there was a good chance Philip was leaving.

"Good riddance," she said.

Perhaps Clive had realized that Philip was a mistake and she was much more of an asset. Philip would no longer be bullying her to write the story about Natalia. And for whatever reason, he'd finally given up.

This thought provoked her to turn on his computer. What else was hiding amongst the disorganized pile of papers, the unorganized files on his screen? October glanced past the screen to the door, in case Clive arrived on time, which was rare. If he did arrive, she had access to his files anyway and would simply pretend to be working. Could she find any evidence that might explain what Clive had planned?

Her cell phone rang, and she jerked at the sound.

Clive's number appeared.

October glanced around the room, looking for him as if he'd been there all along and caught her in the act. She stacked the envelopes on the desk the way she'd found them and glued the envelope back in place with some ChapStick she found next to Clive's computer. Before she answered, she paused to catch her breath.

"Hello?" she said, then cleared her throat. "I mean, hey Clive, what's up?"

"Do you have a story?" he said.

She wanted to say "Where's my money? And why is Philip getting paid?"

"I don't—"

"Fine, whatever. This week sucks."

He hung up before she could say anything else.

It was clear that Clive wasn't going to help get the paper finished, so she opened the file corresponding to the edition for that week. Volume 11, Issue 26, June 2025. When she saw the title and the byline, her stomach flipped like one of Summer's pancakes.

Chapter 34

The Article

Strangers Among Us By Philip Van Sloan

HONEYCOMB BEACH: Natalia Murrow, the celebrated author of the horror novel *Fingers of the Fallen*, has been basking in the sun at Honeycomb Beach, Florida, her cherished retreat. Her dark trench coat, piercing eyes, and enigmatic demeanor starkly contrast with the residents, who favor bright pinks and oranges while sipping mai tais.

However, *To Horror with Love*, Murrows first novel, wasn't Murrow's creation as her fans believed. The novel's premise was originally conceived by her brother, Charles, who submitted the idea to a publisher before Natalia claimed it as her own.

Using her connection, Ms. Murrow, who was close friends with the publisher, rebranded the concept under her name. This act of deception undermines her reputation as the brilliant author her brand portrays.

But there's an even deeper secret lurking in Honeycomb Beach. Atop the Island Café, while the town sleeps, a clandestine group of well-known authors, including Murrow, convene to pen their drafts in secret. Richard J. Osburn, also known as Vail Stillbreaker; Dax Cooper; and Korta the Greek pen their novels right under our noses. These literary figures, who write fantasy, ghost stories, horror, and cozy mysteries, blend into the town by day, seemingly aloof to the residents who unknowingly support their luxurious hideaway.

The citizens of Honeycomb Beach deserve transparency about who frequents their establishments. Are these authors exploiting tax loopholes, deducting every cup of coffee as a business expense while hiding from the very readers financing their lifestyles?

Isn't it time we uncovered the truth about what's happening in our community and stop buying books from authors like Murrow who plagiarize?

October's jaw dropped, and her fingers froze at the keyboard.

What was Philip doing? And how did he get this information? She reread the story. Something struck her as odd.

Korta the Greek.

In her notes, she failed to name Korta by her last name because she didn't know it. Philip had stolen the names of the authors from her laptop. She'd never thought about proper protection, two-way authentication, or face ID. She had never meant to disclose the details of the group and, in hindsight, should have deleted it earlier or saved it somehow away from Philip's view.

Struggling with what to do next, she sat in Clive's chair and stewed. Her muscles felt tight; her body wanted to run around in circles in a rage, and it all played out as she sat there, her adrenaline heightened by the mad rush of emotions she couldn't name. Philip had violated her by stealing her work, even just the names of the authors, to make his case. That was bad enough, but to seek out revenge by writing a hurtful article was an abomination. It was unethical. And something she had intended to do when she met the group of writers for the first time.

She forgave herself since she didn't follow through, but the guilt was still there. It wasn't her or Philip's story to tell. Yes, Natalia could be blunt and often hurtful at times, but that didn't matter. The *Honeycomb Beach Times* was no place to air that kind of dirt, even if it was true. But was it? Did Natalia steal her own brother's ideas?

The outrage that might come from this article made October even more defensive. As far as October was concerned, Philip had no evidence as to what Natalia had stolen or what relationship she had with her brother Charles. Philip said he was working on something, but she'd never seen him with references or research materials.

She considered the thousand dollars that Clive had given him for this story. Like a shady deal they had between them, a tabloid piece with no facts. At least there were no pictures of her and Dax climbing down the side of the building or of Dodge in his feather boa.

If Philip was interested in writing the story about the Island Café, then why didn't he? He'd used the names but failed to use more of her details, so clearly, he was aiming his anger at Natalia. The only thing that she knew was that they had fought, and Philip had said that Natalia had ruined him.

October clicked through the other articles that were submitted for the issue about the stray dog sightings, fireman's drills, and the broad swath of sunny weather ahead. She'd written the Café piece as a headline story but without the use of Philip's story, which she would rather die than print, there was no story for another page. She had Jeb Howard's personal interest story, and the small call to action piece she'd written about the tourists, but they needed something bigger. The eight-page paper was void of anything truly newsworthy. And without a full paper, the issue wouldn't go to print, and her advertisers would leave.

She would be looking for another job, and any prospects of traveling to Italy would be gone. Did she deserve success now? Her mantra withered before her.

Chapter 35

Rewrite

October highlighted Philip's article and then deleted it. The blank screen glared and hurt her eyes.

Every fiber in her being wanted to find Philip and give him a piece of her mind. The impending deadline threatened her job, not to mention her dreams of Italy. If the twenty-sixth edition of the paper made its way into the hands of the locals, they couldn't read this despicable piece of hatred. She was certain she wasn't going to save the paper, but she would save the names of those in the group and Natalia's reputation and keep her word to Dax.

She recalled the feeling of empty-headedness on her first night of the secret writing group. Staring down at a blank page of paper with no story ideas was the most daunting thing she might ever have encountered. But now, she knew, she had what it took to write something quickly. If she could write one thousand words in fifteen minutes, then she could replace Philip's article with a new one.

There was no way that October could keep Natalia out of it now, but instead of making her sound like an evil woman without scruples, she would make her shine. Unfortunately, Natalia's whereabouts on Honeycomb Beach would be disclosed, but it was better than the alternative. She started to type.

Queen of Horror Natalia Murrow Finds
Inspiration by the Beach

HONEYCOMB BEACH – Natalia Murrow, the mastermind behind the blood-curdling series The Blood Thirsty, has been spotted enjoying the serene beaches and moonlit nights of our coastal town this summer. Known for her spine-tingling tales such as To Horror with Love, Bloody Danger, Sharpen Your Blades, and Fingers of the Fallen, Murrow has taken up residence here, much to the delight of her fans and the intrigue of locals.

Witnesses report seeing the famous author frequenting the cozy Island Café, where she indulges in Bridgette's flavorful Ethiopian coffee—a blend as rich as Natalia's extensive backlist. Despite her fame, Natalia remains an unlikely tourist. She relishes her privacy, which the community respects, allowing her to recharge, soak up some sunshine, and fuel her creative well in peace.

Natalia's love for all things eerie began with her childhood passion for playing dress-up. Today, her writing process is a ritualistic affair, complete with long cloaks, red nails, and dark eyeliner—elements that help her dive into her imaginative worlds. It's this dedication to her craft that keeps her stories fresh and thrilling.

Our town has become a temporary haven for this literary giant, who balances her need for solitude with the simple pleasures of seaside living. Her presence among us is a testament to the town's charm and the welcoming nature of its residents.

For those eager to delve into Natalia Murrow's terrifying tales, her books are available at the

local library or online at NataliaMurrow.com.
Whether you're a longtime fan or new to her work,
Natalia's stories promise to deliver chills and
excitement.

Stay tuned as we keep an eye on any future
sightings and updates from the Queen of Horror
herself!

October sucked in a breath once she completed the piece. It appeared to be an accurate representation, but she didn't know everything about Natalia, and like a work of fiction, she fudged a little. It was wrong, and she might regret her decision, but at least the article showed Natalia in a positive light. She reread her version, which took up more space, rounding out the entirety of page three. Natalia might be pleased with the free advertising, but October swallowed hard, knowing Natalia's disposition, and her desire to be alone. She would not be pleased. There was nothing to be done. There were no other stories to tell. October saved her work, fitting it within the pages, not on the front or back where it could be seen so easily, but with such a small newspaper, page three might as well have been a billboard.

Chapter 36

Identity Revealed

T he front door opened while she sat at Clive's desk. She quickly shut down the computer and adjusted the envelopes once again, making certain that everything was as it had been when she got there.

"Did you get the story?" Clive said when he entered his office. He appeared haggard, having aged overnight. Didn't he shave anymore?

"Just finished adding another piece," she said, hoping that he wouldn't want to read anything now. "It's all good."

Philip had arrived as well, and his body blocked the doorway.

October bristled at his dark shadow, like a devilish aura surrounding him. After reading the spiteful story about Natalia, she disliked him even more than she had before.

When she left Clive's office, he sidestepped, giving her room to exit the small space, but then he followed her to the desk on the other side. He threw a large backpack onto the desk that he'd been inhabiting for the past few days, and October crossed her fingers he was leaving soon.

Ignoring the noise next to her, as Philip dug his hand into his backpack, she refused to engage even to mention that she knew he had stolen the information in her files.

She made a list of every advertiser that had canceled and the others that still had accounts. She'd convince them to stay. Her instincts were that once Philip left, and he appeared to be moving in that direction, Clive might get the energy to help her proof the newspaper before the deadline and get it published as always.

Her phone calls were brief.

She made a quick call to James, telling him about the bigger ad, but some of her other clients were on the fence about renewing. She was met with many a "No," "Sorry," "Maybe next time," or the brush-off of avoiding the call.

How was the paper going to keep going if they didn't have the money for printing? They had also lost some volunteers who had delivered the paper for years, but some of them were old and just weren't up to the task anymore.

As she was preparing to dial another number, Philip stood in front of her, arms across his chest, hands deep in his armpits. He leaned back and stared at the ceiling as she took the call, but when no one answered again, she hung up.

"What do you want, Philip?"

He was no longer a threat since she'd rewritten the story but more like a nonvenomous snake, slimy but harmless, especially now that she'd cut off his head.

"Just wondering how long you're going to be working here, that's all," he said.

"Really? I would ask you the same thing."

This threw him off for a moment, but then he showed teeth.

"You and this small town are hardly newsworthy. But I know there's a story you're not telling. It's your job to tell it."

"I don't know what you're talking about," she said.

He shrugged, pulled a stick of gum out of his pocket, unwrapped it, and shoved it into his mouth. "If that's how you see it, but I don't care about your paper anymore. No one does."

He tossed the little foil wrapper on the desk and then walked around the corner into Clive's office. She couldn't see the pair of men but imagined the two shaking hands and Clive handing the money to Philip, who would take out the bills just to make certain that he was getting paid what they agreed. He'd just gotten paid for services rendered, but October had changed the story. Clive was paying him for nothing.

Philip returned to his desk holding the envelope and shoved it into the front pocket of his backpack and zipped it. He nodded to her, hoisted the heavy bag over one shoulder, then headed out the front door.

She ran to Clive's office door.

"Did Philip just quit?" she said.

"Your lucky day," Clive said, looking like his best friend had just told him he was moving to another country. She didn't understand what he saw in him.

She grabbed her purse and tailed Philip like a sleuth in one of those old mystery films her mother had always watched, keeping far back as he walked down the street and toward the condos past the dunes. He sang something, but he was a terrible singer, and the birds flew out of his way as he passed. She followed two blocks, hiding behind a car parked at Claudia Bloom's realty, and pausing briefly behind garbage bins, a sturdy palm tree or mailbox, until Philip had passed the Beachside Grille.

He took the stairs down to the beach. She waited at the top and took off her shoes, then headed down barefoot, her cries silent as the sand scorched her toes.

She hovered around the tall sea oats and watched Philip remove a large envelope from his backpack and then a packet of cigarettes before he tossed the bag in the sand. He sank down and leaned on the thick leather and slid on a pair of sunglasses. She couldn't see what he was reading, but he'd taken out a large stack of papers and flipped through them while dangling an unlit cigarette between his fingers. And then, he cried out.

"*Ahhh!*"

She jumped back. Was he losing it? And what for? He'd tried to ruin Natalia's name. Hardly the type to air his frustrations in public. October looked up and down the beach, and other than the flock of royal terns, she was the only one to hear him.

He patted down his pockets and pried out a blue lighter, lit the cigarette, and shoved the lighter back into his pocket.

"Rubbish," he cried out again. "Pure rubbish."

October watched from the dunes but close enough to witness Philip rub the back of his neck before he started jamming some of the pages back into the backpack until cramming didn't work, so he started shredding the papers right there on the beach. He held up a page, then lit the edges and watched it burn before letting go, the fire going out as it blew through the air. He laughed to himself, and it scared October to witness this, as he continued to light the remaining pages. She watched as he staggered around in a circle as if he were drunk. Maybe he was.

After he'd ripped the entire pile of papers to bits, half of them burned, he held up one remaining page.

"I've had enough of you," he yelled into the air filled with seagulls who mistook the pieces of paper for food.

Instead of shredding or burning this one, he wadded it up into a ball and threw it like a minor league pitcher toward the ocean waves.

The sea oats scratched her legs, but she remained still until Philip took off running up the beach with the backpack strapped on, arms pitching him forward. October rushed from the dunes in search of the remaining page. The wadded paper floated like a beach ball. She waded in and stretched out her arms, unable to reach it.

The water was warm as she lunged further in, the ball bobbing farther away. She sank up to her knees keeping her gaze on the wadded-up paper as it continued to wash away from shore. She could have given up but knew it might give her the answers she needed about why Philip was there, why he was so mean, and possibly it would make her understand the terrible behavior that he'd brought to her town.

The wad of paper kept traveling beyond her reach. With every wave that came in, the wad went out.

October was no newbie to swimming, but the idea of plunging under the waves fully clothed didn't appeal to her. The paper was only a few feet away, and her desire to grab it outweighed her displeasure of getting fully soaked. She held her breath and plunged.

"Got it," she said when she popped back up like a joyful child who'd caught a fly ball in little league. She kept her arm above the water as she swam back to shore. The last wave pushed her onto her knees, but she never let go. The paper was soaked but hadn't come apart. She sat on the beach and unrolled the scrunched paper with her fingers. The letter was typed; therefore, she could still read it even with it being drenched.

Dear Charles,

We are sorry to inform you that we are passing on your next memoir. Your writing is flat, and the topic doesn't interest us at this time. Perhaps in the future.

Everworth Publishing

"Charles?"

Natalia had written a dedication to Charles. Something about him losing his soul. He wanted revenge. It was now clear who Philip was. Philip Van Sloan was Natalia's brother. Charles.

Chapter 37

Charles

October sat on the beach and reread the letter several times until it fully sank in.

Philip Van Sloan was Charles. He had to be. How would he have said those terrible things about Natalia? Why would he have argued with her early in the morning that day? Did she steal his ideas? It made sense as to why he appeared in Honeycomb Beach at the same time Natalia was there, but why try to sabotage the newspaper?

She searched the beach, and Philip was gone.

October was soaking wet when she returned to her desk. She toweled off with a napkin from yesterday's lunch. The paper she had rescued was soggy and crinkled, so she smoothed it out, without ripping it. It was evidence of who Philip was, but it didn't mean anything.

Why go to all the trouble of pretending to be Philip Van Sloan? She scratched her head.

None of it mattered now. He was gone, and the paper was in trouble. But the week was going by, and though there were enough articles for the next edition of the newspaper, the articles didn't show her best work. She and Clive weren't ready for tomorrow's publication. And Philip had been in the way, and Clive could have cared less.

October slammed the laptop shut, then pushed herself away from her desk, rolling sideways. She stared at the poster of the Italian countryside, which would typically provoke feelings of warmth, adventure, and success. Now she simply glared at it, as if it was a dream that mocked her and would never come true.

She stomped into Clive's office, tired of pretending, tired of being nice. Ready for a fight, she was met with a man sound asleep in his chair. Instead of calling out his name, which she'd done more than enough, she grabbed onto his bulky shoulder and shook it, forcing him to wake up.

He groaned.

"I need to discuss something with you," she said.

His eyes were barely open. Finally, he sat up, shook his head, and stared at her. This wasn't at all the man that she had known when she'd started at the paper. A few years ago, he had been eager to take on the responsibility and hopeful that the *Honeycomb Beach Times* would live on.

"What do you want?" he said.

"Clive? What's wrong with you?"

He leaned back in his chair, his face flushed from falling asleep in the pool of sun that burned on his desk, the window wide open.

"Nothing's wrong with me."

She stood above him, wanting to knock him out cold.

"You didn't pay me today. You've always paid me on time. You know that I am saving for Italy, and I'm crushed that you think I'm not important. And why did you give Philip money? Sue me. I looked at your envelopes this morning, and I see that you aren't paying any of the bills, but Philip gets a stack of cash. I need an answer."

October's heartbeat had hit its highest point, even higher than when she ran miles in college. She trembled at having lost respect for her boss and at having the audacity to speak to him like that. It was inappropriate. And opening the bills and the envelope with Philip's cash was a low point.

She wasn't sorry.

Clive rubbed his cheek with a hand. Then he pushed his chair back, opened the desk drawer, and pulled out a white envelope.

"This is for you."

She took it.

"What is it?"

"Open it."

She did as he said, and there was a check. For double her paycheck.

"What's this?"

"I owe you. You've been doing all the work."

"But you haven't paid the bills."

"It doesn't mean we don't have the money. I'm just tired of it. Honestly, I don't want to do this anymore. This was my dad's dream. I tried, but I hate it."

"So that's it? You're just giving up? What about this week's edition?"

His eyes were tired and glazed. He closed them briefly and opened them again.

"I don't know," he said. "I just don't know."

Chapter 38

One Last Round

October left work early. As hard as she'd tried to write interesting stories, it all seemed like a worthless cause now that Clive was sick of it. She headed for the café to sip a roasted coffee from another world and dream of another universe where she had a career she loved and a boss who cared.

The café was dotted with a few locals she recognized, and she spotted a man and woman near one of the windows she hadn't seen before. It was too late for the tourist story, and asking questions of the couple who were enjoying their coffee would be rude.

The story she'd written about Natalia was still on her mind.

Would Natalia hate her for the rest of her life? Would she be barred from the group now that she'd intentionally written the story? Even if it was to replace a smear piece? It was more than she could bear.

She cursed Philip and Clive. And Alice too. October's boring life was working for her, but she didn't know it until now. If only it could all go back to mundane. But would she want it to?

The large chalkboard behind the bar was full of choices from all around the world.

"I'll try the one from Papua New Guinea," October said.

When her mug arrived, she paid for her order and then headed to the back deck. She stopped abruptly when she noticed Philip eating and sipping coffee, appearing unaffected by his actions that morning. She turned to leave but hesitated. Confronting him seemed pointless, yet something urged her to stay. If Rose could board a pirate ship after leaving her husband, October could have one last go around with Philip.

She stopped at the cream and sugar station, added a touch of stevia, and then strolled out onto the deck.

"May I?" she said. He looked up, and she could see the shock on his face, but he covered it quickly with his grin, the one she couldn't stand. Where she sat, he couldn't leave. Not until she got to the bottom of it.

He took a bite of his meal.

"Do you play the piano?" she said.

"Me?" he said, wiping his mouth, dabbing the corner of his lips. "An odd question, wouldn't you say?"

"I don't know. I was just noticing your hands." His fingers weren't slender or graceful like Dax's. They were thick little nubs like half-smoked cigars.

He extended his fingers and analyzed them. "My fingers don't fit the keys. My piano teacher told me so."

"You took lessons?"

"For a short time. My sister was the pianist."

His assessment of his fingers was accurate. They were thick wedges that might not have fit on the piano keys, but he had perfectly manicured nails. She let him chew on his sandwich, wishing he'd choke on it.

"You're leaving us," she said, glad that he was.

"My job is done."

He smiled, and the glimmer in his eyes was like that of a naughty child who'd gotten away with something.

"What job is that, exactly?" she said, then grasped the large mug in her hands and took a sip. This maneuver kept him from seeing her shaking hands.

He tipped his head back and laughed.

"The newspaper will reveal it all soon enough."

"I was wondering," she said, "did you know Alice?"

He clasped his hands and leaned onto the table. October leaned away.

"Alice?"

"The one that wrote the articles before you came. She quit the day you got here."

"Oh, yes. Clive mentioned her."

"What did he mention?"

Philip was playing games with her, but she would be a strong opponent.

"Just that she was leaving, and he needed someone to pick up the pieces."

This rattled October because Clive had never told her Alice was leaving and she should have been the one that he turned to for help. Not Philip. And she didn't believe that was the only thing that Philip knew.

"Did you know that this building has a staircase in the back that leads to a trapdoor?" he said.

October heard herself gasp.

He grinned. "I wonder where it leads." He'd known about the Secret Scribes all along, attempting to make her write the story, but she couldn't. Maybe she was the coward.

"Here's your check," Bridgette said.

She laid Philip's receipt down in front of him and removed the plate full of crumbs and silverware. Philip took out his wallet and handed Bridgette a credit card, even though she knew he was carrying loads of cash. October tried to see the name on the card but couldn't make it out.

"I understand you write memoir," October said. "Who is your publisher again?"

She hit a nerve. He winced and took a napkin out of the dispenser and wiped his mouth again, then crumpled it up in his hand. Before she could inquire further, Bridgette returned.

201

Philip took his credit card, scribbled a signature on the receipt, and pushed his chair back.

"I hear it's hard to get a publishing deal," October said. "Quite competitive."

His eyes became cold. He knew she knew.

"I think we've said enough," he said.

"Where are you headed?"

She leaned back, appearing casual but still curious to understand why he'd come to her town in the first place.

"Not that it's any of your business," he said, "but I'm heading to the Keys. I find it much more stimulating there. This place is a bore."

October scooched in, letting him pass, then picked up his receipt. The scrawl was very hard to read, but she could see that his name started with a *C*.

"Have a great time in the Keys, Charles," she said.

Philip didn't look back. Now *her* job was done.

Chapter 39

Dax

S he finished her mug of coffee and walked to Jack's Tiki Bar. She sat down on the barstool, skipped the chardonnay and went back to her regular banana daiquiri. October ached as she thought about Dax and how they'd left things. Would he meet her there or not? If he arrived, she would tell him about the article she had written about Natalia. It wasn't going to be easy, but it had to be done. Then she would be free to join the authors that night without guilt. Natalia may or may not forgive her, but Dax had to. She needed him to know.

She sipped the sweet drink down and when there were only a few sips left, he arrived. He looked like a typical Florida local. Tan, linen shirt and shorts, wearing a pair of flip-flops. He wore a hat and sunglasses. October smiled and looked around for the woman who had recognized him, but she didn't see her.

Dax sat opposite October and reached for her hand.

She melted at his touch. And prayed he'd listen fully and understand.

"I didn't know if you'd come," she said.

"Are you ready to talk about Rose?" he said.

"In a minute."

Their hands slipped apart when he ordered a drink, but she didn't want another.

How would she tell him about the article? She could have given Philip the byline and made him the bad guy, but that would have been a lie. Her heart said to tell Dax, but her head told her to be quiet and let them all find out the next day when the newspaper was published.

"Everything all right?" he said.

"Not really."

Dax got his drink and took a swig. Waiting.

"There's going to be an article in the newspaper tomorrow," she said. "About Natalia."

He put his drink down and stared at her, but through the sunglasses, she couldn't tell whether he was upset or just listening. She continued.

"Someone else, Philip, wrote a terrible story about her. It was revenge. He said that she stole his story ideas. He also listed all the names of the writers in the club. You. Dodge. Natalia, Korta."

Dax took off his hat and ran a hand through his hair, then put it back on.

"You're serious."

"Dead serious."

"How did he get the names?"

She wished she had ordered that drink, some nachos, anything to distract her from this moment and the stern look on his face.

"I wrote an article," she said. "Before I even really knew all of you."

"Before the first night?" he said.

"No. I wrote it when I was supposed to be writing my fictional story. When you gave me the spot. That first night."

"October."

She hated hearing him say her name that way. It was the sound her mother used when she'd done something she didn't approve of. She looked down at the table and curled her hands in her lap.

"I know," she said. "But the paper is failing, and I was supposed to save it. I promise you that story will never see the light of day. I just wanted you to know the truth. Philip must have found my article. Don't worry, I deleted it."

"But you wrote something about Natalia? How is that not giving up the secret?"

He leaned away from her now, and she picked at a piece of chipped pink nail polish.

"It's a good reflection of her. As an author. I have to submit a story to the paper. We don't have anything else to report. As you know, this town is pretty boring."

She hoped it would lighten his mood, but he didn't appear to have softened.

"So, you have to cover something that isn't any of your business. Gee, that's rich."

"I thought you'd understand."

Dax took a swig of his drink as they sat there in silence. People around them chatted, a few laughing amidst the clink of celebratory glasses and a seagull that squawked from the thick rope tied between the pilings.

October couldn't bear the silence between them, so she got up from the table, and since she hadn't ordered anything, there wasn't any reason to stay.

"I'm sorry," she said.

Dax held the drink in his hands and rattled the ice inside, staring at the glass.

"Me too."

And then, she left.

205

Chapter 40

Secret Scribes 5

B y the time the night rolled around, October was ready to face her mistakes and go to the Island Café for what might be the last time. They might not welcome her there, but she would take that chance. Rose was waiting, and writing was a way for her to forget what was happening between her and Clive, and her and Dax. Writing so many words in record time was addictive. Like riding a runaway train, almost off the rails. It was exhilarating when the words came faster than her pen would go.

When she arrived ahead of time, Dodge allowed her in. He and Korta were there, but Dax and Natalia weren't there yet. There was plenty of time, and she was happy that she could sit alone at the table and collect her thoughts. Dodge didn't seem aware of any issues, so she breathed slowly and channeled her characters. She would block out everything about the day and put it into Rose's story. It was gratifying to create something meaningful when her life, or at least her job at the newspaper, didn't seem to matter at all.

Dax and Natalia arrived together.

Natalia strolled by October, imparting a callous stare that wasn't atypical for Natalia, but after what October had told

Dax, and the fact that they may have had time to talk outside, October's guilt got the best of her.

She glanced away from Natalia and met Dax's eyes as he sat opposite her, sizing up his demeanor. He didn't smile, or frown, or give her any indication as to what he might be thinking. If anything at all.

"Hi," she said.

He nodded.

"Now that we are all present," Dodge said, "and on time for once, let's begin."

The pens and papers rattled and shuffled as the authors got to work. October began her new scene and cut off any mental chatter she had about Natalia's knowledge of the article or her fight with Dax.

October heard Rose's voice as she wrote, but the scene wasn't coming together as she'd expected, and her writing was slow.

Where are you, Rose? What's going to happen next?

Natalia shifted in her seat, got up from her table, and stood at the opposite side of the room.

October's focus shifted from Rose to what Natalia was doing, distracting her from her pages. No one else appeared to notice, they were so glued to their work. The movement slipped October up. Her focus disintegrating. She should have kept her head down and listened to Rose. Instead, October and Natalia made eye contact, and now all she could think about was her encounter with Charles and how his article had said that Natalia had stolen from him. Before she knew it, Rose was gone.

"What are you doing?" Dax said, witnessing the unmoving pen and her eyes wandering all over the room.

"Trying to write," she said, but she wasn't.

"You're not going to finish."

"I'm trying."

"Try harder," Dax said, keeping to his writing, but his sharp words were heard by everyone.

The chair became uncomfortable on her back; heat wafted up from the vents, and the absence of air made her lungs beg for life. The window would give her breath. She could escape this incredible tension from within if she bolted from her seat at the table.

Run.

It wasn't Rose doing the talking. She could tell it wasn't the voice of her character. It was her own.

You aren't a writer. You aren't anything. You're not worthy of success. All the mantras in the world aren't going to get you to Italy. You'll never finish a manuscript. You can't save the paper.

Dodge had stopped his own story and threw his pen. It flew at her head, and she flinched when it stung her ear before slamming into the wall behind her.

"Get writing. We are writers. Or you can leave."

Dodge picked up another pen from the table and started back to his draft as if he'd done nothing. As if throwing pens at someone's head was normal practice.

A thick tear welled in her left eye and fell on her blank page. With the back of her hand, she calmed the other potential tears and began writing, just to show she was. She wrote the same word repeatedly so that it appeared she was doing the work. *Fraud, fraud, fraud.* Her eyes stung, stinging more than the pen that had hit her on the head. Her hand shook, and her writing appeared jagged on the page.

Dax tapped her hand, but she snatched it away.

Finally, she began writing something for her story, though she didn't link it to a previous scene.

I need air. And my stomach growls like a starving child with nothing to eat. I didn't pack anything. How could I have been so stupid? To think gold and jewels would save me. I need the necessities. When the men aren't looking, I crawl toward one of the plates that's been left there. I don't care whether there are flies or bugs. I scoop from the mash and fill my stomach. I am strong and will do what must be done to survive.

I will survive.

I long for my home and the comforts there, my bed, my thick blankets, and all the normalized luxuries I stupidly cast away.

It's been months, and all I see is the ocean. Wide and dark with no hope in sight. My head feels heavy, and the ship almost sings a lullaby, the creaks and groans of the wood putting me to sleep. The blanket I was given is rough but warm, and I tug it around me, like a warm hug, a thing I haven't received for many years living in a dull, isolated marriage. I long for love. For a life to call my own. For family, friends, and safety.

"Time," Dodge said.

October stayed in her seat rather than getting up for coffee, which she badly needed. Her cheeks warmed from having been reprimanded like that. She watched as they all gathered around the coffee pot without her.

Rose would not have stood for this kind of treatment, so October got up out of her chair and marched over to Dodge. He was talking to Korta about something or other, but she didn't have the time to waste being patient.

"You can't throw pens at people," she said, cutting Korta's sentence off.

"I need my writers to focus," Dodge said. "It sets us all up for failure if someone's not keeping up."

"If I'm behind, I can't change that," October said. "I'm trying my best. I'm the author of this story, not you."

Dodge sipped his coffee but kept his stern face, and for the first time since they'd met, she wanted his approval.

He said, "We are an authors' group. Hence the word. *Group.* And you are part of that. We have rules, and codes, for our own sake. And you will need to respect them."

"This isn't a courtroom," she said. Dodge shot a look Dax's way, as he had told October that Dodge was the lawyer, telling her too much.

He kept his voice down, but it was clear the others could hear it all.

"She's just tired," Dax said. "I think we all are. We get prickly at the end. You know this, Dodge. It's nothing."

October was pleased that Dax wasn't among the ranks of those reprimanding her.

"And she's not the first author whom you've thrown something at," Dax said. "I still have the scar to prove it."

There was low chuckling that cut through the tension in the room.

"I want to write," October said, "but maybe I'm not cut out for this. It's too intense, and I just started writing again after ages. And I think I may have to quit."

"What's this all about?" Dodge said as he set his cup down and placed a gentle hand on her shoulder.

October was trying to keep her knowledge about Charles to herself, and the article about Natalia. But the guilt was weighing heavy.

"I met Charles Murrow," October said.

There was a hush. The coffee pot dripped slowly, sounding like a leaky faucet. October cleared her throat before continuing with the bad news. "He said his name was Philip. But I suspected he was not being forthcoming, so I followed him."

The authors stared from one to the other.

"Do you all know him?" October said.

She gave them time to consider what she had said, and then Natalia stepped out of the group and planted herself directly in front of October. Her black eyeliner was thick, as if a black Sharpie had been used to apply it. October stepped back at having her space invaded.

"He confronted me the other day. Startled me with his knowledge of where I was," Natalia said. "We were all to keep the secret to our whereabouts. And that included you." Natalia glared at October. "No one here would have told him where I was. Except you."

October staggered back. It wasn't her fault that Philip had come. She dabbed at her eye, which could have been damp from the terrible lighting, but it might have been another tear. She wouldn't admit to it.

"He's been working at the newspaper, and I think he intended to get revenge. He was using the name Van Sloan."

"Van Sloan. *Ha!*" Natalia said.

"I knew her position at the newspaper would be an issue," Dodge said. "She knows too much."

As the authors spoke amongst themselves leaving her out of it once again, she considered that she could leave the group and they wouldn't even notice, or care. She longed to be part of it, to feel a speck of closeness to her mother for wanting her to be there, and for Dax, a hopeful relationship in the midst. But it was fading away as if it had never really existed. Only a figment of her imagination, just like her fictional story. Just words on a page.

"I can assure you," she said, "that when the paper comes out tomorrow, there will be no article about this club. That's a promise."

"Well, that's a relief," Natalia said.

"Except," October said.

"Except what?"

"The paper is suffering. We don't have a lot to report, as you may have guessed from the lack of things going on around town. There weren't enough articles to publish a full paper, so I wrote a story, about you, Natalia."

Everything that was coming out of her mouth was all wrong. Like terribly written dialogue.

"About the club?" Dodge said, who appeared to speak on their behalf.

"No, but Philip, I mean Charles, wrote a nasty article that had all the details. And it would have been published too if I hadn't found it."

"How would he get the information?" Natalia said. "He knew nothing about this. He suspected, of course, but we never wanted him to find out. Otherwise, he would have wanted to be part of it. Charles always wanted what he couldn't have."

October didn't think keeping her lies was a good idea so had to add, "In the article, he said that Natalia stole his idea for a story, and that's why he never got published."

"Now, listen here," Dodge stepped in. "Natalia has never needed to steal a premise from anyone."

Dodge frowned at October, the deep crease in his forehead growing. If he hadn't already thrown a pen at her head, he would have been prepared to do worse. She shook while they had a stare-down, which she clearly would lose, so she looked away.

"How did Charles find out about our whereabouts?" Dodge said. "You need to be up-front about it."

"I don't know. It appeared I was followed, but I dismissed it. Another employee had handed over notes. At the time, I didn't understand what they meant."

She had been the reason. The detailed lists, their names, their pseudonyms, their clothes, and the code to enter the Island Café. The hours they wrote, how they wrote. She'd known it all and was prepared to use it.

October gulped. She wasn't prepared to tell them about her part in it. "I don't know how he knew," she said. Her shrill voice should have been plenty to give her away.

"It's not your fault," Dax said. He knew that it was.

October had wanted to be the person he believed she was.

She smiled at Dax, grateful for having him in her corner now, but swallowed hard, knowing that the details of the club had been hers to use and that she'd allowed them to slip into the hands of Charles, who wanted revenge.

Their five minutes were up, and Dodge sighed and went to his table.

"We have work to do, fellow authors, if we are to finish on time. We can't let this get in our way. We'll deal with it later."

The authors returned to their tables, but Natalia stood where she was for a moment. October sat down, defeated about how to finish telling Rose's story that night. If writer's block was real, it was happening. When Dodge told them to begin, there wasn't a scene in her head. Rose could have been drowning, and there was nothing October could do to save her.

"Begin," Dodge said again.

This time, the words wouldn't come at all. The hot stares of before burned through her, and the anguish of having made notes about the secret club made her feel sick inside.

"I can't do this," she said to Dax.

"Shhh."

"This isn't working."

Being a writer was more than she had signed up for. She was supposed to see Italy. The Mediterranean Sea. Instead, she was stuck here writing at night with a bunch of writers in secret, climbing ladders, dressing like children. It was foolish. Lillian Sinclair might have been cut out for this, but October Sinclair wasn't writer material.

She stood and placed the pad and pens into her backpack, strode to the door, and opened it. It appeared she could have left anytime she wanted. Why hadn't she done this sooner?

When she opened the window, she heard footsteps behind her.

"Dax, don't try and stop me."

"He's not," Natalia said. When October turned, Natalia was standing close to her, and October could hear her breaths and smell the fragrance of her perfume. "You need to come back inside."

"Why?"

"Get back to your writing. We'll talk about this after we are finished."

It wasn't what October had wanted. She didn't want to be there anymore. Her story was terrible, and Philip had won. He'd written the story and had left. She would have to pick up the pieces.

Natalia led her back through the door, and for a moment, the others stopped writing and stared, but it was such a fleeting moment that she hardly recognized it. Natalia took her seat again, and October did the same, pulled out her writing tools, and stared at the blank page. Dax glanced her way. She avoided his gaze. She was humiliated, but she took a deep breath, closed her eyes, and allowed her character to show her the next scene.

Storm clouds sink heavily in the sky, followed by lightning and thunder. The rain gushes down onto the ship, so I take cover beneath the stairs and protect myself with the blanket that the man gave me.

This is no regular storm.

The boat struggles in the ocean waves, the water sloshing on board, and my stomach can't tolerate the bobbing. I wretch to the side of the stairs, and I imagine my face is a pale shade of green. The wind is some of the worst I've ever seen, blowing the masts to bits, and the ship, once bobbing, is now in a tailspin. I feel the boat keeling so far to the right that I fear we are all going overboard. The men rush for the jib, and one of them falls to his death, his scream mixed with the wind.

I cannot tell how far we are from land. I've been told to get out before we get there, but I doubt that anyone here cares whether a woman has been on board all along. At least they have more to worry about than me. I stand and hold onto a large crate to get my bearings. Are we headed toward land still? Or have we turned in the opposite direction?

"Land ho."

The large ship is falling apart bit by bit, farther toward land, and before I have time to gather my senses, the bow smashes into bits and thrusts me forward until I crash into something hard on the deck. And that's the last thing I see before I sink deep down into icy cold water.

When I surface, I cry out. I have fallen overboard. There is no one to help me now. The thick blanket, once warm and soft, is weighing me down like a bloody anchor. I gasp for air. The water is so cold I can barely breathe. I'm going to die. I am ready to die.

The ship continues to float like a pile of lumber, and mixed with the wood are some of my belongings. The box floats, for now, and I swim to it, abandoning the blanket, watching it float like slick grease on the sea surface. I stare up to the deck and see him there, a shadow hovering above me. He points, but my eyes are filled with seawater, blurry and unclear. I turn my head in the direction and squint, and it's then that I see it.

Land.

I swim, but my dress is so heavy it may take days to get to shore. The waves are so fierce that I must hold my breath for long periods, closing my eyes to save them from the intense salt and seaweed that slashes around me.

October wrote a bit more, and the minute Rose could see land made her excited for what was yet to come. Rose would have plenty of obstacles ahead of her. But she would prevail. The heaviness, the guilt, the confusion of all that had transpired that day had been lifted, simply by writing about something that wasn't real.

When Dodge called time again, Dax pulled his chair closer to October.

"What's going on?" he said.

"I told you."

"Okay, that's fine. But it appears that there's something else. Usually, when I can't write, it's really because something else is bothering me."

She smiled. He knew her more than she realized.

"Something is bothering me. Terribly. That you hate me."

He leaned back with a questioning look.

"Hate you?"

"For writing the article. For allowing Philip, I mean Charles, to get the information. And you lied for me."

"I know you. You're not malicious. Charles, well . . ."

She wanted to know more about Charles. All the authors appeared to know.

"It's still my fault, don't you see? I took notes. When I first came here, I intended to use this as my brilliant story for the paper."

"But you didn't publish it."

"I didn't, but Charles did. As I told you. I deleted it."

"So, you kept your promise."

"Thank you for sticking up for me."

She held her ear that still tingled from the pen, and they both laughed.

They finished the writing for the night, and October climbed down the ladder feeling lighter from getting it all out in the open now, and for telling Natalia about what happened. Dax and the others knew what she had intended at first, but it was Charles in the end who was to blame.

She wanted to walk home alone, to soak in all that had happened that day, without worrying about the rest. Dax went toward the Wild Honey B and B, and the others disappeared into the dark landscape.

October took her time, strolling down the main street, enjoying the calm. Charles was gone, and she wasn't afraid anymore. The sound of gentle waves lapping up the shore slowed her breathing, and when she saw a glint of light about the horizon, she smiled. Maybe it would be okay in the end. She chanted her little mantra to herself.

She had passed Glen's Bakery when bright headlights appeared round the corner. She shaded her eyes.

An early morning car wasn't odd, but this one slowed as it approached, and the window rolled down when it reached her.

"October?"

The voice she recognized. She walked toward the car and peeked in the window.

"Alice?"

Alice grinned. She was wearing a black tank top with sweats and had tucked her ponytail into her Gator baseball cap. She had a tattoo of a heart on her upper arm, one that October had seen almost every day they worked together. "Wanna ride?"

October didn't need one, as her apartment was less than a block away, but she got into Alice's little Cooper and slammed the door. There was a camera between them, which Alice tossed into the back seat.

"What are you doing here?" October said.

"I guess I could say the same to you, but I don't have to. I know."

Alice put the car into reverse, then backed into the beach parking lot and took off south toward the dunes.

"I thought you left," October said. "Clive told me that you quit. And you didn't even say goodbye."

"I'm not much for farewells."

October was still upset that after two years of working together, Alice had just left her like that, but she kept it to herself.

"I found the notes," October said.

Alice's eyes lit up like sparklers.

"I hoped that you would. Last year, a bunch of people came out from the upstairs window of the Island Café, but then I never saw them again. I made a note in my journal to check again at the same time this year, to see if they came back, and sure enough."

Bridgette had said Alice was there one time when she was closing.

"What else do you know?" October said.

"You tell me," Alice said. "Give me the juicy details."

October had sworn to secrecy for the second time that night, and this time, she meant it.

"I don't know any more about it than you do," she said.

October didn't know how much she should tell Alice about any of this. She'd already made a mess of everything.

"Some guy named Philip took your job," October said. "But now, he's gone too."

Alice kept her eyes on the dark road.

"Did you tell him anything about the club?" Alice finally said.

"No."

Alice used the word *club*. No one had used that word. Only October.

"Why'd you quit?" October said.

"The job was getting boring. Plus, I got the scoop that Clive was giving up the paper. Why stay on a dead horse?"

"Who told you he was giving up the newspaper?" October was embarrassed that Alice had known this, but she hadn't.

Alice shrugged. "He did."

"Clive?"

"Look, we were tight. He told me a lot of things. I pretty much did his job for him. We'd have a scotch after work. Nothing serious, just a drink."

"Were you two—"

"No. Just friends."

October almost mentioned her and Clive's friendly relationship once, and how it had taken a turn lately, but decided against it. They had never had drinks, and October had no idea what was going on outside of her advertising clients.

"Philip was a writer," October said, prodding Alice. What else did she know?

"Was he?" Alice pulled the car into the newspaper, switched it off, and turned off the lights.

"What are we doing here?" October said.

"Mind if you let me in to the place? I want to grab my hibiscus plant. Sorry I didn't tell you I quit, we never talked anyway."

October blushed. She'd thrown the plant away.

"Okay," she said anyway.

For two young women, using the same desk for as long as they'd worked there, it was rare that they spoke. October had tried many times to get to know Alice, but she didn't reciprocate. Both of them were out of the office anyway. Alice getting stories and taking long breaks, and October getting ads.

"I would have liked it if you'd said goodbye," October said.

Alice laughed, and it made October uncomfortable.

"Alice," October said finally. "What's going on? Why are you driving around so early?"

"I was on the beach. Got a great picture of a leatherback. I swear it was the size of my car."

"Fine. Don't tell me."

"I'm serious."

Alice grabbed her camera from the back seat, switched a few dials, and then held the photo up for October to see it. A large leatherback.

"It's gigantic," October said.

"Told you."

October gazed around Alice's car. It held all the magazines that October remembered on her desk. Her laptop was thrown over a couple of beach towels, and there was a suitcase.

"Are you going somewhere?"

Alice didn't answer but leaned back in the seat and stared up at nothing.

"The paper goes out today," Alice said. "Is it ready?"

It was, but October wished some of the stories were better.

"It still needs proofing," she said.

October grabbed the handle of the car door and opened it.

"I could take a look," Alice said. "I always did it for Clive."

It wouldn't hurt to have another pair of eyes on it, since Clive would probably print it as is without any editing whatsoever.

"That would be nice," October said.

And Alice beamed.

Chapter 41

Running the Show

Alice went directly into Clive's office, and October followed her there, wondering how much of the newspaper Alice had run without October even realizing it. Clive had let her have access. Alice turned on the computer and sat down in his chair.

"Mind if I open the window?" Alice said. "It's hot in here."

October grabbed her laptop from her desk and joined Alice in Clive's office as the ocean air trickled in. Two women running the show. No more men laughing about writing gritty stories about strangers in town.

"What do you think?" October said to Alice.

Alice clicked around the page layout software, and October was proud that Alice could see her article about the Island Café with the photo of Bridgette on the front page. Her byline included.

"Looks pretty good. Would have been nice to have a few other juicy pieces, rather than the boring stuff," Alice said.

It wasn't all boring, but October didn't want to appear defensive. There was the Island Café article, the Jeb Howard piece, and the one buried on page three about Natalia. She was right that the other stories that filled the pages were pretty bland.

"I told Clive that we should use stories from the archives. Do you think that's a good idea?" October said.

"Hell, yeah," Alice said.

October took the mouse and clicked open the file on the screen that held the articles they'd run in the past.

"You have a knack for this," Alice said.

"I'm just trying to help."

"I never saw this side of you before. You used to just sit by yourself, barely talking."

It wasn't true. October had attempted multiple times to make small talk, but Alice had been too busy talking on her phone or going out for lunch. They didn't have the same friends or the same interests. And Alice had quit without even mentioning it. October shrugged it off.

"Here," October said when she found an article she wanted. "We'll run that piece. You wrote the story a few years back about the new construction of the wing for the Oaks. Let's update it with more information and use it."

"That place used to be hideous," Alice said.

"Not anymore."

October had seen the updates firsthand when she interviewed Jeb Howard. The soft and beachy colors, the contemporary feel, and the updated carpets gave it a youthful appearance. Then she cited a website that rated the Oaks as one of the top ten fifty-five-plus retirement communities in Florida.

October started typing on her laptop while Alice clicked around the screen. She crafted the article with detail and facts and made the Oaks a highlight of the newspaper. Voilà, she had a story. Alice scanned it, made a couple of grammar corrections, and replaced one of the small stories with the new one.

"It's good."

There was still room for something else. October had an idea.

"Can we use your turtle photo?"

Alice sent the photo to October, who quickly found another article about leatherbacks, writing as fast as she could to update the year's nesting totals along with new information she gathered from the Honeycomb Beach Sea Turtle Conservatory's website. She gave Alice credit for the photo.

"There's one more article that we might replace if we had something," Alice said. "Otherwise, the segment about when the town plans to finally repair the crack in the riverside sidewalk remains."

"What if I write a fictional piece?" October said. "Something that might continue in the next issue?"

Alice rolled her eyes. "We don't have that kind of time, and even if we did, we don't have a story idea."

"Actually, I do."

October leaped up, ran to her desk, fished out the pirate story she'd been working on from her backpack, and took it back to Alice.

"I've been working on this. Have a look."

Alice took it and started reading, and without saying a word, sat down in Clive's chair, flipping to the next page. October bit her lip, as she'd never shared her story with anyone, even Dax. She talked it through with him, but up until that moment, she hadn't shared a word.

"October," Alice said, looking up from the work after she'd finished. "This is good."

October smiled with pride.

"You think so?"

"It's great. And I can't wait to see what happens next."

Without asking for permission, Alice pulled herself up to the computer and started typing the first section of October's work on the page, filling in the space they needed. It would fit perfectly.

To be continued.

"We did it," October said. "The paper is ready to go. I couldn't have done this without you."

Alice stared at the screen.

"What's wrong?" October said. "Did you see an error or something?"

"No. I was just . . . It's nothing."

It was six in the morning when they finished. Clive would be there shortly to take care of the rest. He might have been late all the days leading up to publication, but he'd never missed press time. October's job was done.

"I wish Clive wasn't going to sell the paper," October said. "Maybe you could come back, and we could convince him not to."

Alice stepped out of Clive's office and into the small area where she used to work and took a look around. The long table was empty, her desk accessories all stuffed in the back seat of her car. She studied the poster on the wall.

"Think you'll ever get there?" she said.

"I hope so. One day."

October and Alice walked outside, and October locked up again. She would go home, shower, and change, and know she had finished the paper. She had saved the day.

"So, you won't come back?" October said.

"Nope. Heading to the Keys."

"Guess everyone's going there these days," October said.

There was a small part of October that was envious of Alice. To have no real plans but to seem oddly elated by it.

"Well, good luck," October said.

The two walked down the path toward the sidewalk, and Alice went left and October went right.

As Alice skipped away, she waved goodbye and October realized she'd never looked for the hibiscus plant.

Chapter 42

Front Page

October slept.

Her mind was blissfully void of Rose, Dax, Clive, or Philip. The work had been done, and she could finally rest for a few more hours, tucked in her bed. She smiled, eyes still closed, and pulled the light coverlet up to her chin.

Cinnamon drifted in the room, and the smell of toasted coconut along with it. She inhaled and opened her eyes, her mouth salivating.

There was a knock at the door. She pictured Summer outside with a plate of her cinnamon coconut buns.

"Can I come in?" Summer said.

"I'm awake."

October rubbed her eyes when Summer entered the room holding a small plate with one perfect roll and a steaming mug of coffee.

"You made these?"

Summer smiled. "Glen's Bakery. I went over to get the newspaper."

October took a bite of the hot bun and closed her eyes again.

"Yum," she said. "But yours are just as good."

Summer sat on the bed and handed October the latest edition. The papers were always at the stores early, and then later, they'd go to the rest of the residents. It had always been that way. Clive's father thought it helped businesses.

"We've got to celebrate," Summer said.

"Celebrate what?"

Summer began reading October's story about the Pirate Princess.

"When have you had the time to write fiction?" Summer said. "I love it."

Summer still knew nothing about the authors' club, and once the week was over, she'd tell Summer everything about it, and maybe even broach the subject of not going to Jack's Tiki Bar all the time.

"I've been writing after work," October said.

"Oh. I thought you were in the secret authors' society."

October froze.

"How did you know about that?"

Summer showed her the front page featuring a picture of her and Dax. Holding hands.

"I can't believe you didn't tell me you've been dating Dax Cooper!"

October wanted to explain to her friend having found out about it this way, but she couldn't speak as she stared at the headline.

`The Island Café's Secret Rendezvous`

`by October Sinclair`

October slapped the newspaper on the bed with so much force that the cinnamon roll fell on the floor.

"This isn't . . . I can't believe this."

"Dax Cooper?" Summer said once again. "Is he as dreamy in person as he looks?"

Summer wasn't mad. At least she had that.

"Summer. This is serious."

The byline was something that October had wanted when she wrote the very first article about the Island Café. An interview with Bridgette. But her original story, a nice piece about the roastery and café, had been replaced with this one instead.

"I'm confused," Summer said. "I thought this was a good thing." It should have been a celebratory occasion to have her byline on the first page, as well as stepping out with one of the most hunky authors in the writing world, but it was the worst thing that could have happened to her.

"I didn't write this," October said.

"Well, it's a good story. It makes this issue a lot more interesting than some of the others. And the story you wrote about the character Rose makes it even better."

This was a nightmare. October had to go and find Dax, Dodge, Natalia, and Korta. They had to know that she had kept her promise.

"I know who wrote it," October said. "The question is why."

Alice had been so eager to help October with the paper. Why had October believed that she was just out taking photos of turtles so early in the morning? Alice had watched October go to the Island Café that night. And she had waited there until October emerged all by herself. She had intended to go back and change the story after they left. Alice must have come in through the window in Clive's office. October had taken the bait, thinking Alice was being nice. October tossed on some clothes and shoved her feet into flip-flops.

"I've got to talk to Dax," she said and ran out of the room and slammed the front door behind her.

Chapter 43

Apology

She ran as fast as she could and, to anyone passing by, looked like a typical athlete, which she had been in college, speeding down the sidewalk like a lean gazelle. October lunged up the stairs, taking them two by two, passing Oreo's food bowls by the rocking chair. Her first inclination was to knock, but no one was going to answer. It was a bed and breakfast; she was welcome inside.

In the large foyer, old hardwood floors gleamed, and the aromas of freshly baked bread and crispy bacon mingled with the musty scent of antique rugs. Courtney, the proprietor, appeared holding the stack of newspapers and smiled at October as if she was welcome.

"They just arrived," Courtney said and placed the stack on the table nearby.

October stared at the pile, wanting to take them somewhere and burn them.

"Is Dax here?" October said, looking around now, hoping he had left or moved back across the country before he could see what she'd done.

"I see that you know him," she said as she pointed to the first page.

"It's innocent."

"He hasn't come down for breakfast."

Oreo rubbed his body on her leg and purred so loud she could feel the vibration on her shin. Any other day, she'd stay and play with the cat who loved people, but her mind was preoccupied with the newspaper and what it contained. She leaned down and gave him a little pat to please him, and he moved on to Courtney.

Courtney left the pile where everyone could see the front page with the black-and-white photo of Dax and October secretly leaving the Island Café in the early morning hours.

"You can wait for Dax if you like. I've got to get to work."

Courtney headed for the kitchen, and October stood alone in the large room, wishing it would swallow her whole.

"October," Dax said. "What are you doing here?"

She jumped at the sound of his voice and melted at his comfortable demeanor, looking a little worn, hair out of place, yawning.

The kitchen staff chatted and clanked pots in the background. She didn't want to talk there, but she would get it out in the open before she lost her nerve.

"I need to tell you something," she said. "And you're going to be mad."

He brushed a hand through his bedhead hair and watched as she grabbed a copy of the newspaper from the table nearby.

She held up the front page, and he stepped back, his face crinkled in disbelief.

"I didn't write it," she said. It didn't matter who did, and she knew that she wouldn't be off the hook simply because someone else typed what she had already written. This was all her fault.

He grabbed the paper and read the words that everyone in town was now privy to.

"Who wrote it then?"

"Alice. I think. Or Charles? I don't know."

"You promised. You swore to secrecy."

"I know. I'm so sorry," she said. "I've messed up."

It appeared not to be the right thing to say because Dax stuffed the newspaper into her hands and left her there alone again. She watched as he took the stairs back up to his room. Her instinct was that he might come back. Was he grabbing a coat? Was he coming back to say that they'd work it out together? She stood at the base of the stairs, but he didn't return.

Dax wouldn't be coming back to her ever again.

Chapter 44

The Truth

She left the Wild Honey B and B and staggered down the sidewalk like a dog whose owner had tossed it into the streets to fend for itself. She deserved it, but it hurt anyway. She had someone else to tell the news to, and it wasn't going to be pretty. Natalia had a right to know that not only was her name in the paper but also the secret was revealed, and on the front page.

October didn't expect Natalia to give her grace, but she needed to explain. When she reached Natalia's condo, she stood outside the door, running dialogue through her head, trying to find the right words. Natalia frightened her. Everything from her dark eyeliner to her matching black coat.

Just do it.

She knocked on the condo door and stepped back as if the wooden door might explode. It was absurd to be frightened of another person. Confrontation was her real fear.

"Who is it?" Natalia said from behind the door.

"October. From the writing club."

The door opened wide.

Natalia stood in the hallway, fully dressed in a white tunic and skirt, her eyes bright and unlined, her lips devoid of the bloodlike lipstick but replaced with a pink sheen.

"Come in," Natalia said, motioning to October, who stepped inside. "Coffee? It's not the best, but it's hot."

There were suitcases by the front door.

"You're leaving?"

Natalia pointed to the newspaper on the kitchen counter.

"It was only a matter of time."

October didn't say that she was sorry because it didn't matter. She was the one responsible for starting the whole mess, taking Alice's notes and creating enough imagery and research so that either Alice or Charles could use it as their own.

October watched as Natalia swept through the kitchen, with fresh seafoam green, white tile, and starfish decor, then poured the coffee into two small mugs and handed one to October.

"Sit."

October did as she was told, and the two sat opposite one another at the center island bar with a wicker light fixture over it. October relaxed her shoulders, but her hands remained clasped around the mug, tight and rigid.

"I feel so guilty for what I've done," October said.

"You mean for what Charles has done."

October's eyes widened. She promised herself that she wouldn't place the blame on Natalia's brother, but she had wanted to.

"I was the one who originally had the plan to write the story," October said. She explained once again how it all came to be from the first notes Alice left up until the newspaper's publication.

Natalia nodded and sipped her coffee as October continued to tell her story.

"I didn't want to expose the group after I met you all and got to become a fan of the club, but I see now that someone had been following me. For that, I'm responsible and very sorry."

Natalia stared at October with pretty eyes.

"Charles, the one you met as Philip, has always been jealous of me. He is a writer too, and we had, shall we say . . . differences. We didn't always have a bad relationship," she said. "We were close once."

October sipped her coffee to keep Natalia talking. She didn't want her to stop with this story that October had been very interested in. She needed to know why Philip was the way he was. And why he had come to the beach.

"But now, after everything, we just aren't anymore."

October nodded but needed to know more. She waited.

"Philip was an author too," Natalia said. "He wrote a memoir."

"I know," October said. "I followed him to the beach one afternoon."

October dug out the crumpled letter that she'd rescued from the ocean and gave it to Natalia. "He had a letter from a publisher that he wadded up and tossed. I retrieved it. And that's when I learned that he was Charles Murrow, not Philip Van Sloan. And that he had been rejected by a publisher."

"God, not another rejection," Natalia said. "He can't bear it when he doesn't get his way. He hates to lose. And he's always wanted revenge."

She opened the paper and smoothed it out in front of her.

"Years ago," Natalia said, "Charles wanted to follow in my footsteps, started writing stories and sending them to my agents and stalking publishers using my name as his way in. It didn't work. His writing wasn't good enough. I don't like to sound uppity, but he didn't have the talent. After every rejection, he would blame me, saying that I was the one keeping him out of the publishing world. After a while, it calmed down, but then, he asked me to write with him, hoping to gain access to my author friendships and the writing world. I wouldn't let him, of course, knowing how he was. The secret authors' club was just a way to keep Charles out of it. We don't have to write in secret, but he would ruin it. Like he's ruined so many things."

"I'm so sorry. I didn't realize."

"It's not your fault. I'm responsible for all of this," Natalia said. "Charles will never forgive me for his memoir."

"He said you stole his idea about a novel."

"He says many things that aren't true."

October raised her eyebrows, waiting for more. And Natalia easily gave it. Natalia shifted in her seat and cupped her mug. "You see," she said. "Charles wasn't just trying to copy my life by writing books. He lied. He wrote something in his memoir that was so far from the truth that I couldn't accept it. Memoir is written from the perspective of the author, of course, and there are certain liberties, but some of the things he wrote were simply false. And he was very close to getting that one published. But I couldn't allow it."

"What did he write that wasn't true?" October said.

"He told terrible lies about our parents to make his story more interesting. And I couldn't let him do it."

October leaned in as Natalia continued.

"My father was not the man Charles made him out to be. He never hit us, nor did he have an affair. It was pure embellishment on Charles's part. Our life was relatively normal. We didn't come from money, and we did have some hard times. I assumed that was the subject of his book. I think his need to publish was so great that it led him to lie."

"So what happened?"

"I called the publisher. And I told them that he was not telling the truth. Several memoirs have gone too far and gotten publishers into trouble. So they were not going to take a risk on Charles. They pulled it."

"Oh."

No wonder Philip had wanted October to tell the story about the club so badly. He wanted revenge. On his sister.

"The advance for that memoir was sizable. It could have put it on the bestsellers list. And he will never forgive me for using my contacts to get it pulled. And he will probably never get an offer again."

233

"It seems like a lot to go through, coming to Honeycomb Beach, getting a job for a week at the newspaper, just to get back at you," October said.

"Oh, he was here often. I think he had a girlfriend that he visited. I'm surprised that you never saw him."

October tried to think back to when she might have seen him, but oddly, they hadn't crossed paths.

"I don't think he was the one to write the last article anyway. I changed what he had written, and then I think the reporter who recently quit came back and wrote this."

October couldn't understand why Alice would have done such a thing.

"Perhaps, she wanted some revenge too," Natalia said.

October hadn't considered this. But it might be true.

"Charles was always that way. When he didn't get what he wanted, he would do anything. Even if it didn't make much sense. Charles is a charmer. He will go to great lengths to get what he wants. He may have convinced her to write it instead."

"It's possible, I guess. Maybe that's why he faked his name. Philip Van Sloan."

Natalia laughed.

"Van Sloan. As children, Charles and I would watch old movies and scare one another. Edward Van Sloan was a famous actor who had roles in films like *Frankenstein*, *Dracula*, and *The Mummy*. We watched them all. Charles chose the name because he knew that I would recognize it.

"Like as a byline?"

"I suppose. Now it seems that it was a waste of a very good pseudonym.

"You think that Charles convinced my colleague, Alice, to do his bidding?"

"It was already put into place," Natalia said, glaring at October across the table. October warmed with embarrassment. "You and this other girl were putty in his hands."

"I'm surprised that he got the job at the paper."

234

"He is resourceful. When he wants something, he usually gets it. It's always been that way with my brother."

Natalia finished the last of her coffee and took her cup to the kitchen sink. "I hoped that you would come here today," she said. "And I'm sorry that the first time you came I wasn't receptive. I had a feeling that something wasn't right. And I knew that Charles was not far behind. You are not a bad person, October. But you'll have to make this right. The authors will no longer have a place to write."

"But how?"

"I can't tell you that. It's up to you, of course. But you've hurt people. Maybe to you, we were just a bunch of silly writers dressing up and making rules. But our code was our bond. And they were all trying to protect me from Charles. We let you in. If you want to stay, you have to do something about it."

"I could stay?"

"Maybe. I don't know. Even so, you are a good person, and I know you'll do the right thing."

"Will you forgive Charles?"

She chuckled to herself. "We will mend. In time. But for now, I'm keeping my anger. It fuels my fiction. He's probably halfway to Key West by now anyway. Thinks the rich words of Hemingway might rub off on him there."

Natalia snickered and reached across to the table, and October handed her the coffee mug, which Natalia placed next to her empty one. This would be the last time she would see Natalia before she left.

October stood, and Natalia placed a hand on her arm.

"Thank you," October said. "I mean it. I will miss the authors' club."

And then October did something she hadn't intended to do; she hugged Natalia tightly, and tears came to her eyes.

"Goodbye," Natalia said, letting her go. "Keep writing. And your fictional piece in the paper was good. And you know I wouldn't say it if it weren't the truth."

October turned to go.

"There is something else," Natalia said.

"What's that?"

"The article. You said Charles didn't write it, but the girl from your office did?"

"She was with me last night. I thought she was helping me."

"It sounded like Charles to me, but I could be wrong."

October left, and when she got down the stairs, she stopped. *Key West.* The light bulb finally went on.

Alice was Charles's girlfriend.

October returned to the newspaper after saying goodbye and didn't know what to expect. Her job was finished; Clive was selling, and it was apparent that the issue that claimed the whereabouts of the authors was the last one.

The office offered up its familiar creaks; the soft pool of morning sun was beginning to stream through the windows from Clive's office. She didn't think he would appear anytime soon or even at all. The newspaper was over from his vantage point.

She took in the surroundings, her home away from home full of familiar smells, coffee, burned leftovers that Clive had eaten for lunch, the click of the fluorescent lights, and the damp smell that never went away after the rain. It would be sad if Clive sold the place and she couldn't come back there anymore. She'd dreamed of Italy, but now, her town appeared to offer more than she'd realized. And there was something meaningful in what she did, even if it was just ads.

At her desk, she opened up the issue that she dreaded to read for the first time, having only scanned it before, too upset to give it a thorough glance. Alice had either written it herself or simply entered everything that Philip had wanted her to. And like a copilot, ruined the secret authors' club for good.

October pictured Alice and Philip driving over the Seven Mile Bridge to the Keys, laughing at what they'd accomplished together. Not caring whether they'd hurt anyone in the process.

HONEYCOMB BEACH -In our sleepy beach town, where the streetlights dim by ten p.m., a curious phenomenon comes alive right under the full moon. Five well-known authors gather in secret in the dark space of the Island Café, accessible only through a window on the west side. With the café closed and the town quiet, these writers stealthily ascend a side ladder, slipping into their covert sanctuary with pads of paper and pens in hand.

An anonymous eyewitness reveals that the room is sparsely furnished with small tables, chairs, and an abundant supply of coffee. More than enough to fuel creativity from midnight to the early hours of the morning. The authors, who have made this clandestine gathering an annual tradition, write under pseudonyms, adding another layer of mystery.

Dax Cooper, famed fantasy writer of Above the Dragons and the television adaptation of Ember's Reign, wears dragon cufflinks and theatrical garb to write his fiction. As writing is a play, the cast of famous writers dresses cringingly, in feather boas, celestial jewelry, dark masks, and pirate garb. Natalia Murrow, renowned for her chilling horror series and recent bestseller Fingers of the Fallen, conceals her identity with deep makeup and wigs, as she hides more than she's telling, like the truth behind her premise and whether the title is entirely hers.

While the true nature of their late-night activities remains uncertain, the secrecy surrounding their gatherings has sparked speculation. Are they penning their next masterpieces, or is there something more sinister at play? Are they stealing other authors' work, as Natalia Murrow has done, and calling it their own? The intrigue deepens as the café's owner, Bridgette, collaborates with the local sheriff to investigate how the café was accessed without the staff's knowledge.

For now, the hidden world of Honeycomb Beach's secret authors' society continues to captivate the imagination, leaving locals and readers alike wondering what stories and secrets lie within those walls.

October swallowed hard as she read the article for the umpteenth time. Alice took part in this. But why? They did nothing to her. October slammed the paper down on the desk just as Clive walked in.

Clive shuffled toward his office door, but October flew out of her chair and blocked him from going in.

"What is all this?" she said, showing him the obvious front page.

He ignored her and sidestepped around her, threw his bag on the desk, and turned on the computer. She followed him in and slammed the door behind her even though they were the only ones in the place. It was hardly necessary.

"I know you're upset," he said.

"Upset? That's an understatement. The article is one thing, but you haven't been coming to work, you aren't taking charge, Alice is gone, and I know that you paid Charles a lot of money."

"Who?"

"Philip Van Sloan. His name is Charles Murrow."

Clive looked stunned and incoherent. Had he gotten any sleep in the last week? He sat in his chair and drank from a paper cup, then rubbed his head with his large palm, as if a migraine was pounding on his forehead.

"Maybe you should start from the beginning," he said, "because you're not making any sense right now."

She handed him the newspaper.

"Alice left us a little gift last night," she said. "Didn't you read it before you published it?"

"I didn't . . . She called and said she'd take care of it."

"What?"

"I don't know. I thought it was weird, but she was glad to do it."

238

He took it in his hands and flipped through the pages, then stared at the photo of her and Dax. Then he smiled, and she wanted to wipe it off his face.

"How can you be happy about this?"

"This is a great article. It's too bad though. It's way too late. Dad is already committed to selling."

She felt sick.

Clive scratched his head, and she was tired of his inability to grasp difficult concepts. She'd cut to the chase.

"Is this what you paid Charles a thousand dollars for?"

"Charles?"

"Philip. You gave him a thousand dollars."

"You shouldn't have gotten involved in this."

October took a step back. As if she'd been slapped. She was simply trying to do her job. A job that Clive appeared not to want anymore.

"Involved?" she said. "It's my job to be involved. After Alice quit, someone had to do something."

He stared at her as if he had no recollection of what had transpired in the last few days even though he was responsible for all of it. Of course. Clive wanted the newspaper to be late or so badly put together that his father would sell it before he could think twice about it. October figured that he'd be much better as a surfing instructor, not a newspaper owner, but still, it was unprofessional what he was doing. And he wasn't even thinking about her job and that she was about to be out of work.

"Did you fire Alice?" October said, feeling a shred of pity for him. She had an idea that she knew why Alice didn't come back and why Alice might want some kind of retaliation.

"No. I told you I didn't. She texted me that she was quitting after—"

"What?"

"Well, I'll be damned."

October had no idea what had just registered so waited until Clive could put it all together himself.

"I didn't pay Philip for writing a story," he said. "I paid him because he won a bet at the bar that night."

"A bet?

"Yeah. Philip told me that he'd seen what he believed was Alice at the Island Café talking to Bridgette the morning before I met him at the bar, then after a couple of drinks and me telling him all about my dilemma at the paper, that things weren't going that well, he bet me a thousand dollars that Alice was going to quit."

"And you took the bet?"

"It seemed extreme, plus I'd had a couple of beers by then. But I couldn't believe that Alice would just up and quit without even giving notice, so I said sure I'll take that bet."

"Then she quit?"

"I got a text almost immediately after I took that bet. Alice said she was taking off. Going out of town."

"Then what happened?"

"I told Philip my situation and that my best writer was gone. He told me he was a writer himself and that if the paper was struggling, then a good story would save it. He offered to help. So I hired him."

She recalled how Alice had acted the few days before she quit. Quiet, reserved, and frustrated with the paper. But October hadn't put much emphasis on it until now. Alice had found out about the secret club, and if she was Charles's girlfriend, she'd told him what she knew. And the two of them would have some fun with it, tell the story, and then go off into the Key West sunset together with a bunch of money.

Philip had known that Clive would be at the bar that night. He'd also known, through Alice, possibly because of her after-hours drinks with Clive, how unhappy Clive was, making him an easy target.

October knew now why Alice didn't say goodbye. She wasn't finished yet.

Philip had wanted Clive to publish a story about Natalia, the tourist story, from the beginning. It was October's refusal and her inability to interview Natalia that might have pro-voked someone to follow her the next evening to the Island Café. Alice.

Charles, posing as Philip Van Sloan, sought revenge on Natalia and wanted to write a terrible article about her. He'd chosen an easy paper to get even, but what did it prove?

Clive leaned back in his chair and covered his eyes with his fists. October winced at how it had all turned out.

"He told me that he could end the paper. That he would make sure that my father wouldn't want it anymore."

"So the gritty stories?"

"I admit, that was a terrible idea."

"You and I could have run the paper alone," October said. "We could have made some changes, cut costs, digitalized."

Clive pressed his flat palm in the air, halting any more words from her mouth.

"My father is selling the paper, October. It's over. It's not what I want to do with my life. I'm sorry, but this was the last issue of the *Honeycomb Beach Times*."

It only took five minutes for October to collect her things, including her files and laptop. She filled an empty printer box with odds and ends that she kept on her desk. A mug, a fake cactus, a picture of her and Summer at the beach, and she took down the poster of scenic Tuscany, a place that she had little hope of ever visiting now. She grabbed the files that Alice had given her, even though they were already written and the authors' club was no longer going to convene once a week every summer in her town. Just when she'd been excited that her new life was beginning, it was over.

She held back tears, but it was silly. The paper wasn't a great job, and she didn't even like doing ads that much. James the Bug Guy and the rest of her clients would have to be told and given an explanation. James wouldn't mind, as he was just trying to keep her going more than the other way around. It wasn't the paper that made her sad anyway. She had betrayed her new friends.

Clive slithered out the door before she did, his last word was to send out a letter to businesses telling them that they were closing and that she must do it from home because he asked for her key.

When he left, she stood there, looking around at the emptiness. There was no job, no paper, no Dax, Dodge, Korta, or Natalia. There was no lust for travel. The last days had sucked her dreams away. She had almost enough money, but she'd lost the thrill of leaving the beach for something different.

"I've been duped," she said to the walls while she finished putting her things in her backpack. She reached into the drawers of the table one last time to fish out any extra pens or paper clips and found a note written on a small yellow Post-it.

"Sorry! Chalk it up to love. Good Luck." —A

October shredded it with her hands and threw it in the trash.

She left the newspaper, heading back to her apartment, where she tossed the box of things on the sofa and then flung herself across her bed.

Tonight, she would return to the Island Café and pray that the authors, minus Natalia, would still be there for one more writing session. Natalia didn't care that Charles had found her. She knew he wanted to make her look bad to make himself feel better. And with Alice's help, he had done it.

The rest of the authors desired the secret to keep their own writing lives separate. As Dodge had told her, it was more a game than anything else, but she couldn't deny that she'd played a part in ending it. And her mother would have one more reason for telling her that she shouldn't be a writer. That was probably true.

The idea of Rose and her pirate story sat idle. Would she even bother to try to write the whole story? Now that there was no author group or even a paper to publish the excerpts. It all seemed such a waste. And just when she was starting to think that she had a calling. She was right back where she'd started at the beginning of the week.

She slept soundly and only woke when she heard Summer rummaging around in the kitchen. The cabinet doors groaned when they were opened, an annoying feature that they never fixed.

October crawled out from the covers and made her way into the living room.

Summer was sitting in the beanbag chair with her book, munching from a bowl of potato chips.

"What are you doing home?" Summer said. "Are you sick?"

October had to admit that she was tired and achy. But it wasn't sickness that was making her feel that way.

"No. I'm fine."

"You don't look fine."

Summer slid over and patted the leather cushion, and October plopped down next to her friend and laid her head on her shoulder.

"I didn't have the best day," October said.

"What happened?"

"I lost my job. And I don't know where I'm going to get another job in this town."

"You wanted to go to Italy. So go."

Summer looked down at October, who was staring at her now, eyes full of tears.

"I did. But right now, I just don't know what I want anymore."

"You'll figure something out," Summer said.

"There's something else I've been meaning to tell you."

She sat up and placed a hand on Summer's. They were good friends, and she needed to get everything out in the open.

"I've been going to the secret author's club all week long. I'm sorry I didn't tell you. I was sort of initiated and sworn to secrecy. It's a long story."

Summer smiled.

"It's okay. We don't have to tell each other everything."

"But I didn't even tell you about Dax Cooper. You had to find out from a photo in the newspaper."

"I still think that's really cool."

"I lied to you, Summer. I went out all week and I didn't tell you. We don't keep secrets. What kind of friend is that?"

"You're a very good friend."

"And . . ." October took a deep breath before she spoke, summoning courage. "Could we not go out to eat every night? It's a lot of money, and you cook so much better—not that I expect you to cook for me."

Summer wrapped her arm around October's shoulder.

"I'm so glad you said that. I'm getting tired of Jack's tropical nachos."

"Me too."

They both laughed and hugged one another.

"Let's just be honest from now on, okay?" October said, smiling. If they'd told each other the truth, they could have avoided so much.

This led October to believe that if she told the authors she was sorry as she'd told Natalia and Summer, they would come around. All she needed to do was be honest with them.

"Thanks," she said to Summer, giving her one more hug. "I'm so glad we're on the same page."

It was all going to be fine when she told them the truth.

Chapter 45

Uproar

October told Summer she would be writing at the Island Café all night and wouldn't be home until the following morning. Her excitement was reignited and hopeful. They would allow her in. She would be forgiven.

When she opened the front door to leave, voices vibrated through the air, and crowds roared in the streets a short distance from the apartment.

"What's that?" Summer said. They stood on the front porch, peering toward town.

They walked together up the sidewalk to investigate.

When they turned the corner toward the café, October gasped at the size of the crowd. Cars lined the sidewalks, bumper to bumper, and the crowd surrounded the Island Café, coming and going through the hedges on the side of the café where the secret entrance was. Pedestrians extended their arms and clicked selfies and videos, and the once quiet streets resembled a rock concert. October's phone buzzed madly, her social media feeds going berserk. People were everywhere, trying to get a glimpse of the famous authors as they made their way to their secret writing club. She scanned the crowd. Was Dax there? Where were Dodge and the others?

The news story was everything that Philip and Clive had hoped it would be. It sparked a kind of tension that she hadn't seen in her beach town before. It was dark, but the glow of flashing phones and car headlights stained the beach with light.

A few men staggered out of the bushes but rushed away when the police department arrived.

The chief of police lifted a bullhorn.

"Every one of you must go home. This is private property. And you are trespassing."

The announcement sounded like something out of a movie. And October had never seen him use a bullhorn, except at the start of the Beach Trot, a 5K run the locals did every summer.

October plugged her ears as people started shouting. Summer took out her own phone and started taking a video of it.

"Where are the authors? We want to see the authors."

What kind of circus was this? Who were these people? They certainly didn't resemble the townspeople she knew. They would never act this way. Never once had she thought they would be in any danger.

At that moment, she caught Ezra and Jeb Howard taking a selfie in front of the Island Café. There were other people she recognized, some of her advertising clients. She scanned the crowd for James, who appeared to have stayed home. Her hairdresser, Diana, was there with the other girls from the salon, looking as if they were at a boyband concert, holding signs with Dax's book cover, big fans of the Netflix television show themselves. Summer zoomed in on the women who waved when they caught sight of her.

"Go home," the police chief shouted again.

The officers started escorting the citizens away from the Island Café to their cars and out of the area. October witnessed it all with watery eyes, a glimpse of her town through a blurry lens. It wasn't malicious, like some of the riots that she'd seen on the news, but for her town, it was a shocking truth that people could be provoked by the news.

A movement caught her eye. Dax walked with his head down and his hands in his pockets, taking long steps from the café and down the riverbank toward the B and B.

"I'll see you back at home," Summer said.

October nodded and sped up, not wanting to call attention to him. When she caught up, she placed a hand on his arm. The sudden movement jarred him, and she pulled away. He stared for a moment, and she pleaded with her eyes. He looked away and walked even faster, but she wouldn't let him leave her behind. She tugged at his sleeve, but he kept up the pace until they had almost reached the back door of the B and B. They stopped there, and finally, he looked into her eyes.

"I'm sorry," she said, wiping her nose. "I can't believe this is happening."

"Maybe I should just stay. Sign autographs."

There were people following them now, as if they all knew who he was. How would they respond if he stayed? He wasn't prepared for this ambush.

"Go," she said, pushing him forward.

A group from the crowd appeared on the riverbank, so Dax jogged away. The group, speeding up now, passed her with their signs, all chanting. She stood in the middle of an empty parking lot with a few of the garbage bins and a couple of seagulls waddling around aimlessly.

Her town had changed. And so had she.

Chapter 46

Goodbye

After much corralling, the police officers were able to contain the locals, who dispersed and went away without seeing what they'd come for. Some drove off quietly while others walked back to their homes, their movement short lived. October sat on the steps of her favorite coffee shop and looked out at the main street, watching it all happen like a bad dream. When the thick dust of the event settled, her town appeared different than the boring place of beauty she'd once known. Now it was a blur of bad manners, curiosity, and chaos, all at the expense of Natalia's reputation and way to get a glimpse at the others who only wanted to remain private.

This was certainly not what she had intended when she'd first come up with the idea for the article. She'd simply wanted to prove she could write a "real" news story. Maybe her town wasn't ready for the real news. Maybe they were better off hearing the small stuff, like dogs that helped tow surfers out of the water, or how friendly their neighbors were by stepping up when the town was in need. That's what she wanted to read about each week. Not gritty stories like this. Maybe without the newspaper, or the articles that needed to be told, the town could be washed clean.

She sat on the steps until Kirt, the chief of police and her father's longtime friend, walked past and recognized her.

"October? You okay?"

She smiled and felt a tug in her chest. Her father barely tried with her anymore, so seeing the chief, who had come over on weekends when she was a child and grilled with her dad in the backyard, made her feel lonely.

"Not so great," she said.

He sat next to her on the stairs.

"Hell of a night," he said.

She nodded, leaned forward, and placed her elbows on her knees.

"I'm so mad at this town," she said. She didn't admit to him that she was even madder at herself.

He smiled and patted her on the shoulders.

"People do strange things sometimes. They're not bad people. Just curious."

He was a nice man, and maybe she would have done the same thing if she hadn't been part of the club. To get an autograph from Dax Cooper or Natalia Murrow, or to snap a selfie with one of them. She had them to herself. They were her friends. And she was sad to see them go.

Kirt stood. His tall stature and slightly large belly filled out his uniform. He wore a captain's hat, and his gun was tightly in the holder at his waist. She prayed he would never need to use it.

"Why don't you get going?" he said. "It's late."

"I'd just like to sit here for a little bit if that's okay?"

He nodded and tipped his hat with a finger, then strolled down to his patrol car, got in, and drove away.

The night was silent again as she sat there, not scared but not completely fine with the silence either. She hoped it would all be safe once again, but there was something that made her worry that it might not always be. Honeycomb Beach was a special place, and she wanted it to remain that way.

What am I going to do? There must be something I can do.

She stood and brushed off the dust from the steps but then paused. A noise came from the side of the building. A click.

Following the sound, she found herself behind the hedges staring up at the window. There was a light on.

She grabbed the ladder and climbed up, checking for the straggling onlooker. No one was there. All the locals had gone home, and Kirt along with them.

When she got to the top of the ladder, she attempted to lift the window but found it was locked. She knocked and gazed at the doorway, hoping someone would emerge. Before too long, Dodge presented himself, walking toward the window, but instead of opening it, he stood on the opposite side of the glass, peering at her with intense eyes.

"Can I come in?"

He stared, and the part of Dodge that had scared her in the beginning, the part that threw the pen, the part that commanded the attention of the room, was staring back now, not the sweet teddy bear of a man who wore a pink feather boa.

"Please."

He opened the window but didn't help her inside. He stood silent while she navigated the windowsill and righted herself. Dodge didn't have on his usual writing attire. Instead, in gray trousers and a white shirt with rolled-up sleeves, he looked like any man she might see on the street. He looked like the lawyer he was.

"To what do I owe this privilege?" he said.

"I came to say goodbye. And that I'm sorry. For everything."

He sucked his teeth before turning toward the door, which he walked through, leaving it open behind him. October followed him inside and nodded to Korta, who was putting things away. The coffee pot had been boxed up, and the rich aroma of the grounds still hung in the air. Candles stood tall in a row, ready to be stored away. The lamps were unplugged except for one that was necessary and would join the others as soon as Dodge and Korta were through.

Dodge made his way around the tables, collecting pens that had been left there, pages that were torn out of their pads and wadded up, remnants of the writing journey. It made October sad to see the place returned to an abandoned attic. Where there was once levity and joyful play of words was now a joyless room where creativity had died.

She cleared her throat, to remind Dodge she was there. He cleaned up the last of the pages and instructed her to take them and place them in the garbage bag near the door. She was holding pieces of drafts of Dax and Natalia, famous authors whose first drafts were more poetic and profound than most writers could hope to achieve. She wanted to sneak a page into her pocket for a souvenir but was afraid that Dodge would notice.

"You have no idea how hard we tried to keep Natalia's identity safe," he said.

"I spoke with her before she left. She told me all about her brother Charles."

He shrugged as if it made no difference, which it didn't anymore.

"I'm sorry that this happened. And I'm so sorry that my town acted like they did. I didn't expect that."

"People are drawn to drama. To chaos. Why do you think it is so important to have the right balance of conflict in a story? It's engaging."

October understood now how important it was for writers to have solitude for their craft. She was never as good at coming up with story ideas if she was stressed or had too much going on. This respite was special. And she would miss it.

"Where will you go?" she said.

"Oh, we'll find another place. But we'll be hard-pressed to find a place as beautiful as Honeycomb Beach. You are very fortunate to live here."

She didn't realize that until just then. When he said it.

"I want to travel," she said.

He grabbed a bunch of pens and placed them all in a clear plastic bag.

"Then travel."

"Maybe."

There wasn't anything more for her to say, so she stood there and stared at the attic space and framed a picture of it in her mind. It would always be at the top of the Island Café, but she would never come up here to write again.

She said goodbye and left them there to finish their work, safe now that everyone had gone home and no one would find them there.

"Please tell Dax goodbye for me," she said,

Dodge nodded, but it wasn't his job to tell Dax anything. October doubted that Dax would ever contact her. It was the end of their relationship.

"Don't give up writing," Dodge said. "Make your mother proud. All she wanted was for you to find your passion. Writing or otherwise. Latch on to something and make it yours. No matter what it is."

Lillian Sinclair would never be proud of this. And October knew it.

Chapter 47

The Island

October returned home, and it was still before midnight. Summer was awake.

"That was wild," Summer said. "It was like the Fourth of July on steroids."

"It was awful," October said. "I said goodbye to my writing friends." A little choke took hold of her throat.

"Wanna watch Netflix? *Ember's Reign* is on."

"I think I'll crawl into bed."

October went into her bedroom, slipped into her pajamas, and got out her pad of paper from the writing club. She could type the words more easily on her computer, but she was so used to writing this way now that she couldn't think of not using a pen.

She sat at her desk and lit a soy candle she'd received as a birthday gift from Summer, the gentle smell of an ocean breeze. She waved the match and watched the little stream of smoke float up toward the ceiling. Then she turned on some instrumental music and set the timer on her phone.

"Fifty-five minutes," she said. "Begin."

The dark, murky waves wash aboard the small boat I was able to procure after the ship crashed on a series of large rocks. Many of the men fell overboard, squabbling over the last remaining boats, tossing each other out. I must save myself and get to shore and hope those who showed me kindness find safety. I cut the rope from the main ship, climbed into the boat, and began plowing my way toward the shore.

I'm still miles from land. The waves crash even harder, and my body aches from the chopping surf, the days of sitting endlessly waiting to arrive, and the stress of what is yet to come. But I know there is hope. There is a future.

It takes another full day for me to arrive on the beach of the coast where palm trees lean heavy in the great wind. The ship has almost sunk in the ocean, and the small specks of boats bob behind me as my boat gets closer to land. I wish for the safety of those on board, that they will not perish. The man who helped me I pray for.

When my feet feel the soft beach sand, I cave under my heavy limbs and fall to the ground. My small boat is safe on the sand, and my things are in it. Nothing is important to me now except finding a safe place to sleep until I can regain my energy and wash this terrible ordeal from my skin.

I press my body up from the thick, wet sand and turn over. There's a sound coming from the waves. And then I see him.

The man with the red bandanna is struggling to swim; maybe he doesn't know how, so I gather up all the strength I can and step into the sea once again, swimming toward him.

"Don't swim out," he calls, but he's taking in seawater. I can hear it gurgling as he tries to yell.

"Can you swim?" I ask.

He slashes at the waves.

"You're almost to the place you can stand." It's another twenty meters, but he can make it. I stretch my arms out but will never reach. Don't drown, *I think.* I don't want to be alone.

A large wave crashes over him, and I scream.

It takes more minutes than I can count before I see his head come up again, and I cross my heart that he's made it, that the waves didn't take him.

He slashes at the waves again, his long arms like thick rudders.

There's another wave, and this time, he rides it, as if it's a hand giving him grace. Another one and another, and finally, he's close to me, and I grab him with both hands, my fists clenching the ripped white fabric of his shirt. I'm standing in the water, my feet permanently grounded in the soft sand. Together, we stand him right, and I help him to the shore where he falls on his stomach and begins to vomit up the ocean.

I sit near him and put a hand on his shoulder. A stranger, a man I know only in proximity. I won't let him die. Already, I know he's a better man than my husband. And this journey would be lonely without another. Loneliness would almost be worse than death. I didn't come here to suffer. I came here to live.

Chapter 48

Mock-Up

Last night, October was ready to give up. But Rose was living on. October could too.

Honeycomb Beach was in desperate need of change. The newspaper that had brought them the boring news of the past was over. October had seen the desire in people's eyes and voices last night. They wanted more. But could the *Honeycomb Beach Times* of the future give it to them without writing negative stories to fuel their curiosity? If people were so hungry to see famous authors on their beaches, then there was a need for news stories that provided them with more interesting coverage. She didn't want to admit it, but Clive might have been right. The stories needed more punch.

October sat at her kitchen counter with her laptop, struggling to come up with a new plan. If she could create stories for the paper the town would enjoy—stories from every corner of it, from the stores to the school, the summer events, and the Oaks antique extravaganza—maybe that would have value.

Even if Clive was going to sell the newspaper, someone eventually was going to buy it. And October wanted to be ready. She was already an employee, and why wouldn't she be hired along with the new staff? She had advertising contacts and had created one entire issue herself, with Alice's help. And she would make certain that Clive gave her a recommendation. He owed her that.

"I'll create a mock-up," she said, almost singing the words. The enthusiasm for creating a paper to bring out the best parts of the town was all she could think about.

With her contact list at the ready, she worked her way down the names and dialed the well-known numbers, hoping she would find some stories that would be a good fit for both her vision and her résumé.

Since she'd already spoken to the Howards, she had established a relationship, so she dialed the number with ease. When the voice of the antique dealer answered, she smiled.

"Mr. Howard, it's October Sinclair from the *Honeycomb Beach Times* again. We did an article about you missing your tee time."

"Very boring."

October took in a breath. She was proud of the article but allowed herself to be unaffected by his tone.

"The other day, when we visited, you showed me some of the treasures you'd found on the beach, and I have an idea. What if we do a series and track those things in each edition?"

"Who is it, Jeb?" A woman yelled in the background.

"She says she's from the newspaper again."

"Tell her I liked the fictional piece."

"She doesn't care."

"Tell her anyway."

October laughed at the banter between them, pleased her fictional story had had some impact.

"Would you have time today for an interview?"

She didn't have time to pussyfoot around the idea, nor the time to be shy. She would need as many stories as she could acquire and then start writing and formatting the whole thing on the computer.

257

"Today is fine," he said, but she could sense hesitation in his voice.

"I'll be there this afternoon."

"I have a tee time."

"I can come now," she said.

"Make it quick. I've got an hour."

Mrs. Howard was thrilled when she arrived once more at the Oaks. She found Mr. Howard hitting golf balls over a long green carpet with a hole in the end. His demeanor was cool, and instead of saying hello, he simply nodded and got back to his focused attempts at putting.

"Would you like a scone?" Mrs. Howard said.

She didn't, but the woman handed her a small plate patterned with tiny red and yellow roses that held the triangular wedge filled with chocolate chips, along with a linen napkin. October followed Mrs. Howard out to the balcony already set up for tea with a backdrop of a tranquil ocean, the perfect shade of turquoise. October stood at the railing, and took some interest in a beach volleyball game, and smiled when a young girl slammed the ball over the net for a point.

"We're so excited to be part of the paper," Mrs. Howard said, though Mr. Howard didn't have much interest. He was talking to himself about his stance.

"Tell her about the treasure," he said from the other room.

"I'm getting to it."

"Don't forget to mention the collection."

"I will, I told you."

October chose a chair opposite Mrs. Howard, set down her plate, then took out her pen and paper to take some notes.

"My father used to tell me pirate stories, about buried treasure," October said, hoping to start the conversation. "What have you found lately that you think might interest our readers?"

"We've found some interesting pieces throughout the years. When the hurricanes come, treasures come with them."

Before Mrs. Howard got to it, Mr. Howard came out of the living room onto the balcony with a box. He set it on the table between the two plates, shoving Mrs. Howard's teacup out of the way.

"These are all of the coins we've found so far."

The box was full of them.

He took one out and held it between his thumb and forefinger, holding it up to the sun.

"This one's a pretty rare 1981 Susan B. Anthony coin. Found her just down there while I was fishing. Course I take my metal detector out there too." He searched around in the box for another to share. "Here's a mint Eisenhower coin. From 1977. That's worth a bit."

"Show her the newest one."

He put it back in the box but then left them to return to the living room and, in a few seconds, came back with one coin in his palm.

"You said you liked treasure stories. Well, here's a goodie."

October looked at the coin he held in his open palm. It was an old coin that was jagged and rough.

"What's this one?" she said, jotting some notes.

"This is a silver coin, and if I'm right, which I am, it came from a ship that was lost during a hurricane in 1715."

"The Spanish Treasure Fleet," Mrs. Howard added.

"Twelve Spanish ships were heading for Spain when a hurricane off the coast of Florida demolished them. There's lots of treasure out there in the ocean. I found this baby on the beach."

"How much would that be worth?" October asked, and Mrs. Howard smiled wide.

"Oh, I don't know. A few hundred, maybe a thousand. I don't care. I'm not selling it. It's part of history."

"Would you be willing to share some of these photos and descriptions with me? For the paper?"

"Love to," he said. "It beats the stupid things your paper has been printing lately. I don't think that anybody cares anymore with social media. It used to be a good paper, full of news about the residents. Now it's just fluff. The piece about the authors was—"

"Distasteful," Mrs. Howard said, taking a sip of her tea.

October didn't mention that she'd seen them taking selfies.

October stayed for another hour while the Howards took her through more of their treasures, and she ate her scone and enjoyed it. From that moment, she promised that she would get to know her town and the people in it. She'd found they had something to offer. And for that, she was grateful.

When she was ready to leave, Mr. Howard, who insisted, after spending time with them, that she call him Jeb, handed her a twenty.

"I'd like to place an ad in the newspaper. Might be helpful for our business."

October smiled but shook her head.

"I'm afraid that Clive is going to sell the business. There won't be a paper anymore, or at least, until someone buys it. I'm sorry."

His eyebrows rose.

"Why did you come here for a story then?"

She explained her intention to make a mock-up and convince the new owner toward a different type of paper.

"That's a fine idea," Mrs. Howard said.

She handed the money back to Jeb, and he took it and wished her luck.

The story about the treasure hunters would be a good article and something that the newspaper could continue with each week, but it wouldn't be enough to fill the eight pages. She had her fictional piece, the advertisements, and would no doubt have several editorial pieces at her disposal after the authors article, and she would use the constructive ones. Everyone loved a good letter from a resident who had something on their mind.

When she drove out of the Oaks, she turned south toward the golf course. It might have more money to advertise, plus there must be something going on there, an event or a school team she might report on.

When she arrived, there were several cars in the parking lot, and one of the staff was helping a couple with their golf bags.

She headed inside to the golf shop and waited for someone to assist her.

A lanky man with a white pair of pants and a striped green-and-white golf shirt came to the front desk.

October introduced herself.

"I was hoping to do an interesting piece about the golf course. Maybe a personal interest story. Someone who's learning to golf or maybe a team of golfers."

"I don't think we're interested," the man said.

"Oh."

The door opened, and Jeb Howard entered. She smiled as he approached the desk. Maybe he would put in a good word. October stepped aside as Jeb paid for his tee time.

"I see you got in the paper," the man at the desk said, chuckling.

"That I did. And I'm going to be in it more now too. Thanks to her."

The man stared at October as he handed Jeb his change.

"Here's the man of the hour," Jeb said when the door opened again. "James, I hope you brought your driver. The guys we're playing against are heavy hitters. We've got to hit some greens."

James the Bug Guy strolled in wearing a pair of plaid pants that resembled a bold Scottish tartan and a maroon golf shirt. He beamed when he saw her there. "October," he said and shook her hand. "So nice to see you."

She smiled and remained where she was at the end of the counter, watching the men pay for their round.

"My ad worked wonders this week," he said, mainly to Jeb and the man at the desk. "I got two more clients. October knows how to generate business."

He gave her a wink.

"You don't say," the man at the desk said.

"I was hoping to do a story," October said, interjecting. "But he's not sure about it."

Jeb Howard chewed on a tee.

"I'll tell you what," said the man. "A young lady's golf team might be starting up soon. It's not fully formed, but we've been discussing it with the school to see if we can get some kids interested in the sport."

"Kids these days like to surf," Jeb said, not helping her cause.

"You've gotta get the kids interested," James said. "They're the future of the golf course."

"Maybe the paper can help," October said. "How about we find one student who would be interested, and we can do a nice write-up. Get some photos of them swinging the club, a little putting drill with you? How would that sound?"

He looked to Jeb and James for support. They both nodded.

"Sure, what the heck."

She shook his hand after arranging a date for a photographer to come out and get some shots. October would interview the girl when they'd found one interested, and she'd do a little piece about the girls team and their love for the game. This one inspired her too. Maybe she'd pick up the game herself. And James said he'd give her some pointers if she were ever interested.

As she drove back toward town, her head was full of new ideas. And she'd decided that she'd add a crossword puzzle as well, which would take up some room. It was about time for lunch, so she stopped by Jack's Tiki Bar to see about another story. She splurged on a deck burger with pineapple slices and sat on the pier under a turquoise umbrella, eating her lunch.

"Can I get you anything else?" the waitress said as October was finishing up.

"I'm from the newspaper, and I'm trying to get some more stories. Anything fun happening here this month?"

"We always have new bands popping up, you know since the Surf Kings hung up their guitars. There's a new band called the Summer Boys. Maybe you could do a story about them."

October remembered the band and that Summer was dating the bass player, and she might set up an interview.

October jotted down the name of the band and the dates that they were playing.

"Do you think Jack would like to include a coupon for a free drink or something in this week's paper? I'll put it under the piece about the band.

"I'm sure he would. And he knows that you are here almost every night after work. He's happy for your business and told me that when I saw you again, to tell you this one's on the house."

October beamed at how well her day was going. She enjoyed the rest of her free deck burger on the pier, watching the river and the boats heading out. There were things about her town that weren't boring after all if she was curious enough to find them.

She was going to have plenty of ideas for the next owner of the *Honeycomb Beach Times*, secure her job, and continue to add money to her bank account.

For the first time in a long while, she was happy and liked being in Honeycomb Beach doing something positive. Dodge had told her to find her passion. And maybe this was it.

Chapter 49

Confrontation

T he day was full of nonstop interviews, taking pictures, and prioritizing the articles for the mock-up newspaper. She took everything she'd compiled back to the condo and sat on the floor with all the notes splayed out in front of her. Would this be what the new owner of the newspaper would even want? Her enthusiasm was diminishing. Maybe this was all just a huge waste of time.

Needing a good, strong cup of coffee, October shoved everything she had worked on into her backpack and headed to the café for something that would pick her up. She hadn't returned since the town erupted over the article, and she would apologize to Bridgette for the paper's involvement in the story and for creating such chaos.

When she arrived, there were a handful of locals there, and the wonderful aromas that October had memorized by now filled the space.

Bridgette appeared at the counter with a familiar smile.

"I'd love something from Italy," October said, closing her eyes. "Espresso?"

"Sounds like just what I need."

Bridgette handed her the coffee mug, and October held her gaze.

"I hope that the authors' club article didn't hurt your business," October said. By the looks of it, nothing had changed.

"You know what they say, any news is good news."

October smiled, but then she had to know.

"Did you know about it happening? I mean, there had to be a key. And there's a trapdoor to the upstairs."

Bridgette smiled. Of course she knew. But unlike October, Bridgette had kept the secret.

October searched for a table where she could spread out her newspaper notes and sip her coffee while she put everything in order. The piles of information would keep her busy. She should have ordered a double or maybe even a triple espresso to keep her going.

The door opened, and in walked Clive with an older gentleman, slightly gray, agile, and dressed in a navy jogging suit. October had only heard about Clive's dad and hadn't worked for him when he ran the paper. Her mother and father had enjoyed the paper when he was in charge, and she hoped that the new owner would bring it back to its past glory. With her help of course.

As the men took their seats near the window, both getting out their cell phones, not speaking to one another, she got up from her chair and walked over. The two appeared so deeply involved in their screens that they didn't even notice her standing there.

"Excuse me," she finally said. Clive looked up first and then his father, who adjusted his reading glasses.

"October," Clive said. "This is my dad. Milo."

She smiled and extended a hand, which he took after he stood. A true gentleman. He offered her a seat, which she decided to take even though she wasn't exactly certain what she would say to them. But she knew that if she allowed this opportunity to go by, she might chicken out.

"Mr. —"

"Call me Milo," he said.

"Milo. Clive tells me you're thinking of selling the newspaper."

Thinking was an understatement, but she wanted to have a chance, and maybe she could still convince him that he shouldn't. Maybe she would be able to help him find a suitable candidate to run it.

"I told you he's selling," Clive said, appearing happy about it.

"Well, in that case," October said, "I have some ideas. For the next owner. I've been working on a mock-up to show them. Something that I think will make the locals very happy. I have stories and photos I could show you. If you have the time."

Milo took off his reading glasses and pressed his chair back as if it would make it easier for him to see her. He crossed a leg over his opposite knee.

"I'm sorry. You must be confused. I'm selling the building. And the paper is finished."

Where would the new buyer work from then? Her head was spinning.

"But why?"

"People don't care about the small things anymore. Dogs, beauty shops, little kids' surfing events. It's all very trivial."

He was right, and Clive should have taken responsibility for it.

"That could change," she said. "With the proper . . . staff."

She stared at Clive, who didn't seem to take it personally. He was thrilled that he no longer had to do the job he hated. How awful that he didn't even care that Alice and October didn't have jobs anymore. She'd wasted her time with the mock-up.

"I always assumed someone would take it over," Milo said, "but I don't think it's a good idea anymore. I'm not interested in overseeing the new person, and it will be easier if I just get rid of the building and allow another business to come to town."

"But the news," she said.

"Ah," he waved a hand. "The locals can tune in to the *County Bulletin*. The bigger stories. This was small potatoes." He spoke in a flat monotone voice, and October felt bad for him for losing something he must have loved once.

"This was your business," she said, hoping to appease his sorrow for having to let it go. "I think someone would love to take it over. We just need to find the right person."

"I've looked. And Clive had no business running such a thing."

Clive looked up from his phone, but even that didn't make him look upset about it.

"I put out the latest edition myself." October decided to leave Alice out of it. "So I can do it again. Until you find someone. I'd like to keep my job, Mr.— Milo."

He rubbed his chin and circled the foot he had perched on his opposite knee, and she watched how his hairy ankle bulged in and out with every roll of his shoe.

"You seem to have a stake in the game then. What do you propose I do?"

"Like I said, I could help you find the next owner."

Clive looked up from texting and stared at his father, and their eyes met. They had come up with the solution, but they weren't letting her in on it.

"October can run the paper, Dad," Clive said.

"Me?"

"Are you qualified?" Milo said.

She shifted in her seat. Whatever she said next would make or break her future of ever going to Europe to travel. It would be a huge commitment, but there were more creative ways to run the paper that didn't involve an office.

"I am. And I would like to buy the business from you. But I don't need the building."

Milo took his well-oiled ankle off his knee and set it down. Clive appeared to be interested in what more she had to say as well because it was the first time he'd put his phone on the table since she'd taken a seat.

"Well, tell me," he said, leaving it completely open.

October took a long deep breath. She hadn't considered buying the newspaper until that very moment, but she did have a much better idea about how she would run it.

"First," she said, "I don't need a building. It's a rather old-fashioned way to run a paper nowadays. I can do all this online."

"Go on."

"I agree that the Honeycomb Beach news stories need to be updated, but they don't need to be 'gritty,' she said, this looking directly at Clive. "I love this town, even with all of its boring parts. And I will be the first to admit that nothing much happens. But that's the best part of living here." She didn't think she would ever say such a thing. But right then, it was so true. She knew that it was her home. And even though she wanted to travel, the idea of leaving for good didn't make her happy anymore. "Honeycomb Beach isn't newsworthy," she said. "It's people worthy. The people who live here make this the best place to live. Individuals who create art, write stories, sing songs, design fashion, make kites, bake cupcakes, create signature drinks, brew coffee, have an interest in language and cats, and provide accommodations for visitors. That's the news that people want to know about."

She let out a sigh after not having taken a breath since she'd begun speaking. Her face was flushed, and adrenaline surged through her body. And this time, it wasn't just the coffee.

"The advertising budget is sinking," he said.

"This could be a profitable business model," October said. "Advertising partnerships form the backbone of generating revenue. And I already have those contacts. They want to stay, and I will make it worth their money."

Milo chuckled under his breath, but she wouldn't be swayed. She could do this.

"I plan on transitioning the entire newspaper from the office to my home."

She had just considered this new business structure. And her home could be anywhere that she took her laptop. The café, the beach, and even Italy. Her smile widened thinking how perfect this scenario would be. She would be free to work anywhere. And her budget would allow her to travel.

"What about employees?" he said.

"I could contract someone to do the articles, but I also have experience now. It's only eight pages, but I foresee expansion. The idea of doing it the old way is redundant and unnecessary."

Milo laughed at her calling him old.

"You have great fortitude and energy," he said. "I like that in a person."

Clive slumped.

"Thank you," she said.

"How about I have my lawyer draw up the paperwork in the morning? See if we can come to an agreement."

She couldn't dicker with him. October only had so much money, and buying a newspaper that had already been established was going to take all of her funds. If she could do it right and get her advertisers back, she'd be looking at a decent salary and working for herself. And she could do what she pleased, like continue her fictional story each week.

"This is all that I can pay," she said, jotting down her savings on a napkin.

If it didn't work out, she had just lost everything, but she was willing to risk it.

Milo didn't show Clive the number but took it in his hand and put on his reading glasses. He appeared like a gambler in Vegas, holding his cards. There was no telling as to what the number was. It was a secret between him and October.

"I think I can work with this," he said.

"Really?"

He stared, and she diminished her enthusiasm to a slow boil. He was giving her a gift, and he didn't want Clive to know it.

"I mean, that's very kind," she said.

"I'll call you in the morning. And we can sign the papers."

Chapter 50

Home

O ctober loved her new job.

She sat at the counter, worked out the stories, and called her contacts, who were impressed by the news and ready to work with her again.

As she pieced the paper together on the new software that she purchased with the last check that Clive had given her, she had one last section to fill.

Months have passed. We've found shelter and some food from the palm trees, including coconut, mangoes, and papaya, with the help of Caleb, who still wears a bandanna, and his long hair rests on his shoulders. We've set up a camp using palm fronds and created a shelter to keep out the afternoon rain.

There are others on this island whom we've come to know, who have welcomed us here like family, and we've become acquainted with some of them and tell stories to one another. I don't mention my husband but pretend that I was coming to visit a sister and then encountered the storm. I didn't intend to lie again, but it is safer this way.

I am considering opening a shop to sell items like clothes or food, though I have not yet finalized my plans. My goal is to contribute and make this place my home.

Caleb and I have developed a friendship. There is a noticeable connection between us that goes beyond mere acquaintanceship. It is important to adapt and find contentment together as we learn to live here.

As we sit on the beach eating a mango, Caleb places an arm around my shoulders, and I'm quite satisfied. He protects me but also realizes that I am perfectly capable of fending for myself. We talk about building a small cabin off the beach in time.

Everything seems perfect until Caleb points out toward the sea.

"A ship."

My stomach flips.

Daniel?

Caleb stands and watches the ship; it's days from making landfall. We have some time.

"What should we do?" I say.

"If it's him? We stand and fight," he says to me.

"We stand and fight."

And as the sun beams down on us, and the ocean creeps in, covering our feet, there is nothing to fear. We have time; we have our friendship, and we have our freedom. And no one can take that away.

October smiled at the story, knowing that Rose would be happy now that Caleb was by her side, but that the silver button from her dress would be found later, causing more conflict and providing more to entertain her readers with. And then she typed . . .

To be continued.

She heard a knock at the door and got up to answer it, having allowed the door to be unlocked once again, during the daytime.

The mail carrier smiled and stuffed a large envelope into her hand.

"Have a great day."

She tore open the tab, slipping her hand into the envelope, pulling out the contents.

It was a legal document, based on the large envelope and a legal firm in the return address. She took the envelope to the sofa and sat down to read through it. It wasn't about the paper; she'd already finalized everything with Milo last week. This was something different.

The documents were about her mother. There was a trust.

Lillian Sinclair had set it up stating that as soon as October was able to find her true calling, whatever it was, she was to receive the remainder of her mother's assets from her book dealings and the future royalties from all her self-published books.

The sum was formidable.

Her heart swelled, and emotions blended between disbelief and elation as she held the documents in her hands. Her mother had already given her enough, but now, she would be able to do all she had dreamed of. Now she might even do more with the paper than she had imagined. When she got to the bottom of the document, she traced her finger over her mother's signature. Lillian Sinclair. And then noted the name of the lawyer she'd used. Dodge Whitmore.

He'd known all along.

Chapter 51

To Italy with Love

O ctober arrived in Italy and already had the list of her sightseeing destinations. June was the most beautiful time to visit, based on her recent Google search and several magazine articles that she had read at the library, though if it had been completely up to her, she would have found a quieter month where the crowds were fewer and prices lower.

The little boutique hotel she had booked for ten nights was on a quiet side street perfect for spending time on her balcony when she was tired of the crowds. She would visit some of the smaller towns in Tuscany along with sightseeing in Florence, Pisa, Siena, and Chianti, and scout out the well-known outdoor festivals. Her week would be packed if she did everything on her list.

October had brushed up on her college Italian lessons and was looking forward to tasting the local foods at the markets where she could say pomodori, fragole, albicocche, and gelato.

She set up the laptop in her room along with her notepad and favorite pens to write with. Her job at the paper would continue from there, but she had made certain that most of the articles were prepared in advance.

Clive had gone on to surf school, a place to learn how to teach surfing professionally. The job would suit him, one where he could be doing what he loved the most.

After a few months, Alice had resurfaced on the beach and offered to assist October with the news articles again. She'd admitted the error of her ways, trusting Philip, who had moved on to another girl and was now in Costa Rica working on another writing project. October didn't need anyone to help her with the articles, and she loved her job the way it was. She declined Alice's offer.

Bridgette's business was booming, selling out her coffee grinds in a single day, as tourists had gotten word about the so-called scandal in town and come to sample the coffee and see whether they could spot any more authors there. Bridgette could have capitalized on the event by selling silly T-shirts about the secret authors' club, but October was relieved to know that it wasn't Bridgette's style. Knowing how the news worked, people would get bored of the novelty of it, and soon it would go back to being a normal locally owned coffee shop once again.

It was late in the evening and getting dark, so October grabbed her purse that held the letter she had received from Dax. They had not seen each other since that horrible day when the locals surrounded the Island Café hoping to spot one of the authors they knew so well.

October snatched up her necessary items, stuck them in her travel bag, and left the little hotel in search of the nearest café. It wasn't odd for people to be out and about late in the evening here, because dinners were eaten much later than in the United States.

She strolled between brick and stone buildings illuminated by flickering lanterns, some streetlights, and the glow from interiors. She breathed in the smells of cooked meat, tangy tomatoes, and herbs. The cobblestone path clicked under her shoes, and she licked her lips in anticipation of a cup of espresso, which would fuel her for at least a few hours into the evening.

Making certain she was heading in the right direction, she dug into her bag and took out the letter she had received earlier that spring. The map included in the envelope led her to an intimate café, really an Italian bar, called L'Angolo Nascosto, up on the right. Her feet moved as quickly as her heartbeat. When she arrived, there were several café tables and chairs outside, but she entered instead and addressed the barista.

"Un *caffè*, per favore!" she said, making eye contact with the barista, who was dressed entirely in black to match his high brows and mustache.

He wrote down her order and handed her a small piece of paper, and she waited at the bar, a beautiful marble slab, for him to prepare it.

She glanced at her watch, noting that it was nearly ten forty-five. The atmosphere was lively, and as October listened to some of the conversations around her while she waited, she found that her proficiency in Italian was adequate. No one mentioned the lone American at the bar, and her shoulders relaxed.

Several couples had been at the bar before her arrival, but most of them had already gotten their orders and were sipping their coffees and chatting. She was struck by the architecture, the curves, the embellishments around the windows, the carved wooden tables and chairs, and the gold inlay.

When the barista handed her the small porcelain cup along with the saucer and spoon for adding sugar, she smiled.

"Grazie."

He nodded politely.

She knew it was customary to drink her espresso before she paid, so she squeezed between fellow coffee lovers and stood sipping like a local. When the drink was gone, she went to the bar, handed another very handsome Italian man her note, and paid him one euro.

It was time.

Her anticipation for the evening made her heart leap, and the added caffeine aided the rapidity of each beat. She knew to go past the dining patrons, then follow a long corridor toward the back of the main bar area and turn left.

A closed ornate wooden door stood in front of her. She made a tight fist and then knocked three times.

It opened slowly, and a familiar nose and eyes peeked through the crack in the door.

Dodge.

She pushed the door wide and lunged, wrapping her arms tightly around him, and enjoyed the strength of his arms around her waist.

"I am so happy to be here," she said.

"I can see that."

He led her inside and closed the large wooden door, leaving them in a dimly lit room with mellow sounds of Italian music and a pot of coffee on a shelf to her right. The faces were familiar. Dax sat at the table nearest the door, Natalia at her usual corner writing table, with Korta seated at the table nearby. Dodge walked to his table and stood at the helm, like a ship's captain ready to set sail.

She took her usual seat opposite Dax, who touched her fingers lightly with his own. Her skin prickled.

"I'm glad you came," he said, his smile wide.

There was so much to say, but now, it was time to write.

Her anticipation was everything she'd hoped for. She looked around, and the authors nodded, acknowledging her presence, their faces positive that they had made the right decision to allow her another chance. It was Dax's idea to find another spot, and somewhere they could meet without worry, secret or not. Because Natalia and Charles, per Dax's letter, appeared to have buried the hatchet for the time being, and he had a new desire to spend the summer at a writers' retreat in Costa Rica. Natalia was free to be herself, without the wig and dark makeup. Dodge appeared relaxed and dressed casually, and the others had also put on more normal attire for an evening of writing.

The group readied their pens, adjusted their chairs, and opened their notebooks to fresh pages. Dodge stood behind his chair and admired the room as the authors anticipated their cue. He took a seat and pulled his chair toward the table.

October waited for the word she'd been longing to hear. And finally, without any more instruction necessary, Dodge said, "Begin."

Also By

Other books in the series
My Island Getaway Book 1
(previously published as My Blue Agave)
My Island Runway Book 2
My Island Hideaway Book 3
My Island Holiday coming next
To learn more, go to valeriebuchanan.com.
If you enjoyed this book or any of the books in this series,
please leave a review. It helps other readers find my books.

About Author

Valerie Buchanan loves crafting vibrant characters who embrace the journey to discover joy and a deeper sense of purpose. Her work delves into the healing power of creativity, the courage to mend fractured family ties, and the strength to pursue one's dreams. Her empowering stories feature strong female protagonists who embrace self-discovery and purpose, and her work celebrates the beauty of finding meaning and fulfillment independent of romance, encouraging readers to reflect on their unique journey and potential. When not writing, she's skiing, gardening, doing barre workouts, and spending time with her husband. She resides in New York.

Visit for more info at
valeriebuchanan.com

Made in United States
North Haven, CT
23 May 2025

68926412R00164